Feet First

Arlene Springer

RIDGECREST
press

FEET FIRST

ISBN 979-8-9866478-0-7
ISBN 979-8-9866478-1-4 (ebook)

This is a work of fiction. The characters and incidents are a product of the author's imagination, and any resemblance to actual persons or events is entirely coincidental.

Copy editing: Kristin Carlsen
Cover Design: JD&J Book Cover Designs
Interior design: Colleen Sheehan, Ampersand Bookery

Printed in the United States of America

To my parents & brother,
who encouraged & shared my love of nature

Author's Note

THE FALKLAND ISLANDS, of course, is a real place, and all the locations mentioned in the novel are real, with the exception of Watkins Island. World Seabird Research (WSR) and the *Professor Zjukovski* are also inventions of the author. The novel takes place in the early 2000s. Penguin populations, the methods of researching and counting them, and human populations reflect those times. My descriptions are based on a visit in 2007.

Joanie

WHEN I WAS a sixteen-year-old exchange student in Chile, I visited a national park on the southern coast. Here lived Magellanic penguins, the kind often seen in zoos. They were tucked in burrows in the grass near the shore, waddling across the beach, peering curiously at me with heads cocked, as if asking something of me.

A ranger lived in a tiny cabin at the edge of the forest, a man with round brown cheeks that scrunched up around his eyes when he smiled, which was often. He told me how he would fall asleep to the sound of penguins braying like donkeys and wake to have coffee overlooking the morning-pink waves. As he spoke, I felt myself rising as if on a wing of air, understanding, with my still shaky Spanish, that this ranger was the happiest person I'd ever met. Living here with the penguins and the crashing surf.

That day I made up my mind I too would be a ranger someday, alone in nature, guarding wildlife.

But the years went by. I became a Spanish teacher, got married, had a couple kids, got divorced, and never got back to my dream. Until now. Thirty-five years later I'm on the cusp of making it all come true.

ONE

Tuesday, December 9

Every year, as spring warms the southern air, animals begin to return to the Falklands from the farthest corners of the sea, crossing thousands of miles of open water to arrive at the same crowded slab of rock or humid, dingy burrow where they were born. It is a journey of optimism and hope - and of sacrifice.

—*Kevin Schafer,*
THE FALKLAND ISLANDS:
BETWEEN THE WIND & SEA

I SETTLED INTO THE chair that faced the picture window. Cup of coffee on the table beside me, highlighter in hand, *Skua and Penguin: Predator and Prey* on my lap. Before diving in, I allowed myself one last longing look outside. Across an expanse of sheep-cropped grass sat two bright white buildings: the caretakers' cottage and the shipping container with its red hand-lettering that declared it "Bleaker Store." Grassy hills rose behind the weathered barn and its adjoining fencing. Downslope to the left was the bay full of racing whitecaps. That and the shuddering tufts of grass were the only movement in the whole scene but for a pair of oyster catchers strutting about poking their long red bills into the lawn. Out there was where I wanted to be.

But it was high time to finish the weighty tome I'd lugged all the way to the Falkland Islands. The study of the predations of the large gull-like skua on Adélie penguins done decades earlier was basic background to the research I'd be embarking on in a few days. And I'd chosen this particular afternoon to wrap it up. Not only were my cottage mates out for the day, but Dr. William Deering, one of the lead scientists on the penguin count, was due to arrive in the next couple of hours. His first impression of me would be of a studious, serious scientist-to-be.

Before I turned to the book, my eye caught a bright spot of yellow on a far hill. Nothing native to Bleaker Island was yellow, not the cream-colored sheep, nor the penguins in their sharp black and white. Not the caretaker couple in their army green, nor the one Land Rover that made the roadless island its home.

The raincoat of my cottage mate Liz was yellow. I picked up a pair of binoculars and trained them on the spot. It *was* Liz. With her husband, Paul. And they were making their way toward the cottage.

I lowered the binoculars with a shake of my head. Why couldn't people stick to their plans? Paul and Liz had set off after breakfast with their knapsacks and thermoses of tea, saying they'd be out until late afternoon. Yet here they were.

As the two got closer, I saw that Liz was hugging a white bundle to her breast, her head bent protectively over it. Paul, with a guiding hand at his wife's back, peered through the tunnel of his hood and adjusted their route. I opened the book at my marker and managed to digest one small paragraph before the sound of feet came stomping into the mud room. Moments later Liz made her breathless entrance into the living area.

"Oh, Joanie," she said. "I'm glad you're here." She bent over the dining table and gently lowered the bundle, which, I could now see, was the sweater she'd been wearing when she went out.

I held my place with a finger and asked, "What have you got there?"

"Come and see." Liz shrugged out of her raincoat, and Paul, combing his thick white hair with his fingers, took it from her and hung it on a hook on the wall.

I came to stand next to Liz, and she opened the sweater to reveal a mass of fluffy down with a tiny gray beak. Its breast rose and fell rapidly, and when she opened the bundle further, I could see that the down was matted with dirt and congealing blood. Liz's gray-blonde curls were flecked with rain, and her eyes held a well of tears in the lower lid. "It's a penguin," she said.

"She knows that, honey." Paul looked at me. "A rockhopper."

"I probably shouldn't have," Liz said. "Paul tried to stop me— but I couldn't help myself. This giant fierce-looking bird swept out of the sky into the middle of the colony and plucked it off the nest when the parents were changing places, and then it landed off to the side . . ." Her words spilled out. ". . . and I ran at it waving my walking stick, and this other bird was there, and they started fighting and I got in and picked up the chick—"

"What did the big birds look like?" I interrupted.

"Oh . . . like seagulls. But dark brown, and with claws."

A skua! The penguin chick had most likely been attacked by a skua, the predator of my coming research. I'd seen one, but it was only standing patiently by a colony of gentoos. It didn't seem fair that Liz and Paul were first to see it in action.

"She's lucky she didn't get herself pecked bloody." Paul had his glasses off, drying the lenses on a bit of his T-shirt.

Tears tipped onto Liz's cheeks. ". . . I just couldn't stand to see it killed. I know it's nature and all, and I shouldn't interfere . . . But the parents, they looked so . . ."

Paul put an arm around her shoulders. Liz looked at me through shiny eyes. "What should we do?"

Paul and Liz, in the one day they'd known me, had learned I was a thesis away from a master's degree in conservation biology, with an emphasis on colony seabirds. Making me the expert. But these were the first wild penguins I'd seen since I was a teenager. I'd hardly learned enough about them from textbooks and my visits to their colonies over the last three days to know what to do with an injured chick.

Nevertheless, I tried to get a better look at its wounds. Thinking aloud, I went through what I knew: "We should keep it warm . . . Food probably isn't essential right away—penguin chicks often go a day or more between meals." I pulled a sleeve of the sweater up over the youngster, leaving a crack for breathing, and straightened. "Its parents might not take it back, you know, even if it does recover."

Liz looked stricken. Before I could say anything to soften the blow, a sound outside made our heads rise in unison: the Land Rover grinding toward the cottage. The engine shut off, doors opened and slammed shut. Voices. Like children caught playing doctor, we looked guiltily at each other.

"The caretakers," said Liz. "With the new guy."

"Already?" I squeaked. My first encounter with Dr. Deering was not meant to include the presence of Liz and Paul and a dying penguin chick.

Paul started to speak, but Liz interrupted him as we heard voices in the mudroom. "Put it out of sight, honey." He picked up the bundle and whisked it to a far corner of the kitchen counter as smoothly as if he'd been hiding injured penguin chicks all his life, while Liz glided into the hall to intercept the little party. Which was to have been *my* job.

I went back to my chair by the window, determined to carry out my "studious concentration" on the book in my lap. The little party had turned down the hall to see the bedrooms and bathroom, while I stared at the page, trying to care about the incubation period of skua eggs on various South Atlantic islands.

After a couple of minutes, the caretakers left and Liz emerged into the common area. The man with her had a messy combover and slightly askew glasses. Paul stepped forward from his corner of the kitchen as I put my book aside and stood to meet Dr. William Deering.

TWO

The Trouble with Bill

In their tightly packed colonies gentoo penguins often squabble over ownership of stones and rocks used to build up their nests—they'll even steal them if given a chance. Scientists have observed male gentoos can actually buy the favours of a female gentoo with the offer of a nice pebble.

—*Lonely Planet,*
THE FALKLANDS & SOUTH GEORGIA ISLAND

M Y ADVISOR AT the University of Washington had given me a list of everyone who would be on the penguin count. Eighteen in total: scientists, grad students, and volunteers. She'd starred the names of the three scientists, saying, "At your age, Joanie, you're going to need all the help you can get finding a good job." I didn't mind hearing this from her, as she was almost exactly my age and we had become friends. "These are people you'll want to schmooze with, especially Bill Deering. He's retired now, but he's had a long and stellar career. And he knows *every*body."

Now, here he was, standing in front of me. Dr. William Deering!

I shook his hand and said, "I've heard so much about you."

"All good, I hope," said Dr. Deering with a brief smile.

Even if our first meeting wasn't going as planned, I would get to have him all to myself for a few days before he had a chance to meet the other grad students. Liz and Paul wouldn't interfere. In fact, as soon as we'd heard of his arrival that morning, Liz had immediately grasped the situation, though from the sparkle in her eye, I suspected she was giving it more of a romantic than a professional turn.

Before I could tell him that I'd admired his photographs in *Audubon* and had cited his article on the effect of Antarctic ice melt on Adélie penguins for a paper I'd written, a gurgled squeak burst from the corner of the kitchen.

Dark eyebrows rose above his glasses. "What's that?"

Paul cleared his throat, but Liz stepped forward, taking full responsibility. She fetched the sweater nest back to the table, opened it, and told her story, this time in a more organized, less emotional manner. As the ornithologist bent over the chick, I felt relief that it was no longer my responsibility.

The tiny beak was still slightly open, but its panting had slowed. The eyes, which had looked accusingly at its captors just minutes earlier, were now half-lidded. Was it dying? Dr. Deering moved it carefully to look for injuries, just as I had done. Not taking his eyes off the chick, he removed his coat and said, "I doubt if it's going to make it." He looked at Liz, and I fully expected him to say, What were you thinking?

But she spoke first. "I know I shouldn't have. It was just instinct."

He pushed his glasses higher on his nose with his forefinger and looked back at the chick. "Best to put it out of its misery."

Liz stared at the bundle, swallowed, and said, "Dr. Deering, isn't there any . . ."

"Call me Bill," he said. "The humane thing is to throw it back to the predators."

But this Liz wouldn't take. She'd bury it, she said. She'd have a little ceremony. We didn't have to take part if we didn't want to; she and Paul would do it. She put on her shoes as she talked. If Bill wouldn't mind taking care of it, she said with a pained glance toward the bundle, she'd get a shovel from the caretakers and get them to show her a good place. Refusing her husband's offer to come along, she put on her coat, went out the sliding door, and strode off across the lawn, her curls beating about her head in the wind.

The two men and I stood in the calm of her departure and watched her cross to the caretakers' cottage.

After a moment, Bill said, "I take it she wouldn't be crazy about me cutting it open to see what it's been eating."

"Probably not," said Paul.

I cleared my throat and said, "I'd love to see what's in that chick's stomach."

Bill looked at me.

"I'm going to be on the penguin count," I told him. "Paul and Liz, too . . ."

"Volunteers," Paul added.

"I'm also doing my thesis—on gentoos—and I know this is a rockhopper . . . and what they've been eating isn't what I'll be looking at, but it may be my only chance to see something like that."

Bill narrowed his eyes. "Joanie Moore, right? One of the grad students? I thought I recognized your name," he said, "but then I thought I was mistaken." His dome, thinly covered by salt-and-pepper strands, turned a bit pink.

"You were probably expecting someone a little younger," I said, and not giving him a chance to see I'd noticed his embarrassment, I turned to Paul. "What do you think?"

Paul was still watching his wife, who was standing at the door of the caretakers' house, holding her hair down with one hand and gesturing with the other.

"It doesn't hurt to ask," Paul said, looking, in fact, like it might.

I volunteered to do the asking and found Liz behind the shipping container store scraping at the rocky soil with a shovel. I told her about our plans for the chick and reassured her that by examining the contents of its stomach, we'd be adding to the body of scientific knowledge, and the chick's death wouldn't be in vain. She saw my point, or anyway, she said she did.

I trotted back to the leeward side of the cottage to find Bill. He had put the chick out of its misery and was waiting for me. "Care to do the honors?" he asked, holding out a pocket knife. Was he teasing? Testing me?

Here was my chance to make that good impression! I pushed back my sleeves along with my hesitation, knelt, and took the knife. "Here?" I said, placing the point of the knife just below the throat.

Bill said he thought that would do, but it would work better from the other end. The skin was tough, and puncturing it was the hard part, what with me picturing a geyser of blood going straight for my face. That didn't happen, and I sawed up and down in a straight line. Then, doing my best to appear deft, I plucked out what I assumed was the stomach, cut it open, and dumped the little pink pile on the ground. Bill declared it a job well done. He poked through the pile and said, "Mostly krill. Not as much as I'd expect."

He said he'd pass on the ceremony, but I went inside and found some cotton balls and twine to tidy up the body for burial. I knew my participation in a penguin funeral wasn't winning me any points with Bill Deering, but supporting Liz was more important. Besides, I already had the feeling Bill was at least a little impressed with me.

He and I spent the next couple days tromping over the hills and cliffs and beaches together, just the two of us. He knew his birds, and having been in the Falklands before, he knew these birds— not only the penguins and their predators, but the ducks, geese, swans, gulls, and the small birds flitting about the cottage and in the scrub. He was a man still in love with his life's work, and I felt I was learning more from him than I had in my four years in school, and I told him so. We spent evenings drinking wine and playing cards with Paul and Liz. I again managed to put finishing *Skua and Penguin* on the back burner.

Two days after Bill's arrival the two of us were on our way back to the cottage for lunch, and he started making plans for us for the coming six weeks. I'll show you this, we can do that. It dawned on me then that Bill Deering was developing a romantic interest in me.

Which was the last thing I wanted! Having a boyfriend did not fit into my plan. A new chapter of my life was starting, and it was to be about *me*, focusing only on my new career, not compromising and making my life fit with anyone else, especially a boyfriend. And while I respected and admired Bill Deering, that was as far as it went. Had I over-schmoozed and given him the wrong idea? I had to change the course of this, and the sooner the better.

That afternoon was my last chance to get out by myself before we went back to Stanley, so I told Bill that those were my plans. I said again how much I'd learned from him, but just needed to spend some time alone. Bill was a bit stiff in his wishing me a pleasant afternoon.

With some effort, I managed to banish worry about Bill, and let the wind and wildlife take over. Walking along the craggy cliffs east of the cottage, breathing the salt air and feeling the squishy peat under my feet was just what I needed. I spotted a flock of ducks bobbing beyond the crashing surf, scanned the duck section in my book, and discovered them to be flightless steamer ducks, unique to the Falklands. I even found shelter from the wind among some giant tussock grasses and scribbled out a to-do list, which included a new schedule for finishing my reading and time to prepare for the phone interview I would have back in Stanley at three o'clock the next day. I decided I wouldn't ask Bill to be a job reference until I was sure we were on a firm, professional-only footing.

༷

Liz, however, had become quite an advocate for this friendship between me and Bill, and brought up the coming interview as we lingered after dinner over the brownies Paul had made.

And wouldn't you know it, the head biologist at Big Bend National Park was a friend of Bill's. He offered to email and put in a word as soon as we got back to Stanley. I protested that it wasn't necessary, but the three of them persuaded me I'd be crazy to not accept the offer.

I went to bed that night with the uneasy feeling that I was just getting in deeper.

༷

On Friday we all flew in the little red eight-seater for twenty minutes over the roiling ocean back to Stanley and then dispersed to our various lodgings. At Kay's Guesthouse, where I had spent my first two nights in the Falklands, the call from Big Bend came in at three o'clock, as arranged. The head ranger began the interview saying, "So! I hear you're a colleague of Bill Deering."

Wow. Not only had Bill already contacted the guy, but he'd called us colleagues. I stifled the urge to say that I'd only just met him, and agreed that he and I were working on a penguin count together.

When the interview was over, I jotted a few notes in my job-search notebook. Big Bend National Park was in the desert, an environment I'd always been drawn to. The job I'd applied for involved monitoring the canyon wren. Hardly a seabird, but a bird, nevertheless. It paid well and there were benefits. And being in the U.S. would add a security not as easily found in an international job.

There was nothing wrong with the job, except for one thing: it wasn't the one I wanted. My dream job was resident biologist in Parque Nacional Isla Magdalena, in Chile. When I'd heard about it a month earlier, I was sure it was a sign. If I got the job, I would live by the sea in my own small cabin and study the impact of human visitors on Humboldt penguins. Almost the exact job I'd dreamed of since I was a teenager! I'd heard that they were keen to hire someone from the U.S., and I'd completed my application before leaving Seattle. I would learn if I'd been selected for an interview during my seven weeks here.

Tempting as it was to sit back and wait for the Chile job to land in my lap, though, I was realistic. I would cast a wider net by spending evenings conducting a vigorous online job search. By the time the count was over at the end of January, I should have some interviews lined up. I *had* to. I'd carefully budgeted enough money to get me home from the Falklands, but little more. If I didn't have at least an interview by then, I would have to sign on as a substitute and try to get back my old job teaching high school Spanish. Twenty-six years of that had been plenty, thank you very much.

A phone call from Bill interrupted my thoughts. He asked me to join him for a pint that evening at the Rose Hotel. I accepted reluctantly and only after I got him to agree to let me buy. It would be my way of thanking him. We'd be even, with me owing him nothing more.

We spent a pleasant enough hour and learned more about each other. Bill had spent the decades after a brief marriage so wrapped up in his career that he hadn't been involved in any serious relationships since. He didn't exactly say, but I gathered that now he was retired, he was ready to find someone to grow old with. When I told him about my ex and my son, it was starting to feel like a first-date sort of conversation, so I emphasized how happy I was to finally be on my own.

As he walked me back to Kay's by way of the harbor, he kept finding ways to prolong our time together, pointing out the giant lupines in one yard, a mother and son stacking peat in another, and reminding me the research vessel that would be our home should arrive in an hour or so. Did I want to stay out and watch for it? It was nine thirty and the sun had recently set, but the long twilight of the Falklands summer would keep it light until past eleven. I wouldn't have minded staying out, but it was time to cut things short, so I said I needed to do some more reading.

But he wasn't done. As we neared the street the guesthouse was on, he stopped again and said, "I wonder if you'd do me a favor."

I looked at him warily. "What's that?"

"I've had some concerns about the results of the last count," he said. "The one five years ago."

"The WSR count?" WSR is World Seabird Research, which counts penguins in the Falklands every five years, the count we were about to embark on.

"Yes." He glanced over his shoulder as if making sure no one was listening. "I suspect the populations had dwindled more than it was made to look."

"Really? But how—"

"I don't know how. But something's not right. I'd like you to keep an eye open for me—people, data—anything that seems off to you."

Was this a way for Bill to keep me close? I mean, if the findings had been off, I would have heard something, wouldn't I? WSR and other Falkland Island penguin counts had been on my radar ever since I'd been accepted on the project. But if all he was asking was that I keep an eye out, how could it hurt? "Any people in particular?" I asked.

"The only person here this year that was here then—other than me—is Ian Hargreaves. He wasn't lead scientist then. I don't necessarily suspect him . . ." Bill shrugged. "So . . . everyone at this point."

Ian was head of the project, so I knew him from letters and emails. "Well, sure, if you want," I said.

We started walking again, around the corner and up to the gate into Kay's yard, where we stopped. "Oh," Bill said again. "Food service on the boat won't start until Sunday morning. Would you care to join me for dinner in town tomorrow night?"

I declined, saying I had plans to meet with my research partner, Finn. The weekly plane from Argentina was due the next day and would bring the rest of the researchers, including my as yet unmet partner. The plan to meet Finn for dinner was true, if you overlooked the part where he didn't know about it yet.

Bill accepted my explanation graciously, but as we were about to part, he leaned close—for what? A hug? A kiss? I maneuvered to make sure it was only a brief hug, slipped through the gate, clicked it shut, and said a bright good night. I turned before he could say more, hopped up the steps, and let myself into the kitchen, firmly closing the door.

I leaned against it. All I wanted for the next six weeks was to do good work on my thesis project and find a job in my new field. To make this happen I needed to continue the razor focus that had carried me to this point. But here was Bill, drawing me into some intrigue. And trying to move us along to the next step, the dinner date.

THREE

Everyone but Finn

The first time the youngsters leave land, they do it with well stocked fat reserves to ensure they survive the first critical period in the sea on their own. This is when mortality is at its highest.

—*Susanne Äkesson,*
PENGUINS

SATURDAY, MY LAST day in Stanley for six weeks, was bright and crisp and, again, ferociously windy. I was finally, after a full week in the Falklands, grasping that the near-constant twenty-five-knot winds I'd read about meant it really did blow almost all the time. I packed my bags, left them in the parlor, and went out for some last-minute shopping—a notebook, stamps, and postcards, though I wasn't at all sure I'd have an opportunity to mail anything after today. On an impulse, I picked up a fuzzy stuffed penguin at a gift shop: about a foot tall, plump and huggable.

Just before noon, I crossed the road that runs along the harbor and plopped all my belongings down on the sidewalk to catch my breath and have my first look at the *Professor Zjukovski*, which had arrived overnight. Bracing against the wind's onslaught, I took in the ship that was now moored three blocks away at Stanley's main pier.

My new home was seventy-two meters long and had five decks. It could sleep fifty, but on this expedition it would hold just twenty-seven, researchers and crew included. It was bright white, gleaming in the sun. A broad red stripe ran the length of it, giving it an air of a package waiting to be opened. I could hardly wait to explore its every corner.

If not for the list in my pocket, that's exactly what I would have done next. But, feeling I'd lost my focus what with this Bill business, I'd set myself four tasks for the afternoon:

move to ship
thank Big Bend for the interview
find Finn
finish Skua

Today, I promised myself, was the day I'd finally be crossing the last item out. Then and only then would I explore the ship.

An aggressive slap of wind sent the stuffed penguin off its perch on my pack and tumbling down the sidewalk. I ran after it, and brushing its white chest off, I trotted back to my luggage, saying, "You can't wait either, huh?" Clamping the penguin between my knees, I hoisted my backpack over my shoulders.

Save for the crew member who checked my name off on a clipboard, no one was about. I tiptoed up the stairs as best I could while lugging a duffel bag and backpack, aware that Bill was likely already aboard. My cabin was on Deck Four, one below the top. I dropped my luggage in the breezeway in front of the door and took a moment to gaze at Stanley from this new angle. The Falklands' capital is home to two thousand people, living in a cluster of white houses with roofs of green or red or yellow that sat snugly in a few rows along the harbor. A seagull swooped up with a cry. I could have stayed there soaking it all in, but turned instead to my cabin.

The room was small, but not claustrophobically so, and I set the bags on one of the two single beds, propped the penguin on a pillow, and unpacked, tucking everything neatly into the tiny dresser and closet. When this was done, I stepped outside for one last peek at the afternoon. In the time I'd been inside, rain clouds had blown in and replaced the sunny sky, and slanting drops were beginning to pelt the deck. I went back in, closed and locked the door, and pulled the shade across the one tiny window, thinking it was only a matter of time before Bill came looking for me. I dug out my book, highlighter, pen, and notebook, and set myself up cross-legged on the bed. It was twelve thirty. I had two hours to conquer the reading.

Not fifteen minutes passed, however, before a bumping and scraping caused me to raise my head. Voices, right outside the door. Paul and Liz. A nearby door opened, Liz gave a delighted squeal, then more bumping and dragging. A door shut, and the voices were muted.

Just as I was refocusing on the reading, they came out and the voices faded down the breezeway. I turned back to page 382 in *Skua*. "This timing is achieved through a complex interaction of endogenous and environmental components which Baker (1938) first recognised as being of two sorts: ultimate factors, such as food . . ." (–Euan Young, *Skua and Penguin: Predator and Prey*)

Not the stuff to capture my imagination at the moment. Paul and Liz were out there exploring the ship. I was a prisoner in my cabin. I fought with myself, even stood and pushed the curtain aside to look out. After a moment, I pulled it shut again and looked at the penguin staring at me with its shiny black eyes. "Okay," I said. "Your name is Prudence, and your job is to keep me on track. Pru for short."

The penguin had no objection, and I sat back down and picked up the highlighter.

Fourteen pages later—the biggest chunk I'd read since Seattle!—Paul and Liz were back. This time they parked themselves at the rail just outside. I managed to focus for a few minutes, but when their voices took on an excited pitch, I marked my place, closed the book, and opened the door.

"They're here!" said Liz, turning from the rail.

I joined them, glancing at my watch. The weekly flight from Río Gallegos, Argentina was due to arrive at twelve thirty. As I'd learned from my seatmate on the flight a week earlier, it was seldom late and never early. After customs and the forty-minute ride into town, my new shipmates shouldn't be arriving until two thirty. It wasn't quite two o'clock.

We looked down two stories to the pier, where people and luggage were piling out of a white van. The sun had returned, and as the group, with flapping windbreakers as bright as Stanley's roofs, hoisted backpacks and duffel bags, I tried to guess which one was Finn.

The number of researchers that were to make up the expedition was eighteen. Six of us—Bill, Paul, Liz, and I, plus two Falklanders I hadn't yet met—were already here, so I should have been looking at twelve people. But I counted only eight. Five of them were men.

I rejected two of these right off as being too old to be Finn—one was tall and white-haired with tanned, leathery skin, the other a balding man walking with a woman I assumed was his wife. As the other three men made their way toward the ship, I studied them. One was probably in his mid-forties; this wouldn't be the Finn I'd come to know from his texts full of "R U sure" and "BTW" and a mention of his mom doing his laundry. The other two were walking together, and with the excited way they looked around, they somehow didn't seem Finn-like either. But one of them had to be, didn't he? The tall thin one with dark hair seemed the right age, but he called out something to the mid-forties man in a decidedly native-sounding Spanish; that man tossed an answer back over his shoulder, also in Spanish.

I switched my gaze to my last hope, a big rosy-complexioned man with blond curls peeking from beneath a brown wool cap. Maybe . . . but as he passed up the gangplank onto the boat directly below us, he spoke to the white-haired man in what I was pretty sure was German. Finn had mentioned in one of his emails that he didn't speak anything but English.

It seemed he wasn't with the group.

I had come up with my thesis topic nearly a year earlier: "Does the presence of human visitors at gentoo colonies improve the success of skuas?" Tourist visits to penguin colonies from Antarctica to South America to Southern Ocean islands like the Falklands have increased exponentially in recent years, so disturbance of wildlife is a growing concern. The premise of my project was that human visitors could make the penguins so nervous or distracted they'd leave their eggs or chicks exposed to attacks by predators, in particular the fierce gull-like skua. Previous studies had produced mixed results. The thesis was a perfect fit with my passion for protecting penguins from human interference.

I'd included the proposal for this project in my application as requested. When I received the news I'd been accepted on the count, I grabbed my son, Bobby, by the hands and danced him around the living room. But then I read on: "By coincidence another applicant has proposed the same project. And he's in your neck of the woods, at the University of Montana. May I suggest you collaborate?" I sank into a chair with a groan.

"What's the big deal, Mom?" Bobby said.

"Honey, he's probably *your* age."

But that wasn't what was bothering me. I got along fine with young people—most of my classmates at the university had been in their twenties. We'd studied together in coffee shops, collaborated on research papers, crammed for tests. One big family of students. The reason for my dismay was that I didn't want to share my project with anyone, especially someone I didn't know.

Before long, though, I'd managed to adjust my thinking. Finn and I had exchanged emails and texts over the months leading up to departure. He wasn't always as prompt in answering as I would have liked, but he seemed to have a grasp of the relevant literature and sound ideas on how to approach the fieldwork. My suggestion that we meet in person in Spokane—halfway—got a cool response. Well, I told myself, he can't be any more excited about having to share the project than I am. We'll just have to make it work.

"Only eight people," Liz said once the group had disappeared into the ship. "Did you see your partner?"

"I don't think so."

"Some of them must have stopped in town," said Paul.

"That must be it." I was miffed. Finn and I had only a day and a half to coordinate, prepare a presentation to the rest of the researchers, and be ready to lead a team first thing Monday morning. One would think he would have come directly to meet me.

Liz said, "Have you explored the ship? It's wonderful. We went all over; everything's here, everything we need. We knew you were in your cabin, doing your reading, and so we didn't disturb you..."

When she paused for breath, I answered the question. "No, not yet..."

But Liz was going on. "Oh, and guess what? We're supposed to make groups for dinner tonight of no more than six. You know how Stanley's restaurants are, and a cruise ship is supposed to be in town. So Paul and I were wondering if you'd like to join us. We'll ask Bill."

"Thanks, but I'm going to wait for Finn . . ."

"But you don't know if he'll even show up." The sound of voices and footsteps reached us from below as Liz said, "You don't want to end up alone for dinner."

I was beginning to think that was exactly what I did want; grab a burger to go and hunker down in my room to come up with a Plan B; If Finn Doesn't Show.

On the other hand, it was my last night in Stanley. The ship was due to sail at eleven the next morning, not to return for six weeks, with no stops anywhere larger than a handful of cottages along the coast. Besides, everyone else would be out that evening getting to know each other. If I wasn't among them, I'd wake up Sunday morning an outsider. And the clincher: when Bill saw me at the evening's meeting, and if Finn hadn't shown up, he'd realize I had no dinner plans.

"All right," I said. "But Bill's probably busy. Let's find some new people to make up a group of six."

Liz was about to say something, but Paul spoke first. "Good idea." He gave his wife that look I'd come to know from Bleaker, reeling her in from her overenthusiastic matchmaking.

Before anyone could say more, a rhythmic thumping and footsteps reached the top of the stairs. It was the tall white-haired man we'd seen on the pier; a small red backpack was snug against his back and a compact wheeled luggage clicked to a stop behind him. He let out his breath with a "Pah!" and said, "This is Deck Four?"

We exchanged introductions. Josef was from Switzerland we found out when Liz asked him about his delightful accent. I invited him to join us for dinner.

"Perhaps also my countryman?" said Josef, when he heard about the groups of six. "A charming lad. And a lovely young American lady we met on the plane. That will be the full house." He employed the expression with confidence.

As Josef headed off down the breezeway and I turned toward my room, Liz was at my heels asking to see my cabin. She stepped inside and after exclaiming how cute it was, with two single beds exactly like theirs, she asked if we could talk for a moment.

"A moment," I said. "I've got to get back to work."

Liz shut the door and sat on one of the beds.

"How did your job interview go?" she began.

"Fine! Thanks."

"And did Bill get ahold of his friend?"

"Yes." And anticipating her next question, I said, "We had a beer last night and I thanked him."

Liz said, "That's nice. I was thinking . . . well, I wonder why you don't want him coming to dinner with us."

I took a breath. "Liz . . ."

"I know it's none of my business, but I was just thinking maybe you should be nicer to him, that's all."

I sighed. "He's getting interested in me. I'm sure you've noticed. And I'm not interested in him, not like that."

Liz was silent for a moment, studying her shoes. "He's a nice man, Joanie. You could do worse."

"But I don't want a man at all!"

"You and Bill have got so much in common, though," Liz said. "And, well . . . he does have connections."

I sighed. "Yes, he has connections." I'd been struggling with that quite well on my own.

"So . . . ," said Liz. "It wouldn't hurt to be . . . friendlier."

"Liz. Thanks for your advice." I gestured to the book. "But I can't even think about Bill right now."

Liz stood. "I guess I'm being a busybody."

"No, no, it's fine."

When Liz was gone, I spent a good five minutes reading one paragraph over and over. Thoughts of Liz and her interfering, Bill and how to handle him, Finn and why he hadn't shown up lurked between every line.

Finally, I snapped the book shut and stared for a moment into the corner of the room. I would never get any reading done until I found Finn. Maybe he'd arrived by now.

I picked up the little notebook with my list of four simple tasks, and still only 'move to ship' crossed off. I ripped out that page, crumpled it and tossed it into the wastebasket. On the next page I wrote a new list:

> *thank Big Bend*
> *read half this afternoon*
> *half tomorrow morning*

I put the notebook on the bedside table and went out to explore the ship.

FOUR

It's Different Here

Penguins are very curious birds. If you stretch out quietly on the ground next to a gentoo colony when the chicks are nearly full-grown, the inquisitive youngsters will waddle over to investigate.

—*Wayne Lynch,*
PENGUINS OF THE WORLD

CIRCLED THE TOP deck and gazed out at the harbor. White-tipped waves were racing past. A bird shot by, almost too fast to identify, but big enough to be a storm petrel. Excitement took me; by this time tomorrow we'd have left Stanley behind. I looked down the long stretch of water to the east, looking for but not seeing the way out to the open ocean. Doing my best to focus on the magical surroundings and not let the niggling worry about Finn intrude. I would think later about all the parts of the project that he had been handling and all I'd need to do if he didn't show up.

The upper deck had bigger cabins—the captain's, no doubt, the lead scientists', perhaps ones belonging to people who'd paid a bit more for a better room. I took the stairs down to Two, the level I'd boarded on. A lot of open deck there, three Zodiacs, a place to launch them. A door that said "Crew Only."

By the time I got back up to Three, I'd seen a few people, crew mostly, but no one who could be Finn. The new arrivals would be unpacking in their rooms. A doorway off the dining room was labeled "Communications," where the computers would be. I might as well send that thank you to Big Bend.

The room was empty except for one man standing in its center facing me. He was holding a globe upside down by its base and gazing at it. When he became aware of me in the doorway, he looked up and said, "Did you ever look at the world this way? It's different." He spoke as if he'd been waiting for me to arrive so we could continue an ongoing conversation.

This was one of the men I'd watched board from above, the one with the curly blond hair. I couldn't help smiling as I walked to the middle of the room. "No," I said. "But there's lots more water in your new "Northern" Hemisphere, isn't there?"

He gave the globe a spin, and I looked up at his face as he studied the oceans and continents whirring by, his head slightly cocked. I took in a strong jaw and a prominent forehead, a frown of concentration.

I looked back at the globe. "Funny how you have to look at it upside down before it strikes you about all the water here."

"Yes." He lowered the globe. "It's different here." He wasn't American. His accent was like Josef's and he was wearing a home-knit sweater.

I took the globe from him and gave it another spin, right side up this time. "In fact," I said, "north of the equator there's forty percent land, while the Southern Hemisphere is mostly water; only about twenty percent land here."

He raised his eyebrows, a hint of a smile at a corner of his mouth. I took this to mean he was interested and went on. "And you've got the Antarctic Convergence here." I pointed to the area just south of the Falkland Islands. "Where the warm northern currents meet the colder currents sweeping up from Antarctica. Which is partly why although London and Stanley are the same relative latitude, London's a lot milder." I was reluctant to stop my little speech and added, "And since the mass of water around Antarctica is unbroken by land, it's windy here all the time."

"Yes." He was grinning by this time. "The Southern Ocean is only place in the world with infinite fetch." He held out his hand. "Hans Schaller, volunteer. You must be one of the scientists."

The room suddenly felt warm, a wash of heat sweeping over my body. I'd only recently learned that it wasn't the room that was warm, but me. Hot flashes had arrived. How many times had I asked my friends, "Did it just get really warm in here?" It took weeks of noes before I got it. Bobby had helpfully pointed out that my skin turned pink at such times. I knew this could be mistaken for blushing. Which it wasn't. Until I felt someone might think I was blushing, and by that time I probably was. Getting older has its challenges.

"Just one of the grad students, Joanie Moore," I said, shaking his hand. I actually *was* kind of embarrassed. A thesis away from a brand new master's degree in conservation biology, I tended to get carried away in sharing all the things I'd recently learned.

One thing I didn't know, though, was what infinite fetch was, so I asked.

"Oh!" he said. "It's a sailing word. It means you can just go and go and go; no land to stop you." He paused. "No . . ." He zigzagged his finger back and forth, eyebrows questioning.

"Tacking?" I supplied.

"Yes, tacking."

"Ah!" I said, and moved toward one of the computers, adding, "I think you're having dinner with us."

"Ah," he said. "With Josef."

After a few words about where and when, we each sat at a computer. I busied myself with my email, aware of him clicking away a few feet from me. I wrote my thank-you for the phone interview and logged off. I would write my friends later.

When I stood, Hans took his hands off the keyboard and looked up. "You are done already?" I told him there was a book I needed to finish reading and said I'd see him later. As I passed through the dining room, I was aware of the impression I'd made: a know-it-all and a bookworm to boot. Plus the blushing.

It was 3:20 and I had just enough time to get my allotted pages done before the five o'clock orientation meeting. But now everyone was out and about, and getting back to my cabin was like running a social gauntlet. Outside the dining room, sitting on a bench, was a sleepy-eyed man with long brown hair. He looked up from his camera and greeted me. He was the ship's doctor,

Javier Martinez, from Spain. Feeling I'd shown off enough for one afternoon, I didn't demonstrate my Spanish. He said no one was allowed to get sick or hurt because he planned to spend his time photographing birds. I asked him if he'd met a Finn Markovich, but he hadn't.

"Did anyone get off the bus in town?" I asked.

Javier thought a moment. "Just Ian and his wife . . . and a young lady."

"Ah," I said, my heart thumping. *Where was Finn?*

Back up on Four, an older couple greeted me with big smiles. They introduced themselves as Yoshi and Michiyo Teguchi. Michiyo had the better English and told me they were recently retired. Back home in Kobe none of the vacation ideas they were considering really appealed to them until they learned about this penguin count that was taking volunteers. They hadn't met anyone named Finn, either.

I'd learned from a chart in the dining room that Finn's cabin was on Deck Four. I found it, knocked, waited, turned the knob, and peeked in. Another room just like mine, but not a hint that its occupant had arrived. I headed back to my cabin to make a list of what forms Finn had prepared and what equipment he was supposed to bring. Before I got there, I passed an open door from which I heard a whirring, and looked in. A woman with a tight cap of gray hair was pedaling away at top speed inside a small gym, mopping her neck with a green bandana.

"I'm Helen," she called, without breaking stride. "Come join me." Well. Getting the blood circulating for a few minutes before getting to work could only help, right? I climbed onto the other bicycle.

Helen was a travel writer from Australia doing a piece on the penguin count. Before the timer on my bike reached five minutes, she had revealed that she had her eye out for a man, someone to spend her golden years with. I told her about Bill and Josef, but she thought they sounded a little old for her. I must have looked skeptical, because Helen threw back her head and laughed. "I'm sixty-six," she said. "I've spent the past five years taking care of my sick husband, bless his heart, but being a nursemaid is not something I'm eager to repeat."

I found her company delightful, and I ended up staying longer than I'd intended. We ended our session promising to be exercise buddies. As I walked out the door, Helen was bending over a large barbell with every confidence she could lift it.

By then only half an hour remained before the meeting. I had a quick shower, crossed "thank Big Bend" off my list, changed afternoon to evening for that next-to-last group of pages, and sat down to think about how to proceed on my research project without Finn. He and I had done a lot of work already. I would train the team in data gathering. Finn was to be in charge of data entry and record keeping. I thought with dismay of the documents he'd developed and was to bring with him.

I brainstormed and jotted notes until I felt slightly more in control. When it was time to go, I told Pru the Penguin, "It's fine. I'm on track."

A boisterous group had filled the dining room. A tall man with bony shoulders was standing at a desk bending over a clipboard, his heavy eyebrows meeting above dark framed glasses. That had to be Ian Hargreaves, our leader. I took a seat next to Paul and looked around the room, confirming we were still one man short. Could the missing man really be Finn?

I shared this worry with Paul, and, heads together, we sorted out who was who.

"There's Josef, who's coming to dinner with us," Paul said. Josef was engaged in conversation with a pretty young woman with an obsidian ponytail and a lavender fleece vest.

I pointed at Dr. Javier, who was speaking Spanish with a young man at the next table. "Maybe that one?" I said, although I was grasping at straws.

Paul shook his head. "That's the doctor and Alejandro, a grad student from Chile. And they don't look like Finns," he said, nodding across the room toward Yoshi and Michiyo. "But how about the guy next to them?"

"Nope." It was Hans, leaning forward, elbows on knees, grinning at something Yoshi was saying. "That's Josef's 'countryman,' as he says, who's joining us for dinner."

There was definitely no Finn.

Ian cleared his throat and introduced himself. "Welcome to the fourth WSR Falkland Islands Penguin Count." After the applause died down, he started his speech. "I'm sure you're aware that penguin populations have declined alarmingly here over the past quarter century, as they have to varying degrees over much of their range. The results of our most recent count, five years ago, showed a slowing of that decline; in fact, some populations were healthier. Our hopes are that this year's count will show a continuation of that trend."

The audience listened attentively.

"Today," he continued, "there are approximately one million penguins breeding in the Falkland Islands. That may sound like a lot, but in the early eighties there were close to *six* million. We may never see a return to such numbers."

A murmur rippled through the room.

"We'll be circumnavigating the entire Falkland Islands over the next six weeks, counting breeding pairs of penguins at various sites. I'll come back in February with another group to follow up on the breeding success.

"We also have four grad students conducting their own research, looking at commercial fishing, cruise ships impact, and penguin-predator-human interaction. At tomorrow's orientation, we'll hear from them about their projects. Some of you will spend part of your time assisting them, just as they'll spend half of their time on the main count."

Four grad students, I wondered, or only three?

As if in answer to the question, a clatter of luggage in the corridor brought Ian's talk to a halt, and all eyes turned toward the noise. A wiry young man came through the door. He was wearing a rumpled tan safari-type jacket and his frizzy black hair was captured in a long, thin braid. Seeing there was no chance of slipping in unnoticed, he stopped. "Sorry. I was detained. Finn Markovich."

I let out the breath I'd been holding all afternoon.

Ian nodded curtly and waited while Finn slid in next to Josef.

While Ian described the count methods in more detail, I studied my partner. He was paying close attention, elbows on the table, hands clasped, his chin pressed against them. A tiny diamond stud winked from his ear. He had to be at least twenty-two or -three if he was finishing his master's, I thought, but not much more. Probably younger than Bobby.

I swung my attention back to Ian. "... five years ago gentoos and Magellanics were holding steady compared to the count done five years before *that*, while rockhopper and king populations dropped, but less than expected."

"Excuse me." Finn raised a finger, not moving his clasped hands from his chin. "Haven't those results been challenged?"

Ian paused, the light from outside glinting off his glasses. "Nothing came of that," he said.

Finn lowered his clasped hands to the table. "But what about the local count that was done last year? I understand there was some controversy over that, too."

What was this? I'd heard nothing about any funny business until last night. And now here it was again. I glanced across the room at Bill, whose eyes were on Finn.

"We'll discuss this in more depth tomorrow," Ian said, closing his notebook with the distinct air of someone who didn't care to pursue the topic any further.

Finn had laid his forearms on the table and leaned back in his chair, soundlessly drumming the fingers of his right hand and looking around the room.

Ian was talking again. "Right now I'd like to do introductions." He looked at his watch. "Then release you to go find dinner in town. It'll be one of your last chances for big city lights." He gave his first smile, and his audience chuckled. Not only did Stanley hardly qualify as a big city, but in the long days of the austral summer the lights wouldn't be needed until eleven o'clock at the earliest.

The lead scientists on the project introduced themselves: Bill and a sturdy French woman with a mass of blonde curls named Yvonne. Then the rest of us had our turns. I had guessed the ages of the group ranged from early twenties to late sixties until Josef admitted he'd fibbed just a little in order to be accepted on the project.

"People think someone of a certain age can't tramp all day over rough ground. I invite you to watch me. In fact, I will turn eighty on this trip."

This was met with whoops and applause. Helen called from the back of the room, "Age is a state of mind!"

People said a bit about their reasons for committing to six weeks counting penguins in these remote South Atlantic islands. They fell into two camps: either bright-eyed young people doing research and getting field experience, or retired folks wanting a meaningful vacation. Purpose-wise, I fit in the first category, but age-wise, I couldn't help notice, I was closer to the latter.

Several women said they were penguin lovers. Hans, my globe-spinning friend, was the only man to do so. "I was in Antarctica last year, and I fall in love with penguins," he said. "So I come here."

When the meeting broke up, Finn and I moved toward each other and shook hands. He offered no explanation for his late arrival.

"Can we have dinner this evening?" I said, and, noticing his hesitation, added, "Or meet later?"

"Uh . . . sorry. I'm getting together with some friends in Stanley."

He had friends in Stanley? "Tomorrow morning, then. We have to be ready to present our project by two." I was hanging on to my last scrap of patience.

"I'm kind of tied up all morning—how about after lunch?"

This was too much. "That's not nearly enough time! We have the whole project to talk about—who's going to be doing what, how we're going to train our team . . . everything."

Finn shifted slightly back. "I really am sorry—I don't see how I can find any more time . . ." He snapped his fingers. "How about after lunch and then Monday morning? Like . . . five o'clock?"

I stared at him, took a deep breath. "All right."

He grinned, shook my hand again, and turned to talk to Ian, who'd been hovering.

I knew it! I thought, fuming out of the dining room.

Bill appeared at my side and steered me to the railing. "So . . . ," he said. "Your partner; see what you can find out about him tonight."

It took me a moment to remember Bill thought I was going out to dinner with Finn.

"Yes. Interesting, isn't it? Where does he get that stuff?"

Bill shrugged. "Anyone could have found information online."

But *I* didn't notice anything, I thought.

Our new companions were passing on the way to the upper decks, and we turned to lean on the rail, looking out.

He said, "It's just as well you couldn't go out with me tonight. Ian called a dinner meeting of the upper echelon."

I told him that Finn was otherwise engaged, and I was going out with a group. "Paul and Liz, the two Swiss guys, and I think that American girl, Marcia."

If he wondered why he hadn't been included, he didn't say. "See what you can find out about Hans and Marcia, then."

"Hans?" I said, remembering how I'd interrupted his delighted wonder over the globe. "And not Josef?"

"Okay, Josef, too. Paul and Liz, while you're at it."

I gave a little tut and shook my head. Bill said, "Look. You know how there will be two locals working with us? I've had a tip from one of them that the *other* local is a person of interest. And that he probably has an accomplice among the researchers."

Person of interest, an accomplice. It was all very cloak and dagger

I probably had that look again, because Bill said, "I suppose you don't believe me; no one does. Just humor me."

FIVE

Not a Hot Flash

Within the penguin family, each species has its own repertoire of displays and calls to achieve this [bond] and to bring the birds into synchrony.

—Wayne Lynch,
PENGUINS OF THE WORLD

As I walked through town in the bright evening sun with my little band of dinner partners, my head was so full of my exasperation with Finn that I barely noticed my surroundings. How would I ever be able to work with someone like that? By being prepared, that's how. And that meant for one thing getting the darn book read. I should be doing that right now, I shouldn't be here, I thought. My latest list was in the purse slung over my shoulder, a feeble beacon struggling to keep me focused.

As we stood in front of Government House, looking up the long drive bordered by hedges of yellow gorse shuddering in the wind, I made an effort to remind myself that this was my last night in Stanley for a long while and I should quit clouding my head with thoughts of Finn. So I turned my attention to Paul, who was reading aloud from his guidebook that until 1982, the tradition was for all visitors to the Falklands to drop in at Government House and sign the register. Then came the attack by Argentina, Britain's response, and the four-month war, and Stanley was catapulted into the twentieth century.

We turned away from the harbor and walked uphill two blocks before turning back toward the center of town, killing the ten minutes until our reservation. As we passed Kay's Guesthouse, I felt I already had a history there. What must it be like, I mused, to live in such a small community, out in the middle of the ocean, three hundred miles from the Argentine coast and more than a thousand miles from any big city, constantly buffeted by wind?

I fell into step between Josef and Paul, and Josef entertained us with amusing tales of his travels. Twice he came to an abrupt stop, fished under layers of clothing into a breast pocket to produce a small notebook and pen, and wrote down an expression Paul or I had uttered. Liz, Hans, and Marcia were walking ahead, Hans in the middle. I watched him idly and noticed that he paid as much attention to the older married Liz as he did to Marcia with her bouncing ponytail.

The Falklands Brasserie, in the opinion of Paul's book, was Stanley's finest restaurant. A server in black pants and white shirt swooped glasses of water onto the table and described the specials. We were seated three on a side of a rectangular table, with me next to Paul and across from Hans. Bill had told me to keep an eye on Hans, and I found this an easy—okay, *pleasant*—duty.

Complexion rosy, eyes robin's egg blue, clothing casual, even a bit frumpy, I noted, taking in that well-worn blue sweater. Probably knit by his mother. Charming. Age, midthirties, no wedding ring.

Next to Hans sat Marcia. Her shiny black hair, at some point having come out of its ponytail, swished around her shoulders. After making a mental note of the dark eyes and smooth olive skin, her age (mid- to late twenties?), and no wedding ring, I observed that she was taking every opportunity to snare Hans into private conversation, lowering her voice and turning from the rest of us. Hans, I saw with amusement, kept bringing the conversation back to the group by leaning forward to toss a comment to Josef, seated on Marcia's other side, or by asking me a question. Here was a man clearly pulling back from a woman's advances. This wasn't exactly what Bill wanted me to be watching for, I supposed, but it was something.

Over salads, we talked about what everyone did back home. Paul and Liz were newly retired, he an electrician and she a nurse, as I already knew. Josef had worked as a contractor, retiring only four years earlier at the age of seventy-five. Marcia had been in school most of her life, just now completing her PhD. Hans worked in his family's chocolate shop in Zurich. I told them about my soon-to-be-completed master's and how I was industriously seeking a job.

"Conservation biology was my master's, too," Marcia said, and looking at me, added, "It's a competitive field. You're going to need a lot of luck."

"Thank you," I said, choosing to treat the comment as friendly. "If I don't find a job soon, I can always go back to teaching high school Spanish. But I'd rather be stuck on an ice floe with a dozen hungry skuas."

Marcia's smile was thin, while everyone else laughed. Liz said, "Well, I for one admire you for making a big change later in life like that. You'll find a job." And they all toasted me and wished me good luck.

"I'm looking for a job, too," Marcia said. So we toasted her as well.

I left the restaurant fully intending to go back to the ship to finish *Skua*. We stood on the sidewalk, full of sea bass and wine and crème caramel, watching red and green lights and foil Christmas trees bob vigorously on lines hung across the street. It made a surreal picture in the low sunlight.

"Must be the big city lights Ian was talking about," said Paul.

We laughed as we turned toward the boat.

Hans stopped walking. "It's too early to go back."

Marcia stopped, too, and said, "Let's hit the Globe!" This was a favorite local watering hole.

Liz, Paul, and Josef said they were turning in early. Citing my vow to get back to my reading, I moved to join them. But Hans touched my elbow.

"Come with us," he said. "Just for a little time."

Josef chimed in, "You're not going to read, Joanie. Go. We old folks will be fine."

It was true. I would have all morning to read now that I wouldn't be meeting Finn until later. And when else would I have a chance to see the inside of a Stanley pub? Besides, Hans seemed in need of rescuing. So, resisting the urge to reach in my purse and revise my list, I joined the young people.

The Globe was alive with music and forty-some people shouting to be heard over the others. A crowded dance floor pulsed at the center of the room, and all tables were taken. Our little group stood for a moment until Marcia tugged Hans toward the dance floor.

He resisted, leaned toward me, and said, "Do you mind?"

"Not at all," I said. Which wasn't really true. As soon as I was left alone, I was swept back to my high school gym, hoping and fearing that someone would ask me to dance. Not seconds went by, however, before a tall man with a string tie approached, gave an exaggerated bow, and held out his hand. I followed him into the crowd.

Talking was impossible, but my partner and I smiled whenever our eyes met, which wasn't often, as he seemed to know everyone in the room and carried on shouted conversations with half of them. Whenever I caught a glimpse of Hans and Marcia, she was smiling up at him and dancing close. He was around six feet tall, and Marcia came barely to his shoulder. It was clear it was *her* dancing close to *him* and not mutual, I noted.

I spotted a free table when the song ended, thanked my partner, and excused myself. I waved Hans and Marcia over, and Hans went off to get drinks. Marcia and I exchanged a couple of polite comments and sat looking around at the crowd. By the time Hans returned with a beer for Marcia, tea for me, and Diet Coke for himself, the music had started again, and a young man with ears like sails had taken Marcia away to dance.

"You don't drink?" I had to lean close to ask. He had drunk his own bottle of sparkling water at dinner while the rest of us had gone through two bottles of wine.

He shook his head, smiling. Talking was nearly impossible, so we gave up and sat watching the dancing and the servers with trays held high weaving their way through the throng. When the song ended, Marcia came back to the table, her partner following.

"Come on, Hans. Let's dance." She was breathless, ignoring the young man who was standing behind her, shifting his weight from one foot to another.

"Joanie and I are just going to dance," Hans said, getting up. "And here's your beer."

He ushered me to the dance floor with a light hand in my mid back, and once we were surrounded by the crowd, he turned. "Sorry, I didn't ask. Will you dance with me?"

"Delighted," I said.

And I was. A song started, an odd sort of country-western-reggae cross with a beat that stirred my feet. The crowd had thinned, and Hans took my hands and began leading me in steps and twirls I didn't think I knew how to do. I'd looked longingly at swing dancing in the past, but neither my husband, Warren, nor my longtime boyfriend, Max, were much into dancing, so I never tried it.

The next minutes were a laughing, breathless series of twirls; one hand in his, then two, then one again. He was in control, relaxed, smiling. I could *do* it. When the song ended, I asked him where he learned to dance like that, and he said only "Wyoming" before the music started up. After three more dances, we took a break, and he led me through the crowd by the hand.

Back at the table a little drama was in progress; Marcia was standing by her chair with her coat on, and a man with red hair and a brown parka was leaning toward her, grinning and pointing a finger. "No, I know you . . ." With each nod he thrust his finger. "It was a long time ago . . ."

Marcia fumbled with her zipper, ignoring him, and said to us, "Ready?" She picked up her beer and drained it.

I *wasn't* ready. Not at all. But what could we do but follow Marcia? As we moved away, coats in hand, the man took a few steps in our direction, and Marcia turned. "You *don't* know me. I've never been here in my life."

Outside, she said, "Creep. That's the oldest pickup line." Stepping off the curb, she stumbled, and Hans put out a hand to steady her. She clung to his arm all the way back to the ship.

All was quiet on board. Hans and I had to shush Marcia as we made our way up the narrow metal steps. On my deck, we stopped, Marcia swaying into Hans. They said good night, and I watched him lead her up the stairs to Deck Five.

As I brushed my teeth, I felt a little unsettled that I hadn't properly thanked Hans for the dancing. Just that. Not that I cared what was going on upstairs.

"Why should I care what a couple of kids are up to?" I asked Pru.

The penguin shrugged, noncommittal.

I studied my face in the mirror, checked the wavy brown hair for any new gray invaders. Still only a sprinkling.

While I was rinsing my toothbrush, there was a knock at the door. I opened it to Hans, standing there, hands behind his back. His blond curls caught the last of the fading light.

"I just want you to know," he said, "I got her safe to her cabin."

"Oh!" I grinned, ridiculously happy. "And *you're* safe, too."

He laughed. "Yes. I'm safe." He stepped back, gave a little bow, and said good night.

I closed the door and leaned on it, noticing that my cheeks felt warm. I knew hot flashes pretty well by then, and this wasn't one of them.

SIX

Let's Pretend

Penguins have adapted to the widest range of climates of any species on earth. The differences in the species at the extremes of the climactic range, the Galápagos penguins in the north and the emperors in the south, show how natural selection has enabled penguins to adapt physiologically and behaviourally to a vast range of climates.

—*Jonathan Chester,*
THE NATURE OF PENGUINS

I AWOKE FEELING SO rested, the sun cutting so boldly through the one tiny window into my cabin, that I was sure I'd slept late. A look at my watch told me it wasn't yet five o'clock. At this rate, getting up for my early meeting tomorrow with Finn would be a piece of cake. I tossed back the covers and piled on enough clothes to conquer the chill. As eager as I was to get out for one last visit to town and to get the shampoo I'd forgotten the day before, I was determined to finish *Skua* before doing anything else. Thanks to last night's diversions, I still had thirty-two pages to go. I would just run downstairs and grab a cup of coffee, come back, and lock myself in my cabin, and not come out until I was done.

Sitting in the dining room at a table by the window, coffees before them and chatting away as if they'd been up for hours, were Paul, Liz, and Hans. One other table was occupied by two women: Pepa the cook and another crew member, heads together in a quiet conversation. I got a cup of coffee, put a piece of bread in the toaster, and crossed the room for a brief greeting to my friends. Just until the toast was done.

As I slid onto a seat next to Liz, Hans turned a sheet of paper so I could see it. "We are supposed to make groups of three or four to help with dinner or cleanup three nights a week. Want to join our group?"

"Sure," I said, setting down my coffee. "Maybe we should mix it up a bit more, but what the heck, I like you guys."

"I like you guys, too. Especially you, honey," Liz said, patting her husband's hand, "but maybe you and I ought to split up."

Paul pouted and said it was fine; he'd start his own group.

Liz looked at me and Hans. "Maybe Marcia could join our group."

"Let's get a new person," Hans said, glancing at the door as if she'd come through at any moment.

But it was Doctor Javier who came into the dining room, his long brown hair mussed, eyes puffy. He sat down with a coffee, and after listening silently as we invited him to be a member of our group, grunted his agreement. We wrote our names on the chart. Hans, Liz, Javier, and I would help with dinner prep on Sundays and Fridays, and cleanup on Tuesdays. We would start that evening.

The conversation moved on to plans for the morning. Liz and Paul were going to find a church and see about attending a service.

Hans was going to walk the two miles down the harbor to see the shipwrecks, and he invited Javier and me to join him. This had been on my original list of things to do in Stanley—I had a separate list for fun things—and I figured I could fit a quick trip in after my reading was done, so I agreed. Javier declined, saying he needed to pick up some last-minute medical supplies.

Which was how I ended up spending the morning with Hans.

Paul and Liz stood up, pulled on coats and gloves, and Javier went to refill his cup. Hans drained the last of his coffee and looked at me. "Ready?"

Going out into the sunny morning with this big cheerful man was a lot more enticing than being holed up with that book, which wasn't exactly coming to an exciting conclusion, but I was determined to stick to my plan. "I've got to finish my reading. Can I meet you at eight o'clock?"

"Seven thirty, okay? We can meet at the Brasserie. They have triple cappuccinos. And pastries." He wiggled his eyebrows seductively.

I laughed and agreed to meet him at seven thirty. What was half an hour? I'd read fast, maybe skim some parts. I picked up my coffee and went to top it off, only then noticing my toast, gone cold in the toaster.

I arrived at the Brasserie windblown and breathless and a bit miffed at myself for not staying to finish reading the last seven pages. But I had this thing about being on time, which trumped my adherence to lists and plans.

Hans was sitting in the middle of a sofa in the little lobby, elbows on his knees, hands clasped, as if in worship of the white porcelain cup in a saucer that sat on the low table before him, an untouched swirl of tan in the white foam. As if he *knew* I'd be right on time.

As I slipped out of my coat, he said, "Help me with these," indicating a plate with two croissants and a cinnamon roll.

The server appeared, and I ordered a double decaf cappuccino and sat down across from Hans. The wind had left his hair mussed and skin flushed, and he had a look on his face as if something exciting might happen at any moment.

Which made me feel slightly breathless, like *I* was about to be exciting. I reached for a croissant and nodded toward his cappuccino. "Your first?"

"Yes. I just arrived. I was up on the hill sitting on a bench, looking at the town."

"What did you see?"

The server placed my coffee before me, and we took our first sips. "A couple of Land Rovers, one Volkswagen. A man with a briefcase and . . . what do you call it? Pants, but . . ." He indicated pants coming up over his chest.

"Overalls?"

"Yes, overalls." He cut the cinnamon roll and put half on my plate. "A fishing boat was leaving the harbor. And two dolphins swimming around the *Professor*." Hans, as far as I knew, was the first to call the ship "the *Professor*," short for *Professor Zjukovski*. It was something we'd all be doing by the end of the day. He bit into his half of cinnamon roll and licked his fingers. "And I had a conversation with a cat."

I smiled as I picked an end off my croissant.

"What?" he said.

"Oh . . ." Had I been staring? "It's just . . . you seem to enjoy the moment."

He laughed. "Ah. Yes. Well, why not?"

"Why not indeed."

"Did you finish your reading?" he asked.

"Not quite. I need to get back to the boat before ten thirty to finish it." I glanced at my watch as if ten thirty were imminent; it was 7:43.

"What's all this reading?" A teasing smile. "Why is it so important?"

I bristled; I'm aware my strict adherence to my plans, my lists, might make me seem a bit obsessive. Something must have shown on my face, because he said, "No, I really want to know."

Not ready for the question, I looked out the window, then back. "It's all about my project, the project I'll be doing here . . . And it's about the whole rest of my life, really . . . getting a good job. Getting the reading done is all tied to my master's thesis, to my project. And the project is tied to getting a good job."

He watched me, sipping his coffee.

I went on. "Going back to school in sciences . . . it was so far removed from anything I studied before . . . It's been a challenge. I guess I'm nervous about doing well."

He nodded.

"So, I need to finish the reading and get ready to talk intelligently about my project this afternoon."

"What *is* your project?"

"Does the presence of human visitors at gentoo colonies improve the success of skuas." I rattled it off as I'd done dozens of times.

"Huh. Interesting." He popped the last bite of croissant in his mouth. "Do you think it does?"

"I think it has to. This book I'm reading concludes there wasn't enough impact to worry about. But the study was done in Antarctica and way before the boom in tourism. When they had fewer than twenty visitors a day. Now it's probably over five hundred a day at some sites. You know, you were there."

"I saw many skua attacks," he said. "I was on a small ship, only forty-nine passengers. So our landing parties were not so big. But." He shook his head. "Of course it would have an impact."

I nodded. "So. That's why the reading's important. Maybe I sounded casual about all this last night, but really, it's everything to me. I gave up my old life to go after this one thing I've always wanted . . ."

"And what you've always wanted is . . ."

I shrugged. "To work in conservation. To help animals survive on this human-dominated earth." I'd gotten passionate, gone overboard, maybe. But Hans was nodding.

We stopped on our way back from the shipwrecks at a picnic table to eat the yogurt and bananas we'd picked up to round out our breakfast. A tidy lawn sloped toward the breakwater, and tufts of grass along the edge wiggled in the breeze. The water in the harbor was gray-green and choppy.

We'd admired and photographed the shipwrecks. In the nine-teenth century ships that couldn't make it around Cape Horn limped back to Port Stanley, many to finish their days here. Hans knew their history from a book he'd been reading and had given me the story on each one. He was a great storyteller, talking about Antarctica, where he saw thousands of Adélie penguins, and how—according to the ship's naturalist—more gentoos were arriving, and the ice-loving Adélies were moving out, heading further south as the ice receded. The very thing I had described in a term paper, Hans had seen in action.

As we ate yogurt with plastic spoons, side by side on the bench, facing the water, our backs against the table, I told him more about my project. He was a good listener as well as a good talker, asking questions, listening to the answers. I'd been half hoping this crush I seemed to be developing would fizzle as I got to know him better. But so far, I wasn't having any luck.

The conversation moved to the night before and Marcia. I said it seemed he had himself an admirer.

"I'm not interested in her."

"Someone at home?" I asked.

He shook his head and moved on to discuss other people on the boat: Finn's questioning of Ian about past counts, Ian's response, Helen, Bill. I found myself telling Hans about the three days on Bleaker Island with Bill and how he'd begun making plans for everything we would do together over the next six weeks. How I'd accepted his offer to put in a word for me on the telephone interview, how now I felt tangled up in that.

"It's a bit of a delicate situation," I said. "A reference from Bill Deering is golden. And it *is* a competitive field . . ."

"But he barely knows you."

"Right. I mean, we did spend a lot of time together on Bleaker. But he hasn't seen me work yet."

"You just have to wait until he does. Then you can feel okay to ask him for a reference. With no strings."

"I hope so." I looked out at the harbor. "But I'm in the thick of my job hunt . . . I could really use Bill Deering on my side right now."

"Well," said Hans, "then I guess you have to be a little more friendly to him." Exactly what Liz had said.

"It's not nice to use someone that way. I can find a job based on my own merits." I could hear that I sounded prim.

"Mm . . . ," Hans said. "But it's only for six weeks. You have your little affair, then you go away to your job somewhere and . . . Adios." He was grinning.

"Oh, now you're teasing me!" I said. "Trying to see if I'll sell my soul to the devil."

He grinned, elbows on knees, hands clasped, head turned toward me.

I shook my head. "Bill's earnest. I'm pretty sure he's looking for a life mate."

"And you don't want a life mate?"

"I already had one." Two, I thought, if you counted Max, the boyfriend I'd had for seven years before going back to school. "I do better without." I steered the talk back to Hans and Marcia. "So what's wrong with Marcia? She's pretty cute. And seems quite interested in you."

His jaw set. "She's not nice."

It was perhaps an early judgment, but I had to agree with him; Marcia had been skeptical about my chances for getting a job in my new field and rude to her dance partner. And the red-haired guy in the pub. I'd seen nothing that seemed very nice yet.

Hans turned on the bench to face me, his face alive again, his mouth slightly open. "I have an idea. You and I hang out together for a few days . . . we pretend to be a couple until Bill and Marcia give up."

"Hah! They'd never buy it. I mean, the age difference and all . . ."

"Pah! Age difference! What are we—ten years different?"

It was time to set him straight. "I'm fifty-one, and I doubt that you're . . ."

"No!" he said, pulling back to look me up and down. "I thought you were maybe . . . forty, forty-two."

"That's very sweet of you." If I'd thought that revealing my age would turn this flirtatious conversation in a more businesslike direction, it wasn't working.

"No, really," he said. "Guess how old I am."

I turned my palm up and squinted. "Thirty . . . something."

"Thirty-three."

"See. No one would believe we're a couple."

I turned to watch a cormorant land on a weathered piling. The bird spread its wings to dry and stood posing, black feathers ruffling in the wind. Hans pulled his camera out of his pocket and took a picture.

Still looking at the cormorant, he said, "They will believe it. I look older than I am, you look younger . . ." He looked at me again. "Anyway, who cares what people think?"

"Well, yes, but the idea would be to make people—certain people—believe we *are* a couple."

He grinned, shrugged. "I think we could convince them, easily." A gust of wind lifted a curl of hair from the side of his head so it stood straight up. I resisted the urge to smooth it down.

Past Hans I spotted three of our shipmates walking along the sidewalk toward us. "Speaking of a six-week fling, here comes Marcia."

"Ah," he said, not taking his eyes from mine. "Think about it. It will help me, too."

The three—Marcia; the French scientist, Yvonne; and Ian's wife, Caroline—had spotted us. I waved.

"There you are!" Marcia said, as they got near. "I thought I'd see you at breakfast, but Liz said you'd already gone." It was clear the "you" was Hans. "Want to go see the shipwrecks with us?"

"Oh," I said, "We're just coming from there."

"We are waiting for the visitor center to open," Hans added. He apparently didn't wear a watch and had noticed that I did. He pushed my sleeve back with his finger, brushing my skin with the lightest touch.

"It's time." He stood, picking up the banana peels and yogurt containers and stuffing them in the bag. He crooked his elbow toward me and said, "Shall we?"

I took his arm—what else could I do?—and amid a chorus of "See you at the meeting," we turned to stroll down the sidewalk.

As we moved out of earshot, I, still feeling his touch on my wrist, said, "Well. Maybe that was enough for her to get the picture."

"I don't think she'll give up so easy," Hans said, glancing over his shoulder. Almost to himself, he said, "She doesn't know me."

Hmm. Sexist me. I've always thought guys more or less lost their heads when a woman that looks like Marcia showed an interest in them. But this was pretty much the way I was feeling about Bill: he didn't know me; he didn't care who I really was.

We arrived at the visitor center door, and I said, "At least Bill has known me about ten times as long as Marcia's known you."

"Yes."

Suddenly aware that I was still holding Hans's arm, I removed my hand and stepped back. "I need to get back to the ship. Thank you for a wonderful morning. See you at lunch."

SEVEN

Just Friends

Not everyone agrees that there are 17 kinds of penguins. As in all branches of biology, there are "lumpers" and "splitters"—those who tend to ignore differences and those who tend to emphasize them.

—*Wayne Lynch,*
PENGUINS OF THE WORLD

"THERE YOU ARE." Bill had found me at the rail outside my cabin. The *Professor* was pulling away from the pier, only half an hour behind schedule. The white houses of Stanley slid away, bright even in the rain. The boat gave two blasts; a woman and a child walking hand in hand along the breakwater waved. I waved back.

"This is an exciting moment, isn't it?" I said. "Our little home, our little community setting off for six weeks on its own."

Bill agreed, but he had something on his mind. "Where have you been keeping yourself?"

"Oh, reading, out on the town, more reading. I finished, in fact." The final seven pages had taken almost an hour, what with images of Hans, his hair in the sunlight, the way he made me laugh. The touch of his finger on my skin. But I'd gotten ahold of myself and soldiered through. If this was any indication of the effect he was going to have on me, it was best not to follow up on his idea of the pretend relationship.

"Congratulations," Bill said, and then, "It almost seems you've been avoiding me. I expected you would find me and give me your report."

"My report?"

"What you observed about your dinner companions last night."

"Oh, right. Well, I didn't observe much, really. Marcia seems to be coming on to Hans, but he's not into it. She doesn't seem to be a very . . . warm and fuzzy sort of person. Josef's a really charming and funny man."

"Yes, I saw Josef come in last night. He said you'd gone dancing."

Ah. Was Bill jealous? It was time to set him straight. I dove in. "Look, Bill. I *have* been kind of avoiding you. Recently, well . . . I've been feeling a bit pressured . . . Like maybe you were interested in more than a professional relationship."

"Uh. . . ," he grunted. "That's me." He leaned on the rail next to me, looking down at the frothing water. "I don't know how to behave around a woman I like, so I act like an idiot."

What do you say to something like that? I couldn't help warming to him a bit.

"So, can we start over?" he said, glancing at me.

"Sure. But I really see us being just friends."

"Fine," he said, straightening up. "Just friends."

"Great." I smiled.

He nodded. "Listen, are you free for lunch? With others. You can meet Audrey Sanderson, one of the locals who'll be joining us. Also that Australian woman, Helen; she'll be there. There's room for one more at our table."

"Sounds nice. I'd be happy to."

This was going to be fine, I thought. Bill had the picture, and I hadn't alienated him. That crazy idea of a pretend relationship with Hans was probably not only a bad idea, but unnecessary. At least for me, anyway.

Pepa passed full plates out through the wide window that opened from the galley. People were filing past, picking them up and finding a place at one of the six tables that were bolted to the floor. As Bill and I made our way to where Helen and another woman were seated at a table in the corner, Hans came into the room and caught my eye. An amused smile on his face, he raised his eyebrows. I gave a little shrug.

The room buzzed with conversation and clanking silverware. The tables were far enough apart to allow for more or less private conversations. We exchanged the usual getting-to-know-you information. Audrey was a woman about my age wearing well-worn brown overalls over a faded pink sweatshirt. She apologized for her attire, and said they'd been separating the lambs from their mothers that morning, and before she knew it, the plane had arrived to take her to Stanley. She and her husband owned an island that had over a thousand sheep as well as a lodge with its own restaurant.

Helen, looking chic with her straight gray spiky hair and a turquoise necklace on her tan neck, asked Audrey a few questions about her lodge, then said, "What do you think about the increasing numbers of tourists and the effect on wildlife, Audrey?"

"Well, no one here thinks that tourism has had much of an impact. Maybe you'll notice something different this year."

"Tourism has increased a lot in the last five years, hasn't it?" I said, eager to hear a local's take on the topic that was so close to my project.

Audrey shrugged. "That's true. Now cruise ships stop. But it looks like penguin and other bird populations haven't decreased all that much."

"Still, there needs to be a better program to remind tourists how to behave around wildlife," Bill said.

Helen sat forward. "Yes! When I was here six years ago, there was nothing like that. No one said anything. I may have seen one poster somewhere telling us how close we could stand, and somewhere else there was a fence we were told not to cross . . ."

"And at Volunteer Beach there's a line of white stones," Bill added.

"One gets so caught up in the excitement of being with penguins," Helen went on. "And they seem so unafraid. But later I realized I may have done things that scared them."

"Such as?" I said.

"One time I was standing at the top of a small cliff with my husband. The waves were smashing down below, the sea just churning. Rockhoppers were in the water trying to land on a ledge. We watched, mesmerized. They weren't landing! Poor things, I thought, the sea is too rough. They'll be smashed against the rocks. Finally it occurred to me—they weren't landing not because they couldn't, but because they were afraid of us! So we moved back out of sight for a few minutes. When we finally took a peek, they were already hopping up to their rookery."

Audrey said, "I imagine that was somewhere that tourists don't often visit?"

"Yes. We'd walked for hours to get there. We didn't see another soul all day."

Audrey nodded. "In areas with more tourist traffic, they become accustomed to people and just go about their lives." She looked up and to my right with a little frown.

I turned to see a large man with a prominent belly standing by my chair, a hand resting on its back, smiling broadly at the group. "Brainwashing our overseas visitors again, are we?"

"Hello, Bernard." Audrey's smile didn't match his beaming. "Bernard McConaghy is a local businessman. He'll be joining us on the count at times." She introduced us, and he shook hands warmly with everyone. Audrey said, "Bernard and I don't always see eye to eye."

He let out a booming laugh. "Do we ever? But that's part of the fun."

Helen invited him to pull up a chair, but he was headed for Ian's table. "I look forward to getting to know each of you soon, however."

Audrey watched him walk away, shaking her head. "He supports oil exploration and unrestricted fishing. Tourism only gets in the way of his interests. And he'll do just about anything to prove tourists are bad for the environment."

This sounded like the kind of comment I'd be passing along to Bill if he weren't sitting right there, watching Audrey and nodding as if he already knew. So. Clearly, Audrey was Bill's informant, and Bernard the person of interest. Maybe there really *was* an accomplice on board.

I stepped out of the dining room to stand at the rail and watch the shore go by while I waited for Finn and our after-lunch meeting. I paced into the dining room and out again several times, looking at my watch. By the time he arrived, ten minutes late and whistling, I was in a snit.

"Look," I said as we passed into the now-empty dining room. "I know you're not too thrilled about sharing your project—I'm not either. But that's the way it has to be. We're going to need to work together."

He looked surprised as he set his pile of notebooks, papers sticking out in every direction, onto a table and sat down. "It's not that. I'm fine working with you. I've just been occupied. And getting hung up yesterday afternoon sort of put my plans back."

He looked so contrite that I was disarmed and, not being fond of conflict anyway, said, "What did happen yesterday afternoon?"

He hesitated, then grinned. Leaning across the table, he said in a low voice, "The sniffer dogs got excited about my luggage. So they took me into this little room and shut the door, just me and this one man and one woman, in uniforms. They were very nice, very British. Went through everything, brought the dogs back in. Turns out it was this little film canister I used to have some bud in . . . I mean like a long time ago, back in the States. Funny, huh? How many airports have I been through with that canister? And they catch it here."

I couldn't help being amused, mostly at Finn's telling of it; he hadn't even noticed, or didn't care, that I was probably his mom's age and might not approve of "bud." Or even know what it was.

"And in this container," he went on, "there was this white powder. They didn't believe me when I said it was baking soda. They sent it out to be analyzed or something. It took, like, all afternoon to come back. Which gave them time to ask about every other little thing I had in my pack."

"Why would you have baking soda?"

"For brushing my teeth . . . I know. They gave me the same look." He shrugged. "I got here as soon as I could."

I didn't bother asking why he was late now, and we got down to work. Finn was surprisingly adept at finding things in his chaotic pile of papers. In a little over half an hour we were ready for our presentation, which was mainly a matter of agreeing on the basic plan and deciding who'd talk about what aspect of the project.

"See?" he said as we got up. "Piece of cake."

As I was about to enter my cabin to spend the next half hour polishing my part of the presentation, Liz caught up with me. "I emailed a friend of ours," she said. "He's with the Forest Service, the headquarters in Boise. Paul and I were talking about you and your job search . . ." She paused while we greeted Josef and Helen, who were descending the stairs from Five. Josef gave us a wink as he ushered Helen ahead of him. Liz, apparently with a highly developed romance detector, said, "*My!* They make a handsome couple!" She turned back to me. "Paul remembered they were expanding their conservation program or something. So I wrote and told him about you."

What was it about Liz? Her advice about Bill and now trying to help find me a job. There was something needy about her eagerness. I reminded myself she meant well, and thanked her. We turned to watch our arrival and mooring in a semi-protected cove at Volunteer Point, a long, low peninsula. Once the *Professor* was secured, Liz hurried off, and I stood for a moment at the rail, letting the salt air clear my head as I looked across the racing whitecaps to the flat green peninsula where I would start collecting data on gentoos and skuas in the morning. Volunteer Point, where we'd spend the next five days, was accessible from Stanley via a two-and-a-half-hour overland trek by Range Rover, and therefore had some of the most heavily visited penguin colonies in all the Falklands.

What a relief it would be to focus on my work. Life had gotten jumbled in the last few days. What the heck was going on? For the almost four years in school I'd not had one unwanted suitor and not one crush. And now? Was it something about being in the Southern Hemisphere? I'd heard that water swirled down the drain in the opposite direction here. Maybe it was turning my ordinary life upside down as well?

I took a breath and reminded myself of all the ways things were ironing themselves out.

Finn. I was feeling a bit more optimistic about working with him since our meeting. Sure, we were staying barely one step ahead of things, but he was good-natured and enthusiastic, and I felt he, too, was ready to focus on our work, now that we were out of Stanley and away from those friends.

And Bill. I'd told him how I felt about him and he seemed to have accepted it. We were moving ahead into a friendly, professional relationship. And I didn't think I'd killed my chances of getting a good recommendation from him, either.

Then there was Hans. The pretend couple thing had been part of his teasing, surely. We needed to get that clear. He would be a friend, someone to go on shore explorations with, to have the occasional chat. A pleasant presence on the ship. I needed to be sure it stayed just that.

I thought, too, about the funny business with the penguin counts of years past that Bill had brought up on Friday night. And how I'd dismissed it. But since then, there'd been Finn's questions at the meeting and my sense that Ian didn't want to talk about it, plus Audrey's comments at lunch about Bernard. It wouldn't hurt to take all that a little more seriously.

I entered my cabin and sat down on the bed to make a list:

> *talk to Hans about couple thing*
> *check Boise F.S. website*
> *go over notes*

I spent the next twenty minutes on the last item, crossed it off, and headed downstairs to the meeting.

Ian began by giving an overview of the coming six weeks. At Volunteer Point we would count colonies of kings, gentoos, and Magellanics. I would be involved in this work as well as my own, so did my best to focus on his speech. In a pedantic, lecturing style that left little room for participation, he talked in great detail about how the data would be gathered. Before long, people were fidgeting and slumping in the hard dining room chairs. It didn't help my concentration, either, that I was nervous about my upcoming talk. Though I'd spent almost twenty-five years in front of a high school Spanish class, this was different. It carried all the weight of my first presentation of myself as a scientist.

No further mention was made of the count of five years earlier, or last year's local count, and Finn didn't bring it up. He was sitting next to Audrey at the table to my right, and more than once I observed them exchanging quiet comments.

When it was Finn's and my turn, we began with a little skit, getting Yoshi to play a gentoo sitting next to its chick (played by Pru) and Michiyo a nearby skua. When Yoshi was distracted by the approach of tourists Bill, Ian, and Yvonne, Michiyo jumped in and snatched Pru. Which caused laughter followed by close attention to the rest of our talk. I was swept up by my enthusiasm and even enjoyed myself. Finn came through as well, giving an informative and lively summary of previous related studies.

The other student projects were fascinating, too. Marcia was studying the impact of cruise ship visits to penguin colonies, and Alejandro, the young Chilean, was looking at the foraging strategies of the black-browed albatross and their conflicts with human fishing activities.

We spilled out of the meeting at five o'clock sharp, as noisy as a classroom of kids released after the first day of school. Hans appeared at my side. It was the first time we'd talked since our morning together.

"Joanie." He bent close so only I could hear. "Are we going steady or not?"

Where had he picked up that expression? My face felt warm; something about him standing close, his voice low, just for me. Even if he was teasing. But I got ahold of myself and remembered item one on my list.

"I don't think we need to do that . . ." We moved away from the crowd to the stern of the ship, and stood looking out across the choppy gray water, the waves turning to lines of white froth as they found the beach.

"Left me for Bill already, have you?" He was looking down at me, his face lit with mischief.

"He and I talked," I said, determined to be serious. "He knows how I feel. We've agreed to just be friends."

"Well, maybe you have him under control, but I still need help with Marcia."

"Just tell her you're not interested. Be firm."

"She's very persistent." Hans glanced over his shoulder and lowered his voice even more. "She wants to come to my room after we get back from the shore this evening."

How worried he looked! Would it hurt to help the guy out, just this evening? "All right," I said. "What do you want me to do?"

"Just hang out in my cabin for a while." He tilted his head, looking at me. "It won't be so bad."

"I didn't think it would be bad; I enjoy your company." I was doing my best to sound like the mature woman I was, talking to her young friend. "It's just . . ." What exactly? "I'm worried about *you*," is what I came up with. "If you hang out with me too much, you may be shutting the door on all the other women on the ship." It sounded lame. There weren't that many women on the ship for one thing, and very few you'd call eligible.

He shook his head. "I'm not here for romance. Just like you. I'm here to count penguins."

"All right." What was the harm?

"Thanks," he said. "Bring your skua book if you want."

"I finished it before lunch."

"Congratulations."

"Thank you. What should we be doing when Marcia comes looking for you?"

He considered a moment. "Sitting next to each other on the couch will be good."

I was getting into the spirit. "And the door will be shut and we can wait a few seconds before we tell her to come in."

"Perfect," he said.

The wind began to fling icy rain pellets against our faces, and the beach grew dim in the mist. After a last look, we went back inside to meet Liz and Javier in the galley for our first night of dinner duties.

EIGHT

Probably a Gentoo

I have often had the impression that to penguins, man is just another penguin—different, less predictable, occasionally violent, but tolerable company when he sits still and minds his own business.

—Bernard Stonehouse,
as quoted by Wayne Lynch in
PENGUINS OF THE WORLD

AFTER DINNER, EVERYONE clustered on the main deck in the steady push of wind, a mass of rattling windbreakers lit by a burst of sun. For those who had arrived the previous day, this evening would be their first chance to see penguins in the wild, and the air was abuzz with anticipation. The crew lowered the Zodiacs, with their hard hulls, inflatable sides, and outboard motors, into the choppy water, got us all into life jackets, and gave a quick lesson on boarding. We piled in, six in the small boat and twelve in the large, each with a driver. A quick zip across the chop, and the rafts ran up on the beach. We jumped, laughing, onto the sand.

Five species of penguins breed in the Falkland Islands, and all but rockhoppers and macaronis are found at Volunteer Point. Ian gave a brief introduction to the appearance and habits of each species as the group huddled around in the biting wind. He pointed up the beach, down the beach, and across the peninsula to where kings, Magellanics, and gentoos could be seen, encouraging us to familiarize ourselves with each species of penguin. We were reminded to stay in small groups and get no closer to the colonies than five meters. We would gather to return to the ship at nine forty-five.

I walked along the hard sand, part of a loose group, toward the kings, the one penguin I hadn't yet seen. The sun was still high in the west, peeking out between heavy dark clouds. I was walking next to Liz. Waves broke with a rhythmic swish, punctuating our few comments. Magellanics emerged from the surf, gave our little group a glance, and trotted toward their burrows in the flat grass at the edge of the beach.

Marcia had attached herself to Hans, and when they stopped to photograph the Magellanics, Liz and I kept walking. Not far ahead was the first group of kings, standing on the beach. They were beautiful, stately, regal. The second-largest penguin in the world, they hold their eggs between their feet and make do without nests, just like the emperors of Antarctica. They were doing this now.

"I don't see any chicks," Liz said. "Do you?"

I trained my binoculars on them and scanned the crowd to see if I was missing some little tuft of brown feathers peeking out from under a parent. I shook my head. "Just eggs. We may be seeing chicks any day."

We sat down on the sand facing the colony. Liz zipped her rain jacket up to her chin. Still watching the penguins, she said, "You and Hans seem to be hitting it off."

"He's great company," I said, so captivated by the kings that I didn't catch any undertones.

After a moment, Liz said, "You don't want to . . . well, it's none of my business, but now is a time when we should all be getting to know everyone, don't you think?"

I lowered my binoculars. "What do you mean?"

"Well . . . and Bill, and your job search . . ."

This was too much. "Oh, for heaven's sake, Liz. 'Be nicer to Bill. Don't spend so much time with Hans. Oh, and let me help you find a job.' Really, I think I can take care of myself."

Liz looked away, and I was immediately sorry, even before she turned back, her eyes brimming with tears.

I apologized, feeling like a heartless oaf.

Liz looked down at her hands with a little smile, then up again and out toward the boat. She brushed away the tears with a fingertip, one eye at a time, and with a little laugh, shook her head. "You'd think if I wanted to mother someone, I'd pick someone my daughter's age, wouldn't you?"

She hadn't mentioned a daughter, not in the entire time we were together on Bleaker. We'd talked about our sons, Liz's thirty-one years old and a physical therapist in Boise, and my Bobby at twenty-three waiting tables in Seattle until he got enough money together to travel to Africa. Half-afraid to ask, I said, "Daughter?"

Liz swallowed and told me that her twenty-nine-year-old daughter had died six months earlier of leukemia. "Paul and I brought her ashes down. We scattered them at the white sand beach on Bleaker." She brushed her eyes again and looked at me. "Laurie came here three years ago. She was just getting started as a science writer; she was doing a piece on rockhoppers and oil spills." Liz shook her head. "She loved Bleaker and said we'd have to see it one day."

"Oh, Liz." This explained a lot—the heaviness behind Paul's goofy jokes, the low-voiced conversations between the two of them, their emotion at the penguin funeral, Liz's studied cheerfulness. Her interfering and her mothering. Tears were in my eyes now. I took Liz's hands and held tight, said how sorry I was. "Losing a child is the hardest thing in the world." I stopped short of saying, I know.

Liz squeezed back, and after a few more tears, we let go and wiped our eyes.

"You can mother me all you want," I said. "But like any self-respecting teenager, I won't listen most of the time."

Liz laughed, and blew her nose.

"As for Hans," I said after we sat silently for a minute, "I'm just helping him keep an unwanted suitor at bay."

"You mean Marcia?" The two were moving up the beach in our direction.

"Yes. Come on, let's walk. And if you help me by distracting her, this whole charade'll be over quicker."

We got to our feet just as they caught up. Liz started showing a great interest in Marcia's spotting scope. Hans and I walked ahead.

"Isn't this amazing?" I said once we were alone. I gazed past him at the penguins; close to a hundred of them, standing three feet tall, a yellow flush at the top of their vast white chests, orange cheek patches like jewels, beaks in the air like the aristocrats they're named for.

"Yes, amazing," Hans agreed. "Although with someone talking and talking it's hard to watch penguins also." He looked back. Marcia was adjusting the scope, and Liz was bent over looking through it. Hans said, "I think if she sees us, you know, with our arms . . . okay?"

So we started walking, Hans's arm linked through mine, presumably seen by Marcia and Liz. I didn't know if Hans was finally focusing on the penguins, but for me it had just gotten a lot harder.

Back on board we settled on the couch in Hans's cabin, faces still flushed from the evening on the beach. His room was larger than mine, though still snug. It had a couch, a coffee table in front of it, one chair, a double bed. "How do you rate?" I said. "Isn't this deck for the scientists and the captain?"

"I don't know . . . Marcia's up here, and Helen also. I guess I'm just lucky."

He unrolled a reddish-brown suede pouch as I watched. Inside was a collection of wood-carving tools. "My hobby," he said, and picked up a wooden bird from the coffee table and held it out. I took it from him and examined it. Five inches from beak to tail, narrow wings spread even wider as if to catch the next updraft.

"A black-browed albatross?" I said.

His mouth opened in surprise, and he said, "How did you know?"

I laughed. "It's the only kind of albatross that breeds here. And it's clearly an albatross."

He peered at it. "I tried. I need to sand it and oil it, but . . . it looks okay."

"It looks more than okay." I opened my book. With the skua book finished and feeling as ready for tomorrow as I was going to, I was relaxed enough to get back to the novel I hadn't touched since the flight down. I yawned. "I'm not going to last very long. I'm not used to dancing till dawn and rising with the roosters. And tomorrow's a big day."

He started carving on a piece of wood that was just beginning to take shape: a penguin. I watched for a while, a finger holding my place in the book. He saw that I wasn't reading and said, "Tell me more about you. I think this morning I did most of the talking. It's my bad habit."

"I've told you about me. What else do you want to know?"

"Oh . . . your marriage, your family, your biggest pain in life . . ."

"Whoa! Is that your typical conversation opener?"

"No. I don't know why I said it. Sorry." He kept carving, his eyes fixed on the wood.

"Okay." I closed the book and put it aside. "I got married when I was twenty-three, my husband, Warren, was twenty-nine. I was pregnant, or we probably never would have married." I paused. And then—why did I tell him what I hadn't told Liz? "Our daughter died when she was two and a half."

My voice caught, surprising me. Sometimes I can talk about it quite dispassionately; I'd thought this would be one of those times, answering Hans's matter-of-fact question just as matter-of-factly.

I pushed on, hoping he wouldn't notice the tear teetering on my right lower lid. "Then I had Bobby two years later. He's twenty-three now. Warren and I divorced when he was still little." I rushed on. "Both my parents are gone, no siblings. So I don't have a very big family. But lots of good friends." I was in control again.

He had stopped carving. "I'm sorry."

I wiped at my eye and shook my head. "It's funny. I can go for years without a tear, and then..." Twice in one evening, I thought, remembering Liz on the beach.

He reached over and squeezed my hand, a brief pressure. "I can't imagine... to lose a child." He took his hand back, picked up the knife again, and began carefully peeling tiny curls from the bird's neck. "My mom died when I was six." He glanced at me and back at his work. "But it's not the same. My two sisters raised me, especially Astrid. She was the older, twelve."

"Oh, Hans, that must have been..." I shook my head.

He shrugged. "I was almost too young to understand..." He smiled again. "But we're not talking about me." He held up the carving he'd been working on. "It's not finished, but tell me—what is it?"

"A penguin," I said, giving it my full attention. "Probably a gentoo."

"You're amazing, Joanie."

I smiled. "It's not me, it's the artist." I took it from him and turned it in my hands. "Have you ever thought of going professional? Selling your carvings?"

He shook his head. "I do it because I like to. Selling them would kill that. You know? The markets, the business, the deadlines..."

I did see.

I stayed almost an hour. Marcia didn't show, and when I got up to go, Hans said he would lock his door and not answer if anyone knocked.

I went down the stairs, hanging tight to the railing as the wind tried to snatch me off into the dusk.

In my cabin I sat on the bed, ran a hand through my hair, and let out a long breath. "Do you see what's happening here?" I asked Pru. The penguin was sitting propped against the pillow, giving me her full attention. But she didn't answer, so I did. "I would rather have stayed up in Hans's cabin. Curled up on his bed, fallen asleep up there. Not that I was invited or anything." I shook my head to make the image go away. "Nothing like this has happened to me in years. And then in the space of little more than a day, I've got this huge, crazy crush."

A knock on the door interrupted my thoughts, and I got up. Who could it be at this hour?

Marcia. She marched into the middle of the room, whirled around, and, black eyes flashing, said, "What are you doing?"

I blinked. "You mean with Hans?"

"Of course Hans. What do you want from him?"

"Friendship?" I said, as if guessing at the answer to a multiple-choice quiz.

Marcia snorted. "You could be his mother."

"Okay, his mother, then."

She shook her head slowly, as if she couldn't figure me out.

"We enjoy each other's company," I said evenly. "We're getting to be friends. And, really, it's not anyone else's business."

"So you're just going to toy with him for these six weeks and keep him from meeting someone more . . . significant?"

"Like you?"

"Not necessarily me. But someone his age."

"Let me ask you; what do *you* want with him?"

Marcia, with her striking black hair, wide eyes, and flawless skin, was not the type you'd expect to be immediately attracted to someone with Hans's less-than-classic looks. And she'd been after him from the moment she saw him. What *did* she want with him?

She didn't answer, but walked across to the bathroom, arms folded, turned, and strode back. "Look, you're a nice lady. I just think you look a little foolish running after a younger man like that. People will think, well . . . You're looking for a job, right? It looks a little flaky to be . . ."

I crossed my arms. "Thanks for your concern. But I'll handle it." I walked to the door and opened it. "It's getting late, so if you don't mind . . ."

Marcia left without further argument, and I felt momentarily powerful.

But once the door was shut behind her, I wondered. *Would* people—like Bill, my valuable job-search ally—see me as flaky if I hooked up with Hans, be it pretend or otherwise? An older woman prowling after a younger man? Well, I didn't feel old, and I really didn't look all that old, did I? I turned to check with Pru. "Look at me. I'm trim, I'm fit. Most of my wrinkles are laugh wrinkles. Nothing really sagging. And besides, I'm *not* running after Hans; he's the one who started it."

I resisted the urge to run upstairs and tell him about Marcia's visit. After pacing back and forth a few times, anger trumped any feelings of doubt.

"A 'nice lady.' Huh! First time I've been called *that*," I muttered.

I got into my pajamas, settled in bed, and, gripping my novel firmly, read myself out of my agitation and into sleep.

NINE

Search Air

The color and pattern [of a newly hatched chick] differs consider-
ably from that of the adult. The distinctive chick plumage immedi-
ately signals the immaturity of the bird, and as a consequence other
adults do not perceive the chicks as rivals.

—*Wayne Lynch,*
PENGUINS OF THE WORLD

I WAS IN THE dining room at five o'clock the next morning, notes
in order, waiting for Finn. He strode in almost ten minutes later
and headed straight for the coffee pot, tossing a "sorry" over his
shoulder. But he had a clipboard and was ready to work, so I didn't
comment. We accomplished a surprising amount in two hours;
how the day would go, the schedule for the week, who would
present the overall plan to the team and who would demonstrate
the observation methods. We also had a little disagreement.

We'd been assigned six helpers, including Bill, who would
also act as our supervisor. We split the six in half, Finn being in
charge of one group and I the other. Neither of us was keen on

having the supervisor looking over our shoulder, but I had the added incentive of thinking it was best to keep Bill at a distance despite his agreeing to be "just friends." Finn and I argued over who would have Bill, and I only won when I said I had personal reasons for wanting to distance myself from him for a while. He cocked his head at this, eyebrows raised, but I just said, "Please," and he conceded.

Stepping out of my cabin after breakfast, I ran into Hans, who was lingering at the railing. He was dressed to go out in a red rain-coat over a bulky sweater and the brown knit hat pulled down to his eyebrows. He held out the albatross, smooth and glisten-ing with a fresh coat of oil. "It's for you."

"Hans, really?" I took it from him, held it up in the morning sunlight. "It's beautiful. I'll treasure it always." I put it in my room, trying not to be thrilled that Hans had given me this gift. I rejoined him at the railing to watch the crew lower the big Zodiac into the heaving water below us.

"Sounds like you'll be out all day," I said. At breakfast, Ian had announced the teams and the plan for the day. Hans would be working on the main count.

"I'm on a team with her." He pointed with his jaw to Marcia, standing on the open deck below, clipboard hugged to her chest, leaning into a conversation with Yoshi. "I wonder if she arranged it. I said I wanted to work with you and Finn."

I had intended not to, but couldn't stop myself from asking, "Did she come looking for you last night?"

"Probably. Someone knocked."

I hesitated. Why? Because her words had gotten to me? "And you didn't answer, so she came to see me."

"Did she? What did she want?"

"She asked what I wanted with you, said I looked silly running after a younger man . . ."

"You're not running after me. If anyone's running after anyone, it's me running after you."

I gave him a glance.

"I mean," he said, "for the pretend relationship."

"Right. Well. I'm pretty sure Ian, Bill, and Yvonne set the teams. Maybe you ought to see how it goes today. It's not like it'll be just you and her."

"I suppose. What are you doing today?"

"We're orienting our team on board first, then going out to pick the colonies we'll be watching and get started. I guess we'll be joining you on the count this afternoon."

"Not me. My group is going far down the peninsula. So I probably won't see you until dinner."

"Let's sit together at dinner, then." I hadn't planned to say that, but he was standing there beside me, radiating warmth, pulling me into his orbit. My mouth, apparently, wasn't listening to my head.

Hans tugged his hat in back, making it rise in front. He looked down at me; a grin filling his face. "Great," he said, and we went downstairs.

Volunteer Point's low peninsula protrudes east, separating a somewhat sheltered bay to the south from the open ocean to the north. My group of eight slogged single file across the stubby grass and squishy moss patches to observe gentoos at the far side of the peninsula, where tourists seldom visited. The knee-high diddle-dee, with its tough, shiny green leaves and red berries, and the undulating low green hills did little to block the wind. Fat gray clouds raced across the sun. I must have put my sunglasses on and taken them off half a dozen times as we made our way to the collection of gentoo colonies on the north beach.

Following the plan Finn and I had put together, Bill gave a brief lecture on the skua and its habits. We then split into the two groups to observe from different angles a gentoo colony that sat on a little rise of sand on the beach. After an hour, we'd get back together and compare notes.

I huddled with Javier, Paul, and Josef on a grassy rise five meters from the colony. Finn and I had agreed that our teams were to act like ordinary well-behaved tourists, approaching no closer than that. We would speak only in low voices and move around as little as possible.

The air was filled with constant penguin chatter as I instructed them on how to tick off the various skua behaviors on the water-proof cards I'd made up before leaving home. I had my own clip-board where I noted how many of us were present, how long we stayed, and the presence of any visitors other than our team. During this first hour no other human appeared.

After a few minutes of watching, Josef said, "There—skua."

We looked where he was pointing. The heavy brown bird was sailing over the colony, perfectly demonstrating the first category of behavior: "search air," or "S.A." on the form.

"Yes!" I said, and put a check in the appropriate box. "So when you're watching with your partner, the spotter should follow that skua with his binoculars, while the other uses his naked eye and watches out for any other activity at the same time."

Josef raised his binoculars, and we watched the bird glide east along the beach over the next two groups of gentoos, turn and head back our way, pumping its wings into the wind.

When it passed again over the first colony, Paul asked, "Is that one S.A. or two?"

"Good question," I said. "I'd call it 'one.' It hasn't landed in between. But let's check with Finn and Bill to make sure we're consistent."

We watched for the rest of the hour, hoping for more exciting behaviors, such as attempted or successful predations from the air or ground. But we saw only a pair of skuas striding around the perimeter of the colony and two more S.A.'s.

The gentoos stuck to their nests, their backs to the wind, a little army of white chests, unperturbed by the lurking threat that could snatch their offspring away in a split second. Several did glance at us from time to time, but the few penguins that were moving around were clearly members of a pair whose partner was sitting on the nest; they were either returning to the clutch or leaving, preening their mate's face, tidying up the nest. Such a peaceful scene, it was hard to imagine a predator attack.

When we were back with the others, Finn disagreed with my interpretation of the skua's over-flight and return. "It counts as two. It left the perimeter of the colony and returned for another pass." He looked like a pirate, standing there with legs spread, earring glinting, and that thin braid batting his shoulder.

"But barely twenty seconds passed," I insisted. "Same bird, same flight." I probably wouldn't have clung to my opinion if he hadn't been acting so darn sure of himself.

He shook his head. "Doesn't matter; Harper and Spaskie did it that way at Crooper Island."

This was the most recent study on skua predation of gentoo colonies, which I had, of course, read. "I don't remember them giving those details," I said.

"They didn't. I emailed Spaskie."

Wow! I was both impressed that he'd thought to do that and chagrined that we'd had this argument in front of the whole team. And that I had lost. There was nothing to do but graciously agree to count it as two.

Throughout this exchange Bill had been silent. He now said, "I didn't know that either. Probably should stay consistent with the way it was done before."

Back on the main beach were gentoo colonies that got a fair amount of tourist traffic, mostly military personnel on their day off, and a few foreign and local visitors who made the trek from Stanley. That morning we saw no one. We split into our same two groups and spent another hour watching.

When I'd been on Bleaker Island, I'd spent hours at a time out in the elements watching penguins. Whenever I started to get cold, though, I would move and get my blood circulating with a brisk walk to another site. But this was different. After an hour's sitting at the new site, I was shivering. My fingers, often ungloved to write, had stiffened into claws. How in the world was I going to sit in one spot for *two* hours at a time, twice a day, in this relentless wind?

We rejoined the others for lunch and huddled in a tight half circle, all eight of us, shoulder to shoulder and knee to knee, to keep warm. I wasn't the only one complaining of the cold, but I was pretty sure no one else was shivering. The little rise we were trying to shelter behind probably cut the wind from thirty knots down to twenty-eight. Sand kept up a pattering on our rain pants and tore a piece of lettuce out of Paul's sandwich.

Bill said to Helen, "I noticed you deep in conversation with Bernard McConaghy this morning."

"Yes! Charming man, really. He told me all about fishing and the restrictions they put in place here a few years back. He's hoping this survey will show they've had a positive effect on penguin populations."

Finn snorted. "I wouldn't believe a word that man says."

I kept myself from looking at Bill as we waited for him to say more, but Finn was intent on getting the peel off a satsuma in one piece.

To encourage him, I said, "Audrey didn't seem to think much of him yesterday, did she, Bill?"

"No, and I didn't have a chance to ask her why."

Finn popped half of the little orange in his mouth. "He was involved with that business of running off the conservationist a few years back."

Paul looked around to see if he was the only one who didn't know the story. "Sounds fascinating. Tell us more."

Finn told a story of a conservationist brought out from England to be in charge of a penguin count here. According to Finn, her final report showed that penguin populations were seriously declining, and pointed the finger of blame at commercial fishing. Fishing being the Falklands' economic basis, this was too much. "They tried to get her to revise her numbers in the official report, but she wouldn't, so they didn't renew her contract," Finn said.

Bill asked, "What makes you think Bernard was involved?"

"I heard. From some people I know here."

The group asked a few more questions, but Finn didn't know, or wasn't willing to share, much more. He ended saying, "And now the great new economic hope is oil."

This was an opening for more questions, but Finn stuffed his lunch sack into his pack and stood up. The rest of us followed. It was time to find Ian and spend the afternoon helping with the main count.

After thawing out in a hot shower before dinner, I found Helen sitting in the lounge beside a box of wine and two glasses. "Chardonnay okay? It's on me." A notebook was tethered to the bar where we were to keep track of any alcohol we took.

I settled into a deep leather chair and put my feet up next to Helen's on the big footstool. "Ahh . . . perfect," I said, accepting a glass. I took a sip. "Not bad, coming from a box."

"Good thing, too; all they've got is two-liter boxes of this one brand of Chilean cabernet or Chilean chardonnay." She set her glass down. "What do you make of Finn's story?"

"I don't know what to think." As friendly as I felt toward Helen, I held back, remembering Bill's words that anyone on board could be an accomplice to these supposed shenanigans. I changed the subject. "It's cold out there in the wind, isn't it? I was shivering when we were sitting this morning. Were you?"

"Not shivering, but cold." Helen ran an eye over me. "That slim figure of yours isn't going to help you in this kind of weather."

We sat for a moment watching the lounge fill up with people until Helen, not letting it go, said, "How could anyone justify skewing the numbers?"

This was more neutral ground, and I spoke generally. "Money, I suppose. Let's say the report shows declining populations. That could be caused by any number of things, but a likely one would be that penguins aren't finding enough to eat near the breeding grounds, due in part to competition with fishermen. So they'd have to go farther and farther away to find food. Which would put them longer in the sea and longer at risk from predators. As well as the energy spent, all those calories used in swimming. They'd be losing body weight, mortality rates of the parents would go up, and chicks would have a poorer chance of surviving." I could have gone on, but made myself stop.

Helen said, "So the blame would easily fall on increased fishing around the Falklands. And as Finn suggested, the latest money earner seems to be oil."

"And people really do remarkable things for money," I said.

"The root of evil and all that," Helen said, slowly turning her glass on the wide wooden arm of her chair. "But it's hard to believe Bernard was involved. He's so jovial and friendly."

This was the second positive reference she'd made to Bernard that day, and I couldn't resist teasing her. "You're not getting interested in him, are you?" It wasn't out of the question. He did have a charismatic twinkle about him.

"Oh, heavens no!"

"Too old, huh?" I said, remembering Helen's wish to find a younger man. Bernard was probably about my age; younger than Helen by at least a decade.

Helen laughed. "Too out of shape." She took another sip. "Speaking of interested—you and Hans seem to be pretty friendly."

Ha! What had Helen seen or heard? The dancing at the Globe? Hans and I arm in arm on the beach? Or perhaps Marcia was talking. I saw then that the seventy-meter *Professor* was like a small town, and that what any of us did or said would soon be common knowledge to all its inhabitants.

But I was getting nothing but delighted approval from Helen, and smiled. "Just friends." I couldn't resist adding, "But he's a sweetie, isn't he?"

"Adorable," Helen said.

As people returned from the field and drifted into the lounge, I found myself glancing up at each new arrival. When I realized I was looking for Hans, I made myself stop by turning to talk to Bernard, who had joined me and Helen. Could I somehow get him talking about previous counts without making him think I was too interested? But before I could come up with a good lead-in, Helen asked him if we could expect the weather to get much warmer.

Bernard said, "Sometime over the next weeks—January *is* high summer, you know—the wind may drop to a breeze for an hour or so. And it might get a few degrees warmer. But we can get hail or gale force winds any time of the year."

We begged him to tell us he was exaggerating, and while he was insisting he wasn't, Hans entered the room, wool cap in hand and combing his fingers through his hair. He came over to our group, which had grown to six and included Bill. Helen and I moved our feet, and he sat on the footstool. He was bursting with stories of penguin behavior.

"We saw two gentoos, they were stealing rocks from each other's nest," he said. "One waited until the other wasn't looking and went over and took a rock and brought it to his nest. He did this for maybe three rocks, until the other noticed him. Then the first one stood up fast and looked to the sea, like he was only looking at the view." Hans gave a convincing demonstration of feigned innocence. "A little later, the other penguin went over and took back the same rock!"

An audience had gathered around as Hans spoke. Not just magnetic to me, I noted. Paul offered to get him a drink.

"Yes, Diet Coke would be great." He asked Helen and me how our day had gone.

Helen said, "We counted 848 active gentoo nests this afternoon. How about you?"

"I think all day something like 1,050 gentoo and 500 Magellanic." Hans called across the room, "Yvonne—what were our final numbers?"

"Nine hundred fifty-two gentoo nests and 486 Magellanics," she called back.

Hans looked back at us, frowning. "I thought it was more." He shrugged. "Well, I was just a holder of rope, what do I know?"

The stories about funny business with numbers were fresh in my mind, and I glanced toward Bill, who briefly met my eyes.

TEN

Just a Massage

Rockhopper penguins preen each other in a courtship display. Mutual care is a way for birds to reinforce their bond and to remove external parasites.

—*Wayne Lynch,*
PENGUINS OF THE WORLD

A FTER ANOTHER GREAT dinner—white fish in a wine sauce, rice pilaf, and roasted vegetables—Hans and I drifted outside to the deck. Neither of us felt like watching the movie that was starting up in the little theater, so we stood and watched the sun disappear behind a thick bank of white clouds. The pale stretch of sand was close enough for us to distinguish Magellanics from gentoos, some just standing around as if in conversation, others still busy with the day's work of bringing in food from the sea. After a few minutes I stretched. "Well. I might as well spend some time on the job search and go to bed early."

"Don't go yet," Hans said. "Let's sit somewhere." He looked around. "There's no place to get away except in the cabins or on the shore."

"Maybe for a few minutes." What was the harm? Not eager to get out in the elements again and thinking it was best to stay out of a cabin with Hans, I said, "Helen and I discovered a place on Deck Two."

I led the way down the stairs. When we got to the open deck, Hans stopped and looked up at the little Zodiac, hanging above us. "It's too bad we can't take it." He examined the pole that held the launching mechanism as if he was really considering doing it.

"We don't even know how to work this thing," I said.

"In fact, I do." He looked down at me, grinning at my surprise. "In Antarctica. I worked on a ship for three months. It was one of my jobs, take people to the shore and back."

"You're full of surprises. But we can't just take one without asking. Besides, I've had enough wind for one day."

I led him down the long, narrow hall toward the stern, our footsteps echoing as we passed closed doors. Several were empty cabins, some were crew quarters, and others were set up as offices or equipment storage areas. Not a soul was in sight. At the end of the hall was a little covered deck, enclosed on three sides. A railing across the front opened to the sea, and a little couch with a plastic cushion tied to it was bolted to the floor.

"This is great!" Hans said, and we sat on the couch. It was like a loge at the theater, with the show being the gray sea before us. The wind was whipping the surface into a spray, but our alcove was still and dry.

He told me more about working on the ship in Antarctica as well as his work on a dude ranch in Wyoming—where he had learned swing dancing—and his importing of crafts from Turkey to Switzerland. I was envious of his adventurous life and said so. As someone who'd buckled down with a career, a husband, and a child shortly after college, I was intrigued by people who'd spent their younger years differently.

I asked him more about his job in the chocolate shop, and he said it was a family business and they were fine with him being gone for months at a time. He still lived at home so he could save his money for travel.

"With your sister?"

"And her husband and two kids. And my dad."

"Oh! And your other sister?"

"She's got her own apartment in Geneva." He looked at me, perhaps feeling defensive about being thirty-three and still living at home? "It's a pretty big house," he said. "This kind of arrangement is more common in Europe."

"I guess so." I hadn't meant to sound judgmental, but before I had a chance to say so, he asked me to tell him more about my day. I told him about my excitement at finally being out in the field working, about my disagreement with Finn.

Hans said working with Marcia had been okay; she behaved herself, treating him as another team member. She'd done the counting, while he and Yoshi had held the rope used for measuring the perimeter of the colony, and Yvonne recorded the numbers.

"Do you really think you counted over a thousand gentoo nests?" I asked.

"I thought yes, but maybe I was wrong. Why?"

"Oh, nothing probably. Finn told us this story today about something that happened on the last count. Someone supposedly tried to change the data to make it look like fishing didn't have an impact. A conservationist supposedly lost her job over it."

"Really."

"Yeah. According to Finn, her findings were not well received. They tried to persuade her to change her report, but she wouldn't."

Hans looked skeptical. "How does Finn know this?"

"He said someone here in the Falklands told him."

"Huh."

"Well, he does have friends here. He couldn't meet me on Saturday because he was getting together with them." How much should I tell Hans? Again, I restrained myself, honoring my agreement with Bill. After all, I wanted to do all I could to help get to the bottom of any mischief concerning the count numbers. But something about Hans made me want to tell him things. I could at least report anything that Finn had said that afternoon, so I added, "He implied he thought Bernard was involved somehow."

"Bernard? He seems like a nice guy. How was he involved?"

"He didn't say."

Hans was silent for a moment, shaking his head. "I really wasn't paying good attention when they said the final numbers out at the site."

"Well. It's probably nothing. Finn's a bit of a loose cannon anyway."

"Loose cannon?"

I laughed. "It's an expression. It means he says—and does—things without thinking about consequences. Only one of the ways he's been difficult to work with."

He asked me to elaborate, and I gave him a few examples before that conversation thread ran its course and we sat watching the sea, patterned with white foam crescents lit by a sun that had emerged from beneath the cloud bank. An occasional feather of wind swirled through the alcove, lifting our hair, and a crumpled paper scudded across the floor, reminding me I needed to go put in some time on my job search.

I turned to Hans, opening my mouth to say just that. But the slight movement tweaked the place between my shoulder blades that had been bothering me off and on since the long flight down over a week ago. What came out of my mouth instead was, "Oh, darn, I thought that was gone," my hand reaching over my shoulder to rub it.

"How about a massage?" said Hans, and the next thing I knew I was sitting on a low stool in front of the couch, directing him to where it hurt.

While he kneaded my shoulders and dug his thumbs in around my spine, I thought about the pretend couple thing. We weren't really doing it, right? But here we were, acting pretty much like a couple; spending time alone, sharing every detail of our day. And the massage. What exactly were we doing?

His warm hands kneaded my back, and we didn't speak but for an occasional "right there" on my part, or "too hard?" on his. I closed my eyes and relaxed. I was very much liking being touched by this man.

But the thought that he couldn't possibly be seeing me as more than a nice older woman in need of a backrub jolted me out of my dreamy state.

I tried to think clinical thoughts, healing thoughts, but when that didn't snap me out of it, I opened my eyes, straightened a little, and started a conversation. "You really don't touch alcohol, do you?"

He didn't answer for a moment, both hands working the outside of my upper right arm. "I had a problem with it for a while," he said. "It's better I don't drink."

I watched through the railing as a giant bird flashed by; an albatross? "Sometimes I wonder if I have a problem, too," I said. "I have a glass of wine or two almost every evening. I have for years . . . It's definitely a habit."

"This wasn't like that."

Approaching footsteps interrupted us.

"Oh. Sorry." Paul had poked his head around the corner, and looked like he might back away.

"It's okay," we said in unison. Hans didn't miss a beat in his attention to my arm.

"Did you forget the meeting?" Paul asked.

"Meeting . . . ," I said. "Oh, darn . . . is it that time already?"

It wasn't exactly a meeting. Bill had mentioned to our team at lunch that he'd give a more in-depth talk on the habits of predatory birds that evening. I'd intended to go after my job-hunting session, though I was sure I'd heard most of it in our time together on Bleaker. In fact, I was pretty sure I'd told Bill, "I'll try to make it," thinking I'd more likely go to bed early.

Paul said, "Bill asked me to find you. We've been looking all over; we were about to sound the man-overboard siren when Helen remembered this place."

I glanced at him with some alarm, but saw the little sparkle in his eyes. I got up. "Well, if it's important that I be there ..."

"I'll come, too, if it's okay," Hans said.

The talk broke up almost an hour later. We all thanked Bill, and I moved toward the door with the others, but Bill called to me to stay for a minute. I thanked Hans for the massage and turned back into the room.

"Well," I said, sliding into a chair across a table from Bill, assuming he wanted to talk about Finn's story and the numbers. "Interesting story of Finn's today, wasn't it?"

"Yes," Bill said. "And it jibes with what Audrey told me."

"Oh!"

"Yep. The conservationist, the numbers discrepancy, her losing her job over it."

"Really. Did you ever ... contact this woman?"

"I tried. It seems she died a month before I found her."

"Bad luck." I took this in for a moment. "Did you ever report any of this to WSR?"

He shook his head. "Only about *their* last count. They looked into it. Or so they said. They found nothing out of line." After a moment, he went on. "And by the time I heard the story about the conservationist, I figured WSR was a bit tired of me."

"Well," I said. "I suppose it could be a rumor, couldn't it? Something that got blown out of proportion? You know how it is in a small place like this . . . I mean, what about the tighter fishing regulations they'd put in place leading up to that count? It would have left more fish, more krill and squid for the penguins in the years before that count. Wouldn't that have made an impact?"

"Some. But not that much, not that soon."

"Well, this is interesting." I thought a moment. "And the numbers discrepancy this afternoon, between what Hans said and what Yvonne said the official count was."

"Yes, also interesting. Did you ask Hans about it?" Bill began straightening the little pile of papers on the table in front of him.

"Yeah; he wasn't sure enough to swear to it."

When Bill didn't immediately say anything, I began to wonder what he really wanted to see me for.

"The plot thickens, you might say," he eventually said. "I guess we just keep our eyes and ears open. And I appreciate you not mentioning what Audrey's told me about Bernard to anyone."

"Of course."

Bill didn't seem to have any more to say on the subject. I thanked him for the way he'd handled the disagreement between me and Finn in the field and pushed back my chair.

He straightened his pile of papers one more time, moved it off to the side, and said, "What's going on with you and Hans?"

So that was it. Shaking my head, I said, "You're the third, no *fourth*, person in twenty-four hours who's found me and Hans interesting."

"Well, it's a little unusual . . . you being older than him."

I shook my head. *"What's* unusual? We enjoy each other's company. That's all."

"It looks like it's more than that . . ."

"Well, it isn't. But what if it is?" What was he basing this on? The massage? My thanks to Hans as I parted from him at the door had been quiet, but I hadn't been trying to hide anything either. "This is quite the fishbowl we're living in," I said.

"Well. It isn't the Love Boat."

"Ha! If it's about being late for your talk, I'm sorry."

He shrugged. "It would have been good for team-building to have you there on time. Your relations with your partner and all."

Finn, when I'd entered, had been sitting front row center. I had a moment's doubt. But I said with confidence, "Finn and I had a debriefing before dinner. We're ironing out any differences. Team-building's going just fine."

He nodded, and before he could say more, I moved to get up. "It's getting late. Was that all?"

"No," he said. "I heard about a job today. You might be interested."

"Oh?"

"A friend of mine works for WSR. He's got a bird job, temporary, ten months. In Central America somewhere. Starting in March. I could put in a word for you."

I was wary, but it sounded like something worth pursuing, so I said, "That would be great. I'd appreciate it."

"Check on the internet: WSR, careers. You'll see a job description and an application." He hadn't really said he *would* put in a word for me, but I thanked him again, stood up, and said good-night.

He stood up, too. "I don't want to see you get hurt, Joanie. Just be careful. Hans is a young man. What is he—thirty-five, thirty-six?"

"Thirty-three."

"It's unusual for someone that age to be interested in an older woman."

"Not unheard of, though." Little hairs prickled at the back of my neck.

"But you've noticed it's not common. There's a biological basis for it—it's related to preservation of the species." The bright lights of the dining room gleamed off his sparsely covered head.

"Right. So an older man with a younger woman is fine, while an older woman with a younger man is . . . what? An aberration?"

"Unsupported biologically. Just be careful."

"Thank you," I said for the third time. "I'll remember that."

I took all this to bed, and lay stewing in the darkening room. What was up with Bill reprimanding me about my friendship with Hans? Not for a minute did I buy his "I don't want to see you get hurt." Just friends—ha! That didn't last long.

And Finn that morning; demonstrating to everyone that he was thorough and on top of things while I wasn't. Well. Every-one had probably already forgotten it except me. I just needed to learn from it and be thankful I had a strong partner.

And eclipsing all these thoughts was Hans; what *was* going on there? As I lay in the dark, curled around Pru, I still felt his hands on my back. I'd been having such a good time with him, connecting on every level, that I'd lost track of time. This was almost unheard of for me, with my penchant for being on time, checking items off my lists, keeping control of my life.

With the thought of lists, I turned on the bedside light—it was finally dark enough to need it—and picked up my notebook, where I crossed off "Mon." and wrote "Tues." I added "Look up Bill's job" and stopped to think.

Maybe I *won't* look up Bill's job! I've already got my application in to Parque Nacional Isla Magdalena, the job I want.

I took a breath and squinted at Pru for a moment. "Cutting my own throat with that attitude, is that what you're thinking?" I said. "Well, maybe you're right."

The penguin was looking a bit smug, as if to say, Of course I'm right.

"Okay, I'll look into that job," I continued out loud. "But I'm not going to quit seeing Hans in order to keep getting job referrals from Bill. That's *my* business."

Was Pru frowning? I didn't care.

To "evening job search"—the other item on the list—I added "6:30" giving it added oomph. I would spend the evening on the computer, checking Bill's job, looking for new leads. No going off with Hans or anyone else.

Because that was what I *wanted* to do, not because anyone told me to.

ELEVEN

A Stormy Wednesday

When going to sea Rockhopper Penguins slide and bounce down banks and cliffs, often falling over large drops without mishap. They often jump feet-first into the water, unlike other penguins that either walk or dive into it.

—*Pauline Reilly,*
PENGUINS OF THE WORLD

O N TUESDAY I flung myself out of bed at five fifteen, ripped from the first deep sleep of the night, crossed the room in two bounds, and turned off the alarm. Why in the world had I volunteered to take the early shift?

I knew why; to show I was as tough as Finn.

With water splashed on my face, teeth brushed, two more layers of clothing added to my torso—another sweater and a thin windbreaker under the raincoat making six layers for my upper body, three on the lower—I went downstairs where I filled a thermos with coffee and a bottle with water and tucked a muffin in my knapsack. By 5:40 I was boarding the bucking Zodiac with my teammates. At the beach Javier and I left Paul and Josef at the nearby tourist-visited site, and walked fifteen minutes across the peninsula to the more remote site.

Shortly after we settled in, there was a mass movement toward the water as one partner of each pair of gentoos set off amid screeching farewells for the day's fishing. Two skuas were in attendance, strutting about the perimeter, watching intently for a chick to be unguarded. But the penguins were attentive, and we saw little predator action other than a few flyovers. I, though of course on the side of the penguins, began to wish for some action—a skua swooping down and flying off with an egg in its mouth, perhaps.

Javier and I exchanged an occasional word, and when he mentioned cleanup duty that evening, my thoughts jumped to Hans and images of standing close to him at the sink, my arm brushing his, and I got a tingling in the pit of my stomach. His hands last night, radiating heat, on my back, my shoulders . . .

"A.G.!" Javier said, and my focus snapped to the colony in time to see flapping and pecking and feathers rising and sailing off in the wind. A skua hopped and flew with a clatter of wings from a group of screeching penguins. I'd missed the start of my first unsuccessful predation from a ground position, or "attack ground."

This was crazy. I couldn't go on letting Hans distract me like this. I wouldn't think about him the rest of the day. And at dinner cleanup I'd make sure my arm didn't brush his. I'd finish as soon as I could and go spend the rest of the evening on my job search. I succeeded with this plan for the rest of the shift and caught

two A.G.'s and one A.A.—"attack air," or unsuccessful predation from flight.

The afternoon proved a bit more challenging in terms of
staying away from Hans, as I was assigned to help on the main
count with him and Helen. Dinner cleanup was even more so.
Not only did I find myself standing side by side at the sink with
him—and the close quarters of the galley made it hard not to
occasionally brush arms—but Javier brought some Gipsy Kings
music and got Liz to put down her stack of dirty dishes and dance
with him. Which of course led Hans to holding out his hands to
me. One dance, I said. Others joined us, and it was three dances
later before I got away to my job hunt.

After I spent an hour working on the application to Bill's friend
at WSR, Helen stuck her head in the computer room. "Take a
break and go to the gym?"

I looked at my watch; almost nine o'clock. "It's too late to get
all stimulated."

"Yoga in my room, then. I've got two mats."

"Wow. You brought two mats in your luggage?"

"One is Josef's."

"Ah!"

Helen smiled.

I looked back at the computer screen. Finishing the application by hand while tucked in bed would work just as well. "Give
me a minute to print this out. I'll meet you up there."

Helen's room was on the top level, and I wondered again why some volunteers and students got these larger rooms. I asked Helen once I was inside.

Helen laughed. "Oh, I paid more. When you get to be my age, you like your comforts."

Did that mean Hans and Marcia had also paid for an upgrade? But Hans had said he didn't know why he was up here.

With mats on the floor, angled by the bottom and side of the bed, we began stretching. I tried to leave my thoughts and focus on going within, being quiet, breathing.

But five minutes hadn't passed before Helen said, "What a good dancer your Hans is."

My eyes popped open. *Your* Hans. "Yes, isn't he sweet the way he's attentive to us older women?"

Helen looked over at me for a moment, then burst out laughing.

I knew suddenly that Helen, at sixty-six, hadn't stopped thinking of herself as a desirable woman, that to her it was perfectly normal that a man of any age would be happy dancing with her. "What I mean is, I guess I'm feeling like I enjoy his company a little too much . . . so I'm trying to convince myself he's just, you know, being nice."

"Why would you want to do that?" Helen said.

"Because. I've got work to do. My thesis, my job search."

Helen just looked at me, that journalist's technique of getting her subject to say more by being silent.

"He distracts me," I said after a moment.

"I'm sure you can figure out how to handle your duties *and* a boyfriend."

"Who said anything about a boyfriend?"

"What else would we be talking about?"

"Oh, Helen. I just don't have room for a man in my life." I went into a downward dog.

Helen followed and we were silent for a few moments, focusing on breathing, until Helen came back to her hands and knees and said, "You know, you can't keep postponing happiness forever."

"I'm not!" What did Helen know about me and my happiness? I sat back on my knees. "I'm happy. I'm happy being here in the Falklands. I'm happy doing a bang-up job on my project. That's what makes me happy."

Helen went into a lunge and, as if she hadn't heard me, said, "A characteristic of truly happy people is they take happiness where it comes."

"Well," I said. "I do." And I, too, did a lunge, right leg forward, left leg back, arms reaching for the sky.

Back in my room, I tucked myself in bed with the job application and spent a half hour tweaking my essay on why I chose conservation biology as a field, interrupted only every five minutes or so with comments to Pru. "Helen's wrong. I'm happy. I'm not postponing anything that I want to be part of my life."

Pru seemed supportive, and I fell asleep before ten o'clock, the essay done, my life feeling more or less back under control.

A stormy Wednesday undid all that. I was out before six a.m. in the worst weather I'd experienced in the ten days I'd been in the Falklands. The wind tore dark clouds across the sky, a slanting rain hammered, and sitting still for two hours was torture. I went in to a late breakfast stiff and cold. Just as I was beginning to thaw, it was time to go out again. At shore, horizontal hail assailed Paul and me from the very direction we had to walk. I trudged after Paul to the site, pushing against the wind, not raising my eyes from his heels, as looking up exposed my face to a stinging assault. The little thermometer attached to my zipper pull said thirty-seven degrees. The wind and wet made it feel even colder.

We settled ourselves near the tourist-visited colony. A lone skua was standing at the far edge, its brown feathers ruffling in the wind, waiting for a parent to let down its guard and leave its chicks exposed a moment too long. This never happened in the two hours we sat hunched by the colony. Our only movements were raising and lowering our binoculars or making the occasional check mark on our forms. We didn't see one human visitor. It seemed all sane skuas and humans were tucked in, out of the elements.

By noon my fingers were so stiff I could barely unzip my pack to put my pad and pencil away. Despite the rain outfit and hood tied tight around my face, little rivulets of waters found their way down my face and into my collar. Paul agreed it was miserable and suggested we go back to the *Professor* for lunch instead of joining the others to eat huddled in the elements. A walkie-talkie was waiting in a waterproof box on the beach, and the researchers had been assured they could call for a ride any time they felt the need. But a culture of toughness kept us away from that box.

I shrugged, hiding my discomfort. "If you want."

"No, no," Paul said. "I was just thinking of you."

So we headed off to find our companions. Surely, getting the blood pumping out to my extremities would bring me back to normal. The wind was at our backs, and by the time we found the group fifteen minutes later, sheltering among a cluster of rocks, I was feeling a little better.

But after bolting my lunch, I was again shivering, so I got up to take a brisk walk. Maybe someone *did* mention in which direction I might find Hans. What the heck, it was good to have some sort of destination. After ten minutes, I came over a rise and saw him, lying on his side, propped on one elbow, in the shelter between two lichen-speckled rocks. His red raincoat against the bright green grass reminded me that Christmas was only a little over a week away. A little patch of white lawn daisies wiggled violently behind him. He was watching a group of five king penguins not thirty feet away. They were standing, beaks in the air, regally ignoring the man. I stood for a moment admiring Hans's ability to sit quietly and observe. I was debating whether to interrupt this apparent communing, when he turned his head and saw me. He sat up and beckoned me over.

I picked my way through the rock-studded meadow and sat down beside him, saying, "Brrr . . ." It wasn't raining at the moment, so I took down my hood and shook the water from my hair.

"You're shaking," he said.

I admitted to being a little cold.

"Lie down and get warm." Hans scooted back against the biggest rock and lay back down on his side, leaning on his elbow. "It's away from the wind here." He patted the grass in front of him.

So natural, like I'd done it a hundred times, I lay down next to him, my back curled into his front. He dropped his arm around me and pulled me closer. It was out of the wind, mostly, but through our layers of fleece and Gore-Tex, I didn't feel any warmth. I couldn't make myself stop shivering.

After a few moments, he sat up and said, "Here. Take off your raincoat."

I did, and we spread it on the grass, dry side up, and lay back down. He unzipped his coat and pulled it over me like a wing.

It was warmer that way, and I could feel his heart beating through his sweater as the wind whistled around us. I wasn't too miserable to miss that there was something pretty sweet about this arrangement.

"I'll be okay in a minute," I said. It was getting difficult to form words with my frozen lips. "Did you see anything interesting this morning? Besides your audience here?"

"I saw how the skua does its kill."

"Tell me."

"Two worked together. One bothered the penguin—a gentoo—from the front until it finally got off its nest. Another came from behind and took the chick before the penguin knew. Then it flew away a couple meters and pecked it open. The other one joined."

I tried to ask how the parent reacted, but I couldn't get out more than one word at a time.

Hans sat up, pulling me with him. "Come on, we're going back to the boat."

"Oh, shit," I said. Here I was, buckling under the elements.

He helped me into my coat and zipped it up.

We made our way across the peninsula, the wind pushing us from the side. I was so weak and stumbly I had to hold on to Hans's arm all the way back to the landing spot. As he reached into the box for the radio, I protested through numb lips that I was much better. But even to my ears it sounded something like "I mush bear."

Hans gave me a look and called the boat; Ian's voice came across saying he'd be right there. As Hans put the radio away, I sank to the sand and sat, legs out in front. He sat behind me, legs spread, and put his arms around me. I leaned against him. "Tell me the ressuh the story," I managed to get out.

"Hmm . . . Not much more, really. Just bloody stuff. A little chick they pull apart and eat. Gray down everywhere. They pick at the bones until there's nothing left." He was speaking quietly, close to my ear.

"And the parent?" I said.

He shook his head a little; I felt this in my hair. "Just stood, watching. Then looked around its feet, wondering what happened."

I wanted to tell him it wasn't fair that he got to see this when I was the one with a space on my form for just that kind of behavior—P.G., successful predation from a ground position—but it was too much effort.

So we were quiet, the wind tearing around us, and as the Zodiac cut a swath through the roiling bay, I was aware only of Hans's breath on my ear, the one warm spot in the cold.

Ian ordered Hans to get me into my cabin, take my clothes off, especially anything wet, down to long underwear, and put me under blankets. He went off to find Javier. I was shaking again from the minute's ride in the Zodiac, but protesting, unconvincingly, that I was fine. We followed orders, Hans taking off my shoes and socks, me tugging at shirt buttons with fingers that couldn't feel, much less accomplish anything. Hans took that job over too. My long underwear was dry and we stopped there. Just as he was tucking the blankets around me on the bed, Javier came in. He took my temperature, pulse, and blood pressure, felt my hands, asked me what day it was, where we were. "Wenssay" and "Perfessor" were my answers.

"You're mildly hypothermic," he diagnosed. He looked at Hans. "One of us needs to get her some warm tea and one of us should get under the blanket with her to help her warm up." He put the stethoscope, thermometer, and blood pressure cuff away while Hans and I watched him, neither speaking.

Javier snapped his case shut and looked up, first at me, then at Hans. "You don't have to take off your clothes. Skin-to-skin contact is only recommended for severe cases."

Hans found his voice. "Okay, I'll stay; you can get the tea."

Once Javier was gone, Hans shed his outer clothes. He climbed in beside me, spooned against my back, his arm around me, just as we were at the rock. This time I could feel heat from him, this time his bare hand covered my icy ones. Inches in front of my eyes was his wrist, with a little forest of gold hairs. How far up his arm did they go, I wondered.

Hans said, "How do you feel?"

"I feel good," I said, not opening my eyes.

He said, "Me, too."

My eyes popped open at this, and I smiled. I closed my eyes again, and the next thing I knew, Javier was saying, "Yours is not too hot." He set a tray on the nightstand.

Hans and I sat up side by side on the narrow bed, the comforter tucked up under our arms. Javier pulled up a chair and the three of us sat sipping tea.

"I feel like such a wimp," I said.

The two men looked at each other, then back at me. "What's a wimp?" asked Javier.

I laughed. "I forget you guys don't know every English word... Weak, not tough, not able to handle things like wind and cold. It's discouraging."

"You'll be fine," said Javier. "We'll just get you some warmer clothes."

Ian knocked at the open door just then and stuck his head in. "We got another call; I'm pulling everybody in." He looked at Hans. "Most of the crew is in town today. You said you know how to drive a Zodiac?"

"Yes."

"If your patient can let you go...," Ian said.

"I'm fine," I said. "Who is it?"

"Josef. I've seen this before," Ian said. "It's the thin ones."

When Hans and Ian were gone, I said to Javier, "At least he didn't say it's the old ones."

That evening, everyone had a story to tell about their battle with the elements. Finn and Bill had refused to come in and were staying out to do the afternoon and evening observations for the skua project. Marcia and the young Chilean, Alejandro, had stayed to help. The three of us who actually got hypothermic—me and Josef and Caroline, Ian's wife—were now celebrities. We ate at a table with Helen and Ian and Javier. Now that all danger was past, we cheerfully vied for the title of worst case. The talk turned to how to avoid future such episodes. Josef was all bluster, saying all we had to do was eat more and "get more fat on our meat." But I could tell his belief in his invincibility was shaken.

All evening I was aware of Hans and his movements; sitting at the next table over, leaving the room for a few minutes, coming back. Catching my eye from time to time. Humming below the surface was the memory of leaning against him on the beach, lying next to him between the rocks, under the blankets in my room. Something had shifted; the pull I felt between us had become almost too strong to resist, and the next time we were alone together... who could say what might happen.

I anticipated this meeting with a mix of excitement and unease. Really, what did I think I was doing? I hadn't completely lost my head. I could still call up all the reasons not to get into something with Hans—our age difference, the distraction from my task and my long-range goals. But a counter-argument was percolating: maybe I *could* manage a little fling as well as my work and my job search. It wasn't like it was the first time I'd done such a thing. There were summers after we'd divorced when I'd left Bobby with Warren and spent a month or two in some Spanish-speaking country to keep my skills up. Twice I'd met someone with whom I'd had a summer fling. This was no different, right? It was only for six weeks. Then I'd go to my new job and Hans would go back to Switzerland. Tears might be shed at the parting, but we would soon get over it.

Bill, Liz, Paul, and I had discovered on Bleaker that we all enjoyed playing cards, and we'd made plans for a game of Spades that evening. As soon as Bill got back from the evening observations and got a plate of food, he joined us. They asked me if I was still up for a game. Absolutely, I said, better than ever. And, in fact, I was relieved to postpone seeing Hans alone. Maybe time would help me get ahold of myself.

We played in the dining room, Liz and Bill against Paul and me, the teams we'd fallen into on Bleaker. The room had emptied, but after the first couple of hands, Hans came in with his carving tools and set up at a far table facing us. People wandered in and out, stood behind one or the other of the card players, asking how the game was played or giving advice. But the big attraction became Hans and his carving. As far as I knew, this was the first time he'd been out of his room with it. People were clearly impressed. Yoshi, encouraged by Hans, disappeared and returned with watercolors and paper. The two sat at neighboring tables and exchanged an occasional comment as they worked. The card players were a louder group, laughing, whooping at successes, despairing at setbacks.

The first game ended at eight fifteen with Paul and me defeated by almost a hundred points. I tried to get away, but they persuaded me to stay for another game. Hans and Yoshi left sometime during the second game. Paul and I won that one, and all but me were up for a tiebreaker. I cited my weakened condition as a reason to turn in early, and we agreed on a rematch for Friday night. "When my partner's not handicapped by hypothermia," Paul said, winking at me.

I left the dining room intending to go straight to my cabin. But when I got there, my feet took me past my door and up the stairs to the upper deck. Hans was sitting with Josef and Helen in the little open area. They were speaking German and stopped to greet me.

Josef and Helen had the only chairs, and I hopped up onto the metal platform next to Hans. "I don't speak German," I said. "So if you're talking about me, go right ahead."

They laughed, a bit too heartily I thought.

"No, no," said Josef. "Just more about the elements."

Josef and I commiserated again on our experiences of the day until Helen yawned and stood. "I'm off to bed."

"Allow me to walk you to your cabin," said Josef.

Helen tossed a few words of German over her shoulder, as they moved away. Did Hans turn a bit pink? It was hard to tell in the dusk.

Though the two chairs were now available, we stayed where we were, side by side. The boat rocked gently and a slight wind batted at us. The water was lit with an odd brightness. I jumped off my perch and walked to the rail.

Up beyond the bow the moon was suspended in the sky, a perfect half, lighting a silver path on the dark sea.

"Hans." I turned. "Come see."

He came and stood close behind me, not quite touching, and let out an "ahhh" at the sight. We watched silently for a few moments, leaning on the rail, turned toward the moon. I could feel his warmth on my back.

After a few moments, he said, "Are you cold?"

"No, I'm fine. Completely recovered."

He was quiet. After a moment I realized what he was asking. And as easily as I'd lain down beside him earlier, I said, "You don't need an excuse to touch me."

There. I'd done it. Let my feelings take charge.

Swept with shyness, I looked over my shoulder to see the effect of my words, but his arms were already around me. I leaned against him, breathed deep to slow my heart. He whispered against my ear, "I think we should stop *pretending* to be a couple."

I turned in his arms and looked up at his face. I meant to say something, but he dropped his head closer and I lifted my face.

His hands lightly holding my elbows, mine at the sides of his waist, we kissed, standing against the railing in the evening breeze and moonlight. It was brief, sweet. Enough to turn me as silvery as the moonlight on the water.

He looked at me, smiling. "I really like you," he said.

"I like you, too," I said.

He bent and kissed me again, longer. I felt a vertigo, like I was standing on the edge of an abyss and wouldn't be able to stop myself from stepping off.

Almost panicked, I pulled back. "Hans, are you sure? I mean, I'm so much older . . ."

He put his finger on my lips. The amused smile. He shook his head. "Please stop that. It's not important. We're just two people who like each other . . . far from home, for five and a half more weeks."

It *can* be that simple, I thought. It *is*. I slipped my arms around his back and breathed deeply, feeling his wide, solid chest, the way my head fit in the crook of his neck. Someone walked by then and neither of us turned to see who.

"You're sure you're warm enough?" he said into my hair.

"It is a little cool, isn't it?"

"Let's go to my cabin," he said.

My heart jumped. His room was two doors away. I hesitated, but he stepped away and took my hand.

Once we were inside, he shut the door and pulled me to him. Our kissing made my bones dissolve. If I'd ever felt quite like this before, it was so long ago I'd forgotten. His hand rested firmly in the small of my back, slid toward my bottom.

I pulled away, breathless; there was something I had to say. I swallowed. "You know the sex part?"

"Yes . . . ," he said, looking at me, amused.

"Maybe we could wait a little while."

Brief pause, then, "Okay, if you want." His hand was on my neck, a thumb stroking my cheek.

"It's just that . . . I don't know. It's been a long time for me. I want to get to know you better . . . take time to build something, so it's not all about sex . . ." I was feeling a little old-fashioned, silly. "Besides, this part'll be fun; the anticipation, the romance."

He smiled, kissed me again. I relaxed, now that the question had been aired, and melted into the feel of his lips on mine. After a few more minutes of this, I was starting to feel like we'd waited long enough for the "sex part." But my head got control again; it was late, work was waiting in the morning. I pulled away. "I guess . . ." My face felt hot. Was it red?

He grinned. "Yes. It's getting late. You better go." He opened the door. "I'll walk you downstairs."

We walked hand in hand. At the top of the stairs were Ian and Caroline returning to their cabin. My instinct was to pull my hand away, but Hans's hold was firm. We exchanged good nights with the couple. As we reached the bottom of the stairs, the captain was just starting up and he tipped his hat. And while we stood by my door kissing, Paul and Liz passed on the way to their cabin. They wished us a good night, Liz rather stiffly.

"How do you say it?" Hans said, "The cat is outside the bag?"

I smiled. "The cat's out of the bag."

TWELVE

Quick Trip to Town

Corticosterone is elevated in naïve birds upon first seeing humans,
but penguins breeding in areas frequented by tourists hardly raise
an eyebrow, and certainly not a corticosteroid.

—*Lloyd Spencer Davis,*
SMITHSONIAN Q & A: *PENGUINS:*
THE ULTIMATE QUESTION & ANSWER BOOK

T HE NEXT MORNING, I was showered and dressed and busy
attaching my Therm-a-Rest pad to the outside of my day
pack—sitting on it would help a little with the cold—when there
was a knock on the door. It was Bill, holding a bundle of gray
down—an enormous parka, a piece of duct tape decorating one
sleeve. I'd seen him wearing it one day on Bleaker Island.

"Javier wants you and Josef to stay in this morning, but if you're
anything like Josef . . ." He held the parka toward me. "It's yours
if you want it."

"Oh, Bill. But what are you going to wear?"

"I've got another."

I reluctantly took it from him and put it on. My fingertips peeked out at the ends of the puffy gray arms. "Really, I can't . . ."

"Take it. No strings attached."

Down in the dining room Javier, Josef, and Paul were lined up at the coffee urn to fill their thermoses.

Javier looked up. "I don't want you going out. It's going to be almost as bad as yesterday."

"We can't miss a day," I said, unscrewing the lid of my thermos. "Finn and I have only these five days to get data at Volunteer Point, and we need every one of them." I spread out my arms. "And besides, now I've got this."

"But what about fashion?" said Paul.

Javier wasn't giving up yet. "This morning will be the worst. You can switch with Finn. Get him up, and one of the others, and you and Josef take the afternoon."

"Finn's not here," Bill supplied, taking a coffee cup from the rack.

"What?" I said at the same time Javier asked, "Where is he?" I remembered then that I had kept an eye out for him the night before, wanting to thank him for sticking it out and gathering the data when he could have come in with the rest.

"In town. He and Marcia caught a ride in with a couple of guys from the base. They'll be back by noon, along with Bernard."

"Really," I said. Stanley was at least two and a half hours away by a rutted, faintly marked track. All yesterday I'd been focused on Hans and had forgotten about "the funny business," as I'd come to call it. It now came flooding back: the numbers discrepancy of Monday, Marcia's unfriendliness, Finn's mysterious friends in Stanley.

Javier started to add to his argument, and I put a hand on his arm. "I'll stay in this afternoon if I'm the least bit uncomfortable. Josef will, too, won't you, Josef?"

Josef nodded, his white mustache the main feature visible in the center of a fur-rimmed hood. I imagined him pulling it up the moment Javier suggested he stay in.

Javier gave up. "Just don't wait until you become blue like you did yesterday."

It didn't take long for word of me and Hans to spread. The first comment came as soon as Paul and I were settled side by side on the windblown slope, binoculars in hand. Paul, eyes twinkling, said, "So. You and Hans."

"Yup," I said. "Me and Hans." A skua sailed overhead and landed next to the colony. I raised my binoculars and watched it for a moment. It watched me back with one sharp eye. I lowered the binoculars. Not caring to elaborate on me and Hans, I said, "What's with Finn and Marcia going into town, do you think?"

"Not another romance, if that's what you're thinking."

I had to agree. It seemed unlikely two such characters would be drawn to each other. I said, "You'd think they could have waited until tomorrow."

Ian had announced at breakfast the day before that the *Professor* was heading back to Stanley the very next evening to spend two nights and a day. An engine part, not strictly necessary, but desired, had come in. It would be installed on Saturday.

"They probably just saw an opportunity and grabbed it," Paul said.

At Javier's suggestion, Josef and I went in for a hot lunch. If it was a plot to keep us in for the afternoon, I didn't mind. My work on my project was done for the day. And the weather was such that the prospect of lunching on the nice warm ship, out of the wind, sounded more appealing than clutching a cold sandwich in frozen hands before joining the main count for more hours of sitting.

The dining room was nearly empty. Josef, Javier, and Caroline were sitting at the big table, and before I could join them, Bill appeared beside me with his tray. He nodded toward a table on the other side of the room, where he had an open notebook and a cup of coffee. "Sit with me," he said. "I want to talk to you."

What now? I thought.

But Bill was all business. He wanted me and Josef to spend the afternoon entering the count data collected so far. Probably in cahoots with Javier to keep us out of the elements, I thought, and valiantly started to protest. But just then a crew member came in from the outside on a gust of wind that scattered a stack of paper napkins over the floor. I glanced out the window, then across to the table where Josef had Caroline convulsed in a fit of laughter. "Josef agreed?"

Bill nodded.

Our help on the count that afternoon wasn't essential, anyway. I asked if the work he had lined up for us had anything to do with the apparent numbers discrepancy on the first day.

"Not just the first day; Tuesday also. I asked Hans to keep an eye on his team members, pay attention to the numbers."

"Has he found anything?"

"He was partners with Audrey. They kept notes about their own data. And he tried to be there listening whenever anyone gave their tally. I've just now had a chance to compare his notes to Marcia's overall data."

I waited as Bill drank from his coffee.

"Marcia didn't make a note of who gave her which numbers. She's supposed to, so that alone is suspicious. At least sloppy. But, no, overall, things don't match up. Marcia's reports show lower numbers than Hans thought people were giving her."

"Lower? But wouldn't she be trying to make the populations look healthier than they are?"

"She would be," Bill said. "By trying to make the reproductive rate look better than it really is."

I frowned. "How does that work exactly?"

"Let's say a colony has 110 nesting pairs now in December. Later, when the February counters come back, 95 of those nests still have chicks. Not a great rate. But if the colony has only a *hundred* nesting pairs now—or we believe it does—later when we count 95 chicks, the rate looks a lot better."

"So she turns in a 100 when the number is really 110."

"Something like that, yes. And who knows what else."

I pondered this for a moment.

"The data I'm having you and Josef enter today is from right here." He cocked a thumb toward shore. "I'm interested to see how those numbers compare to the Monday and Tuesday numbers from the other side of the peninsula."

I nodded and drained my water glass. "So you're having Hans keep an eye on Marcia?"

"He's the one who noticed something amiss that first day."

"So he's in the loop? I can discuss anything with him? Audrey's warnings, your suspicions?"

"I'd rather you didn't. We didn't discuss anything except the numbers. I haven't even told Ian what Audrey said."

I raised my eyebrows. "Shouldn't Ian know that Audrey has suspicions? About Bernard? And whoever his contact is?"

"There's no reason yet. It's not that I don't trust him. But he *was* in charge of the ground crews five years ago. And Hans is a good man for the job. Since he's not a scientist, he probably doesn't have an agenda. He notices things."

I must have smiled. I was beginning to realize Bill himself noticed a lot through those thick glasses.

"So . . . ," he said. "Word on the street is that Hans was still working on your hypothermia late last evening."

I laughed. I was surprised, really, that I'd made it this far into the day before getting the second such comment. "That's right."

Bill folded his hands on the table and nodded slightly, watching me. When I didn't say more, he picked up his tray and said, "Just don't get hurt."

"Not possible," I said, standing with him. "I'm not foolish enough to think it's anything that'll last beyond our time here."

Bill shook his head. What was he thinking? That I could have hooked up with someone more appropriate, like him? That I was being foolish? A silly woman interested only in men?

As we passed into the lounge, where Josef and I would be working, Bill stopped. "Oh. I heard back from my friend with

WSR. He says you should definitely send him your résumé if you're interested."

"Really? Oh, Bill, thanks . . . I didn't know if you were going to tell him about me or not."

"Of course. You're an excellent candidate." He said it as if he were helping out his friend, not me.

For a good part of the afternoon Josef read numbers off the count data, and I entered them. With the small sample we were entering, I couldn't tell if these numbers were off or not. I'd ask Bill later. It was work that would have been tedious but for Josef's delightful company. He teased me about my "young lover," and I teased him about his. I was only guessing about him and Helen at this point, but his response told me I wasn't wrong.

We finished around four thirty, and I took the stairs down to Two, up to Five, and back down to Two to get some exercise before settling down to send my application and résumé to Bill's friend. The second time down on Two, I heard voices down the hall. Men's voices, accompanied by scraping and grunting. I went to investigate, and at an open door to a tiny room I found Finn with Carl, a crewman who often drove a Zodiac, shoving a pile of black rubber into a corner.

"What have you got there?" I asked.

They stood and wiped their hands.

Finn said, "Something I'm keeping for a friend while he moves." Those friends again!

They stepped into the hall and Carl fished through a ring of keys on his belt.

"Do you have to lock it?" Finn said.

"We keep all the equipment rooms locked." Carl locked the door and hooked the keys onto his belt. "Just find me or Ian when you need to get in."

Finn said, "Yeah, but—"

Carl was already moving off down the hall. Finn turned toward the stairs, and I followed.

"What are they? It looks like a pile of old inner tubes."

"They're bags for collecting seawater." He wasn't going to offer a bit more than I asked for, forcing me to be pushy.

"Why does your friend want to collect seawater?"

"He's a biologist. Doing a study on water quality."

We climbed the stairs, me persisting. "Is that why you went to town?"

"What? Oh. No, that was just a spur-of-the-moment thing. Marcia snagged a ride, so . . ."

At the top of the stairs I said, "How long does it take to get to Stanley from here, anyway?"

"Two and a half hours. The roads are hell."

"And two and a half hours back. Wow."

Finn shrugged. "Like I said—just a lark." He cocked his head at me. "Your point is?"

"No point. It just seemed a little . . . sudden. And we *are* going in tomorrow night."

"Yeah, well." I followed him into the lounge, and he said over his shoulder, "So you got hypothermia."

"Yup. Me and Josef and Caroline. And thanks for covering for me, by the way."

"No worries." He went behind the bar and grabbed the clipboard. He grinned. "I hear Hans had the cure."

I burst into a laugh. "You just got back at, what? Noon?"

"More like two."

I shook my head. "This is one big fishbowl, isn't it?"

"Pretty much. Buy you a beer?"

And we took beers to a table by the window and caught each other up on the latest data. I saw that skua success at tourist sites from the data they'd collected Wednesday afternoon was higher than usual. I asked Finn about it.

"Huh. I don't remember anything out of the ordinary." He frowned at the page of data in his hand. "Of course, we've only been watching four days now, we barely *have* an ordinary."

"True," I said. But looming large in my mind was the fact that Marcia had been helping Finn that afternoon. As well as this afternoon. Higher skua success at sites with more visitors, lower at more remote sites. If Marcia was trying to make it look like that was the case, then why?

Finn left me alone to finish my beer, and for the first time that day, I had time to contemplate Hans and me. I had kissed him. We'd made some sort of unspoken agreement to have a relationship. How had that happened? Not twenty-four hours earlier I'd been firm in my resolve to keep him at a distance. But then, one cold day, a few times in his arms, and I'd caved. I drained my beer, set it down, and ripped a sheet of paper in half. What I needed was a list:

more job search
ask Bill about Weds numbers
gym

Feeling somewhat more in control, I allowed myself to look ahead to the evening. A picture of Hans and me on the couch in the alcove leapt into my head and I got an attack of jelly-legs. But I got a grip on myself, deposited the beer bottle in the galley recycle bin, and went to the communications room.

Liz was in a big black leather chair writing postcards. We greeted each other and I went straight to a computer, not being eager to have Liz weigh in on me and Hans at the moment.

After I spent fifteen minutes composing a cover letter, attaching the essay, and sending my résumé to Bill's friend, I sat for a moment. Liz and I hadn't really talked since Sunday night when we'd cried and held hands and I'd told her she could mother me all she wanted. Might as well let her have a go at it. I logged off and went to sit beside her.

She stopped writing and looked up. I said, "So . . . I thought you were going to mother me." I cocked my head. "Don't you have any advice?"

She put her pen down in her lap and folded her hands. "Well, I suppose you mean you and Hans. You know my point of view. And it really is none of my business."

"Well . . ."

Before I could come up with more of a response, Liz changed the subject. "Did you find out why Finn was so eager to get to town last night?" She added, "You were just talking to him."

"Oh, yeah . . . Not really. Nothing special, I guess. Just a whim."

"Hmm . . ."

"What?"

"Marcia seemed to think he was pretty intent on going."

"Really?"

Liz nodded. "When I commented on what a long trip it was, she said she didn't know why Finn was so hot to go, that he asked more than one person. And when he got a ride, she decided to tag along."

"Really!" I gazed across the room, surprised. "Huh. I'm sure Finn said it was Marcia who got the ride."

Liz shrugged and picked up her pen. "She said Finn didn't seem too happy to have her along."

Helen poked her head in the door, wool cap in hand, hair spiking up in various directions, and said, "Is anyone up for a session in the gym?" Liz declined, but I, having spent the afternoon inside, was ready to get some exercise.

"So you and Josef seem to be an item," I said, as we mounted the stationary bikes.

Helen laughed. "How about that? I was looking for someone younger than me, and I end up with the oldest guy on the boat."

"Fit, though." I started pedaling. "And cute."

"And sweet, and attentive, and funny . . . a gentleman. It'll be a lovely six weeks."

I took off my outer shirt within minutes and draped it on the handle of the bike.

Helen said, "And you, who said you never wanted a man again, got one . . . or so rumor has it."

"Yes, well . . . we get along great. Why *not* have a little fling while we're here? It's just that, after all." I paused. "And I really *don't* want a man in my life, not long term. Just for the record."

"If you say so," Helen said.

"No, really. I do better alone. I've got my son, my good friends—some of us are going to live together in our golden years, did I tell you that? Pool our resources, get a big piece of land, build little cottages." I laughed. "That's after working another fifteen or twenty years, of course."

Helen was smiling. "Got it all figured out, have you?"

"Well. Things happen, I know." I notched up the resistance on the bike. "And this thing with Hans is something apart . . . an interlude."

"And Hans?" she said.

"What?"

"He's of the same mind?"

"Of course." What was this?

Helen's green eyes were watching me.

I, ready to talk about something besides me and Hans, said, "What about you and Josef?"

Helen smiled. "He's well aware I don't want to be a caregiver again. And despite his bluster, he's beginning to feel his age. We've both got our lives, our children and grandchildren, at opposite ends of the earth." She got off the exercise bike and mopped her brow. "It's definitely a short-term affair."

I stopped as well, took a long drink from my water bottle. We started on the weights. Focusing on counting and breathing, we fell silent.

After a moment, I looked at Helen. "Of *course* Hans is of the same mind. Why wouldn't he be? I mean, with our age difference and all, he couldn't possibly be seeing it as anything serious."

Helen put down her weights and mopped her neck. "Oh, yes, you're probably right."

Hans came in that evening and made a beeline across the lounge full of people. He squeezed onto the bench next to me, his arm touching mine, all the while carrying on a laughing conversation with Yoshi about Yoshi's first time driving the Zodiac. When Yoshi left the room and the others were more or less distracted, Hans turned and kissed me on the cheek and said, "You look beautiful."

We spent the evening in the alcove. It was the first time we'd been alone together since last night's kiss. I told him about Finn's mysterious rubber bags. We discussed how Marcia and Finn gave different versions of getting a ride to town, how one of them was clearly lying. He tended to suspect Marcia, while I thought it was Finn and probably tied to the bags.

The talk with Helen had gotten me thinking I might want to make sure Hans and I were "of the same mind" as far as our relationship went. But just as I was working out how to bring up the matter, we started kissing, thoughts floated away, and it became easy to put off that conversation.

Friday morning as I settled down to observe the final gentoo colony of the day, I reached in my bag for the GPS. It wasn't there. I dumped everything onto the grass, checked all the pockets. No GPS.

Finn. He'd had the last shift yesterday and should have put it in our shared equipment bag. It was a nonessential, but useful—not to mention expensive—tool, the easiest way for pinning our exact location. I had borrowed it from Professor Brenda back home.

I asked Finn about it at lunch. He said he'd put it right where he always did, in the bottom of the bag's main compartment. He insisted on going through it himself. Of course it wasn't there, and he reluctantly agreed to look for it on the beach that afternoon.

When he reported at dinner that he hadn't found it, we got testy with each other. When did you last use it, Maybe you're the one who lost it . . . , and so on. Of course I considered the possibility of it being my fault. Finn had been putting the bag in my room after his evening shift so I'd have it for the morning; I was ninety-nine percent sure the bag had been there when I went to bed.

With this disruption, the reporting of the missing GPS to Bill, and a session on the job search, I barely saw Hans until the *Professor* was gliding into Stanley's harbor. It was eleven o'clock at night and I stood next to him at the rail—along with everyone else—watching the water turn silver in the dusk. A group went into town for beer and dancing, but Hans and I retired to the alcove. Nagging at me still was the question of expectations of our relationship. We really should be clear about that, I thought. But it was late. We had all day Saturday off, and Hans and I had made plans to rent a car and explore outside of Stanley. During that daylong date I'd definitely find a way to talk about our relationship.

THIRTEEN

Goose Green

As I sit here watching the penguins procreate, the pairs that have mated are easy to spot. It has been raining for the last couple of days, and all the females have muddy tread marks on their backs.

—*Wayne Lynch,*
PENGUINS OF THE WORLD

T HE POPULATION OF the Falkland Islands—minus the thousand or so British military personnel out by the Mount Pleasant Airport—is around 2,500. Most live in Stanley, with five hundred or so in the countryside, which is sparsely dotted with settlements of between two and thirty people. The largest of these is Goose Green, and I'd been intrigued by the name since I came across it in my guidebook at home. Hans, too, was eager to see it, as it was a site that was important during the Falklands War of 1982, when Argentina invaded to take back what they'd always felt was theirs. We had breakfast in town, then walked a few blocks to the car rental lot.

The day was bright, the wind a steady fifteen knots, just a breeze by Falkland standards. A picnic of a roast chicken, macaroni salad, apples, and cupcakes sat in a box in the back of the Land Rover, tucked under a blanket from my cabin. As Hans backed out of the rental lot, telling me how he'd driven a vehicle just like it on the ranch in Wyoming, I caught my breath and held it. People back up so carelessly. Since the seventeenth of March, twenty-five years ago, I've fought with myself every time I'm a passenger in a car that's backing up. Slow down! Look both ways! It's all I can do not to shout it. But nothing ever happens.

This time, a skinny kid on a bike flashed behind us.

"Stop!" I shouted just before we heard a thump. Hans saw the kid half a second after I did, and lurched to a stop. He yanked on the emergency brake and we were both out of the car.

The kid was sitting up, brushing his long brown hair out of his eyes and untangling himself from his bike, saying, "Jesus, man..."

We helped him up, apologizing, asking if he was okay. He was. And the bike? We examined it with him; it, too, seemed unhurt.

The guy we'd rented the car from had run out into the parking lot along with another guy, and we all stood around after the kid rode off, talking about how kids tear around and it's a miracle worse things didn't happen. We got back in the car; Hans started the engine and backed slowly onto the street.

I fumbled my seatbelt on, hands shaking, and sat trying to calm myself by breathing deep.

Hans said, "That was close." He looked over at me. "Joanie! You're shaking. It's okay; nothing happened."

"But it could have."

"I know. But nothing *did* happen."

I looked away from him, out the window, my hands clenched in my lap. I stretched my fingers, trying to relax them. A few blocks up a hill and we were at the highway.

"Right, isn't it?" he asked.

I nodded; he had to look at me to see.

We pulled onto the road, two lanes, paved, not a car in sight; the same road that led to the airport. We drove for several minutes in silence. I looked around the bare rolling landscape for something to take my mind away from the image painted on my inner eye. But nothing could. So I shut my eyes and gave in to it, the picture I'd learned to put away years ago: *Emily, her soft brown curls tangled in pine needles and dirt, her eyes closed as if in sleep, a thin trickle of blood running down the driveway. Warren standing, paralyzed, one hand on the back of the car.*

Hans glanced over and put his hand on my knee. "I'm sorry. I'm not a bad driver. I wasn't so careful back there."

I shook my head and managed, "It wasn't your fault. He came out of nowhere."

He kept his hand where it was, and after a moment, said, "What is it?"

I couldn't talk, could barely breathe, fearing the torrent of feeling. Keeping my eyes on the low brown hills on our right, I took a breath. "That's how Emily died." I looked over at him. "My daughter. My husband hit her backing out of the driveway."

Saying it made me feel heavy, but calmed me, too. A green sign with white lettering came toward us, giving mileage to Goose Green. I read it aloud.

Hans slowed the car, pulled off the highway onto a dirt track, and stopped, turning off the engine. He turned to me, said my name.

I sat, arms crossed, hugging my jacket to my body. "We'd been arguing. He'd just brought groceries home and he'd forgotten milk. I said we'd need it for breakfast; he said we could get by; he'd pick it up on his way home from work the next day. We got into this huge argument over this one little thing. He stormed out of the house to go back to the store . . ." I stared out at a bright white cloud racing across the blue sky. "We both thought she was playing in the backyard."

Hans said my name again, laid his hand on the seat, open. Reluctantly, afraid again I'd fall apart, I put mine in it.

After a moment's focusing on my breathing, I went on. "It was twenty-five years ago. Warren was depressed for a long time. We both were. Of course. I felt like he needed me, needed me to be the strong one, the one who could forgive. I forgave him . . . as much as I forgave myself. But he probably never did forgive himself." I released a breath. "We stayed together for a while. I had another baby, Bobby. But we, our relationship, never really recovered. We separated when Bobby was two."

We sat silent for a few moments. A bus rushed past on the highway, rocking the car. I unfastened my seatbelt and slid over to Hans, under his arm. He pulled me in and I leaned against his chest. I watched the hills rise and fall over the steering wheel with the rise and fall of his breathing.

"I want to say something," Hans said into my hair, "but everything seems . . ."

"No. You don't have to say anything. There's nothing to say."

We stayed that way a little while, until another Land Rover went by heading toward town. I sat up. "Well. We didn't rent this car just to sit here and watch the traffic go by. Let's go see the site of the Falklands War's deadliest combat."

I brushed his cheek with the back of my fingers and smiled. He started the engine and pulled onto the highway. It was then that a few quiet tears escaped down my cheeks.

We stopped at the Argentine Cemetery and wandered among the two-hundred some identical white crosses that mark the graves of soldiers. After stops at memorials to British soldiers, we drove down into Goose Green and walked around the quiet settlement of 30—formerly 250—residents. The main attraction was the community center, where 110 residents had been held by the Argentines for almost a month until British troops freed them. When a squall blew in, we ran for the car. With pelting rain making conversation difficult, what could we do but kiss? When we noticed the rain had stopped, we found a gravel road that led to a protected cove.

We sat on the beach cross-legged, across from each other on the blanket, lunch between us, rain momentarily at bay. Hans asked more about Emily, but when he saw I didn't feel like saying more, he asked me, "And you never married again?"

I shook my head. "I saw a lot of Warren, and it was really amicable. We shared in raising Bobby, did some holidays together. After a while he married again. But I was more or less content with my life the way it was. I had a couple summer romances. Years later I had a pretty steady boyfriend, for seven years. It ended when I went back to school. But I've never lived with a man again, not since Warren."

I picked up a stone with a piece of bright green algae plastered to one round side. "I'm really happier alone. I don't know how to keep my *self* when I'm in a relationship." Remembering my vow to talk about it, I made the effort to add, "That's why this thing with you is so cool . . . We know it's going to end on January twenty-fourth . . . and we can just enjoy it for what it is."

Hans was silent, nodding, then said, "Don't you ever think it might be that you never found the right man?"

"Oh, sure . . ." I gathered up chicken bones and put them in a plastic bag. "It's just that . . . right now, especially, I need to focus. I can't say I *never* want a man in my life again, but I've got to get strong in myself first . . . Does that make sense?"

"Yeah." Hans had shifted to sit with his back against a rock, legs outstretched. I lay down with my head in his lap, and he put a hand in my hair.

"It's your turn," I said. "We've been talking about me. I want to know more about you."

"Like what?" he said, as if there couldn't possibly be anything interesting.

"Mm . . ." I looked up at the blue sky. The breeze sailed high over our heads, and it felt warm for the first time since I'd been in the Falklands. "Like . . . what did you study in school?"

He looked down at me, smiling. "I wanted to be a veterinarian."

"Really?" I waited. "What happened?"

Gazing out at a little rowboat anchored offshore, he said. "I fell in love." He looked down at me. "We were going to be married as soon as I got my . . . what do you call it, after four years?"

"Bachelors," I said.

"My bachelors." He stopped, and it seemed like he wouldn't go on.

I craned my neck to see his face. "And?"

"She met someone else, someone she loved. She told me five days before the wedding."

"Oh, Hans."

He shrugged. "So. I graduated. I felt like I needed some time off, so I started traveling, you know, spending months away each time. I never went back to school."

"What about becoming a veterinarian?"

"That's no longer the dream."

"Is there a new dream?"

"I don't know. Maybe something like you're doing, something with penguins."

After a moment's silence I said, "And . . . you haven't been in love since?"

"Not really." Hans idly tugged the hairs at my temple. "I haven't met the right one, I guess." He was silent again, then laughed. "I suppose a psychiatrist would say I have trust issues."

"What do you think?" I stretched an arm down along his leg, held his ankle.

"I guess. Like you say, this is good, what you and I have. We will have this great time while we're here. With no expectations."

I nodded. There. We've had our talk, I told myself. He's used to this kind of thing, probably has a romance every time he parks himself somewhere for a month or two. I've been worried over nothing.

I sat up on my knees, put my hands on his shoulders and kissed him, sat back and looked at my watch. "We've just got time to see the Bodie Creek Bridge."

Once we left the car back at the rental lot, neither of us seemed to know what to do next. It was too early for dinner, and after I half-heartedly suggested a visit to the museum, and Hans, with just as little enthusiasm a beer somewhere, he proposed going back to the ship. We started walking that way. What would we do there? I thought. Go straight to his cabin with its double bed? But I was feeling distracted, melancholy.

He must have been feeling the same; when we reached the picnic table where we'd sat a week earlier, hatching our plot to be a pretend couple, he said, "Let's sit."

The harbor was choppy, a mild wind ruffled our hair, sun warmed our leeward sides. I broke the silence, saying, "I'm feeling kind of ... I don't know. Sad."

After a moment, he said, "Heavy topics, maybe. Your daughter..."

"You and your broken engagement ... seeing all those graves." I paused. "I guess that's it."

"You don't sound sure."

"That's certainly part of it." What else could it be?

He waited, and finally said, "I probably sounded bitter back there."

"Oh. No. You've been hurt."

He nodded slowly, as if he was thinking about saying more. But the silence went on.

I glanced at him, then out at the harbor. Who is this guy, anyway? I thought. A stranger. A week ago I'd never seen him before.

Hans jumped up, just catching his camera before it leapt to the ground. "Penguins in the harbor. There!"

I stood up, too. There they were, porpoising along. The shiny black bodies leapt rhythmically in little arcs, moving toward the inner harbor. "Gentoos? Or kings?"

"Looks like kings," he said.

"Do kings porpoise?"

"They do. You should see South Georgia. The bay was . . ." He wiggled his fingers. "Like boiling."

As the penguins turned into bobbing black dots, I looked at Hans's face, his lips slightly parted as he watched the penguins disappear. I *do* know him, I thought.

I hooked my hand in his arm and said, "Let's go back to the ship for a little nap before dinner."

The look he gave me made me tingle. "A nap," he said.

"Yes. Your place."

He grinned and we walked back along the breakwater, Hans walking on the edge, holding my hand and pretending, more than once, to be on the point of falling into the harbor.

In the room we kissed. After a moment I realized I was holding myself tight; I was going to be making love with someone new, showing my body to this robust young man, letting him touch me. He was going to see me naked! I pulled back, my heart pounding.

"What," he said, holding my face in his warm hands.

"I'm nervous," I said.

He smiled, his voice quiet. "What are you nervous about?" His thumbs were stroking my cheeks.

"It's been a long time for me," I said. I didn't tell him it was almost four years. Nor did I mention the fact that in those four years, menopause had arrived. And I'd heard from friends alarming stories of what that could mean for a sex life. I said out loud, "I mean, does everything still work?"

"Let's just lie down." He pulled away and took my hand. "We don't have to do anything."

We lay down. The room was cool, and Hans pulled the comforter over us.

"I'm nervous, too," he said after we'd settled in each other's arms.

"You're just trying to make me feel better."

"No," he said. He pulled away from me and lay on his back. "It's been awhile for me, too. And"—he patted his belly under the comforter—"I've put on extra weight lately. Besides . . ." He looked at me. "I really like you."

This sounded a little too serious, so I said, "As opposed to . . . ?"

"No, I mean . . ." He was blushing. "I don't know. I don't want to mess it up."

That blush. He really *was* nervous. Something shifted within me, and I said, "Well. First times aren't always so great anyway, right? We might as well get it over with, so we can get on to the second time."

We both laughed, and still laughing, kissed, and then we weren't laughing and it was warm under the blanket and then the blanket got kicked away in the shadowy light of the cabin. At one point someone knocked on the door and we held our breaths, looking at each other, faces inches apart, even though we both knew Hans had locked the door.

Everything worked perfectly well, it turned out, and when we were lying side by side, hands entwined, I said, "That wasn't so bad after all," in feigned surprise, and Hans said, "No, not too bad," barely containing his smile. "Not too bad at all."

We showered and dressed, and by then we'd missed dinner on the ship, so we went into town to the Brasserie, which was full to capacity. But Paul and Liz were at a table for four waving us over, so we joined them and ordered spaghetti and meatballs. The conversation was lively, with Liz dropping her stiffness over the bottle of wine. I was giddy, still humming, floating with our secret.

We all walked back to the ship together, Hans and I behind, holding hands, and I, speaking for myself at least, looking forward with nothing but unbridled enthusiasm to the second time.

And drifting off to sleep later, my arm draped across Hans's chest, I wondered what it was about this I was so sure I wanted to leave in five weeks.

FOURTEEN

Bobby Who?

The semihelpless state of penguin chicks means that they must be brooded for the first two or three weeks of their lives by having one parent on the nest with the chick at all times.

—*Lloyd Spencer Davis,*
SMITHSONIAN Q & A: PENGUINS:
THE ULTIMATE QUESTION AND ANSWER BOOK

AFTER BREAKFAST THE next morning we moved my clothes up to Hans's cabin. If we were going to be sleeping together, we figured we might as well have my clothes there. Crazily, I imagined sending a quick email to Bobby saying that I was living with a thirty-three-year-old man I'd met exactly one week ago. Of course, I wouldn't. He'd think I'd gone completely bonkers. And of course we weren't really *living* together; I'd keep my cabin as an office.

Liz came out of her room just as the *Professor* was pulling out of Stanley Harbour, and caught us with armloads of clothes. "I was looking for you earlier," she said. "But you weren't in your cabin."

"I stayed in Hans's cabin last night," I said. I wasn't going to be able to keep it secret anyway.

"Well," Liz said, "I hope you know what you're doing." And she headed for the stairs.

"Liz!" I called after her. "What did you want?"

"Oh. Pepa's making paella tonight. She wondered if we could start helping her at four thirty."

After following the northern edge of East Falkland, the *Professor* crossed open water to West Falkland. Though similar in area to East Falkland, its population is around one hundred. We would spend the remaining five weeks following its north, west, and south coasts, mooring at various coves and islands.

Despite the hours on the heaving ocean that drove practically everyone to visit Javier and get dosed with Dramamine, Hans and I had a fine day, watching the distant shore go by and taking breaks for lunch and a nap in the cabin.

In the afternoon I found Bill at a table in the empty dining room in front of his laptop and a cup of coffee. It was high time to catch him up on the latest. I sat down and asked him for an update on the numbers.

"The data you and Josef entered on Thursday? Just as I suspected; they don't seem to have been messed with. Marcia wasn't there that day."

"Huh. Finn and I thought the data he and Marcia gathered on Wednesday afternoon for *our* project showed higher skua activity."

"Hmm . . . well, I suppose it could be a way of showing that penguin populations at tourist sites are suffering. She does seem pretty anti-tourist."

I nodded. "And here's another odd thing. You know how Finn and Marcia went to Stanley on Wednesday evening? They give different stories on who got the ride, each claiming the other was quite eager to go."

"Huh."

"*And,*" I said, "Finn brought these odd rubber bags back with him. He says he's keeping them for a friend."

Bill grunted again, asked me a few questions, and said he'd go have a look at them.

We arrived at Saunders Island around three o'clock, and everyone went ashore, eager to see this place where all five Falkland Islands penguin species are found within sight of each other. The white sand beach of the isthmus, called The Neck, was dotted with several gentoo colonies, each on its own low mound of a couple hundred birds. Along the edge of this beach stood exactly seventeen kings. The bare green slopes that rose steeply to a high rugged ridge west of The Neck were full of Magellanic burrows, and the rocky cliffs to the east were covered with rockhoppers and a few macaronis nesting among them. Black-browed albatross nests peppered these same cliffs. We would spend a week in this paradise.

Monday evening I was at the desk in my room, writing up my thoughts on the project, when there was a knock on the open door. Finn. We'd barely spoken since our Friday evening flare-up.

He walked over and without a word set the GPS down in front of me.

I stared at it a moment, then looked up at him. "Where was it?"

"In my room."

When I didn't say anything, he said, "On the floor, under the desk."

I still held my tongue. Finn stepped to the door, pulled it shut, came back.

"Joanie. I know it wasn't there before. I looked everywhere."

"Okay . . ."

"Someone took it. Out of the bag when it was in your room and kept it until . . . today probably."

I nodded. "I believe you." I wasn't *entirely* sure I did, but I had a feeling he was telling the truth. If Finn was anything, he was thorough and careful about his work.

After he left, I turned to a new page in my notebook and made a list of every person on the ship, researchers and crew included—anyone who might have come into my room and taken the GPS and returned it to under Finn's desk. I crossed out most names and put a question mark by a few. But these question marks seemed iffy at best, and I ended up with a circle around one name: Marcia. Perhaps for no other reason than the woman kept doing subtle little things to annoy me.

When I went up to Bill's cabin to report that the GPS had been found, I said only that I had a feeling Finn was telling the truth and nothing about my thoughts on Marcia. Bill pulled thoughtfully on his chin and told me to be especially vigilant. I would have more time to do so since the gentoo population at The Neck was fairly small, and my team would be spending more time on the main count with the others. Bill added something I didn't know. "Bernard is spending the week with us. Keep an eye out for how he interacts with people, especially Marcia and Finn."

Despite all the funny business, I rather enjoyed playing detective and felt confident Bill and I would figure out what was going on. Before going to Hans's cabin for the rest of the evening, I made a new list with a routine: meetings with Finn, exercise with Helen, two evenings a week on job hunt, one evening of Spades, keep an eye on Bernard and Marcia and Finn. No need to schedule time with Hans; in fact the list was partly a way to keep from spending every spare moment with him. I snapped my notebook shut, locked it in a desk drawer, left the room, and bounded up the stairs, eager for the night to come. I was on top of my project, keeping at the job hunt, and having an amazing romance. It was easy to believe these halcyon days would go on for our remaining time in the Falklands.

Late Tuesday evening, a couple days after I had moved in with Hans, I found him sitting in front of one of the computers in the communications room. I hadn't seen him in over an hour—a rare occurrence when we were both on the ship—and stood behind him, putting my hands on either side of his neck and bending to kiss the top of his head. His hand came up to cover mine, but he didn't move his gaze from the screen, didn't speak. I saw that he was looking at an email, and after a moment said, "What's up?"

He didn't answer, so I sat down in the next chair and watched him.

He clicked the mouse to log off and turned to me. His eyes, normally wide open to his soul, were flat. He said, "My father has died."

He looked so frozen, so unapproachable, that I didn't know whether to touch him, whether to speak. He looked back at the blank screen.

I put my hand on his arm. "Hans, I'm so sorry."

He nodded.

I waited, and he didn't move. Damn, I thought. He'll have to go. Just when everything . . . But I stopped. This wasn't about me. "I guess you'll have to go home."

"I don't know." He stood and walked over to the door, then back. He sat down again. "It was my sister. Freya. I didn't answer yet. I don't know what I'm going to do."

Voices approached, and Finn and Alejandro came into the room, deep in a rudimentary conversation in Spanish.

I said to Hans, "Let's see if we can go ashore for a while."

Ten minutes later we were walking across rocks and up the slope until we found a little hollow in the low scrub, where by lying down, we were more or less out of the wind and in the sweep of the evening sun. I lay on my back and Hans curled around me, his head under my chin.

After a few moments of silence, he pulled back to look at me. "All I can think about is I don't want to leave here." A bitter laugh. "Selfish, right? I don't want to leave the work, the Falklands. I don't want to leave you."

"It's not selfish," I said. "I mean ... it sounds like you didn't have that great of a relationship with your dad." I'd put this together from bits and pieces, though he hadn't really said.

"Yes," he said, up on one elbow now, looking across me at a cluster of tiny white flowers batting at the edge of our hollow. "I didn't. I told you my mom died when I was six, and my older sister raised me, mostly. My father was not much around."

I watched the clouds scudding by as he talked. The blue sky was fading to white, the clouds' underbellies taking on an apricot hue.

"And when I got older ... He was critical of me all the time. I haven't made anything of my life, haven't stayed with anything. I'm not interested in the business. I'm a big disappointment to him."

"But your sisters," I asked. "They'll want you there, won't they?"

"Yes." He lay back down, put his hands behind his head. "They will."

"Then you have to go. You can go for a week and come back."

It was getting cold, even in the protected nest. I sat up. "Let's go back. Go tell Ian and then tomorrow call a travel agent in Stanley and let them work out your trip."

He didn't move and a smile flickered across his face. He said, "Yes, Mom."

I jumped on top of him and, my face two inches from his and with my best steely gaze, said, "If you promise never to call me 'Mom' again, I promise I'll try not to act like one."

He laughed and put his arms around me. "I promise."

We lay like that for a while, neither of us wanting to move beyond that moment.

Hans went to talk with Ian, and I went to the media room and logged into my email. There was a short message from Bobby telling me his plans for Christmas and his birthday on the twenty-sixth. I sent him a quick reply. There were no job offers or interview invitations. I went up to Hans's cabin and got in bed with plans to read until he got back.

It was dark, and I was asleep when he climbed in beside me.

"What time is it?" I said, crabby to be awakened.

"Eleven thirty. Sorry, I meant to be back sooner." He pulled me close, my back fitting into the curve of his body. "I was talking to Ian. His father died last year. He said they weren't very close, so he had . . . confused feelings."

I was awake now and back in touch with what was going on. "That's . . . of course you wanted to stay."

"Yes, it was good." He paused. "He gave me some scotch."

Ah. So that's what I smelled. Determined not to be mom-like again, I kept it light; I turned and sniffed his breath loudly. "Mm-hmm . . . single malt, probably at least ten years old . . ."

He kissed me. "What kind?"

"Umm ... Glenmorangie?" It was the first brand that popped into my head.

"No." He kissed me again. "I didn't notice what kind, but not that."

We snuggled closer. Hans taking his first drink in over two years was probably okay. This was a special situation; his dad had just died and the boss offered a drink as part of a whole package of sharing. A rare and valuable gift.

"When Ian was little," Hans said, "his dad used to get them up at six o'clock in the morning—there were many kids—and make them stand by their beds until he inspected them. The beds, their rooms, their faces ... their ears ..."

I liked the image of two guys, *these* two guys, improbably, talking like that. "I want to hear some stories about your dad."

"Maybe tomorrow. I have other ideas tonight."

"Oh yes? Tell me."

"How about I show you."

I could still count the number of times we'd made love, and each one was distinct; from our nervous excitement of Saturday afternoon, to last night's slow dance. Tonight was about comfort, and ended with him kissing a tear from my eye. Who was comforting whom?

He said, "I wish you could come with me."

I wasn't sure how this was meant and didn't answer.

After a moment, he said, "I'm not asking ... You have your work. And it wouldn't be a good idea."

"No," I said.

"But it would be nice."

As we drifted into sleep, I found myself resisting the crazy urge to tell him I loved him.

The next day, Wednesday, was Christmas Eve. Hans stayed in to put in the call to the travel agent while I went ashore with Finn, Paul, and Michiyo to spend the morning watching skua behavior. As the Zodiac approached the beach, I watched a Land Rover bounce away from us over the rutted track, headed toward the settlement, an hour's ride away, reportedly a cluster of houses with a current summer population of nine.

"More tourists?" I asked Finn as we climbed out of the boat. Tourist facilities at The Neck consisted of one lone building, a Portakabin: a former ship's container remodeled into housing for eight. A group of Japanese photographers had spent three nights and left the previous day, but I saw no sign of activity there now.

"Maybe. Also Marcia and Bernard heading into Stanley." I realized then that I hadn't seen much in the way of Marcia-Bernard interactions in the short time he'd been with us. I had only worked with him once when he joined me and Josef to observe my project. In the evenings he was very much a presence, his voice booming as he made a point of getting to know everyone. But as far as having any particular interactions with Marcia to report to Bill, I could only recall one, which I had told him about.

"Really?" I said. The hour bumping over a rough track would be followed by a forty-five-minute flight to the capital. "I can see Bernard going to spend Christmas with his family, but what about Marcia and her research?"

"No cruise ships here over Christmas. Probably going to see her boyfriend."

"Boyfriend?"

"Just a guess." Finn put on his day pack. "I told you I saw her in town with a guy on Saturday?"

"No. You didn't. What were they doing? What did he look like?"

Finn, tired of the topic, started walking. "I don't know. Sitting on a bench along the breakwater. I was coming down a side street and they didn't see me."

"Anything else?" I said.

"Why are you so interested?"

"No reason. It's just that she's acting kind of strange." I had to hurry to keep up with Finn's long strides along the beach. On impulse I said, "Did you know, for instance, she claimed it was you who found the ride last week?"

He glanced at me.

"Yeah. She said you asked several people."

"Huh." Finn didn't break stride, his eyes on the curve of the hill at the end of the beach.

Suddenly I felt certain it *was* Finn who fibbed about how they got their ride, and not Marcia. But I let him keep thinking I was interested only in Marcia. "So what did this guy look like?"

"I don't know. Medium height. Kind of red hair."

Red hair. The drunk guy at the Globe that first night who claimed he knew Marcia had red hair.

Pepa served up three turkeys that evening and everyone stayed up late playing charades and dancing. Yoshi and Michiyo taught Japanese Christmas carols. Hans, who'd been quiet all evening, announced he was leaving and why. Of course by then it was news to no one.

Christmas Day was a holiday from work. Hans and I, along with Finn, Helen, Josef, and Yvonne made turkey sandwiches and spent the day hiking out to Elephant Point, eight miles round trip. We passed ponds full of waterbirds we hadn't seen before and colonies of nesting kelp gulls. Josef was dive-bombed by a skua, which he fended off bravely with his hiking stick. The "elephants" of Elephant Point were elephant seals, sleeping brown bodies strewn across the beach like giant slugs. When we got back in the late afternoon, Hans's itinerary had been sent. He would leave the next day on the first leg of a two-day journey home.

"Come with me to Stanley," he said once we were in his room. "I'll have the day and night there with no purpose."

"Oh . . . I'd love to. But I shouldn't. I can't really afford it for one thing. The round-trip flight alone is over two hundred bucks. Then there's the room, the meals . . ." My pennies had been carefully counted out for this Falkland trip. Still, the pull of him wanting me was almost too much.

"I'll pay," Hans said.

"I can't let you do that. You're already spending plenty to go home."

He seemed about to say something, but I went on. "I'd have to miss two days of work and with you leaving we're already short one person . . ."

"Yes, you're right," he said.

FIGAS—Falkland Islands Government Air Service—has no fixed schedule. You choose which day you want to fly and where you want to go, and FIGAS gets ahold of you the night before to tell you when they'll pick you up. Flying from one of the outer islands into Stanley on Saturday—the day of the flight to the mainland—is not recommended, as there's a slight risk of the FIGAS flight getting canceled due to wind or fog.

At seven forty-five Friday morning I went ashore with Hans and his bag. The Land Rover was waiting on the edge of the beach. We hugged goodbye, a necessarily short one; the driver had tossed Hans's bag on the back seat, climbed in, and started the engine.

"I'll be with you," I said, my face pressed against his neck.

"Will you stay in our cabin?"

"With that big bed? Absolutely."

One last kiss, longer. He got in the Rover, and I stood watching for the couple minutes it took to disappear around the sandy flank of the hill. He would be back the following Saturday evening, meeting us at our new moorage off the West Falkland mainland.

Javier was waiting by the water, holding the bowline of the Zodiac. He watched me approach, shaking his head, with a small smile.

"What?" I said, knowing it was probably my moist eyes.

He nodded sagely, handed me the rope, got in and climbed back to sit by the motor. I pushed the boat a few steps and jumped in without getting my feet wet; I'd become quite adept at timing the surf. We zoomed back to the *Professor* and breakfast.

Tucked in bed that night, after a long day of counting Magellanic burrows—periodically having to reconvince myself that not going to Stanley with Hans was the only practical thing to do—I lay in bed with the lights out and Pru the Penguin resuming her place as my bed pal.

It was then I remembered; today was Bobby's twenty-fourth birthday. I'd forgotten I had promised to call him.

FIFTEEN

Something That Doesn't Matter Anymore

The distance a parent must travel from the colony to find food generally determines how frequently a chick is fed. Commonly, the interval between meals in kings and emperors may be three days or longer. Adélie, chinstrap, royal, macaroni, rockhopper and magellanic chicks are fed more often than that—typically, every one to three days. The chicks of all the other species of penguins usually receive a meal every day or so.

—*Wayne Lynch,*
PENGUINS OF THE WORLD

'D BEEN AFRAID this would happen. Letting a man into my life had messed with my focus. Forgetting my son's birthday for the first time ever was proof. All night I wrestled with such thoughts. First thing in the morning I sent Bobby an email, apologizing and telling a not entirely untrue story about being in the field all day and not near the sat-phone until it was too late. I left out how Bill had suggested a Spades game after dinner, and to show I wasn't lonely and moping, I'd joined in. At eight o'clock in fact, the time I should have been calling Bobby, I'd just been dealt the ace, king, and jack of spades and been passed the queen and ten by my partner.

When I logged off, it struck me that I hadn't suggested a new phone call date. I had to wonder: Was I avoiding talking to Bobby because I didn't think I'd be able to keep my joy and excitement from bubbling across the line? I wasn't quite ready to tell my son his mother was having a fling with a man a mere ten years older than he was.

I went to stand on deck and admire the new surroundings before breakfast. We'd moved Friday evening from Saunders and were now moored in a protected cove off of West Falkland, surrounded on three sides by steep hills. The gentlest of breezes rocked the boat; a pair of oystercatchers poked their long red beaks among the rocks and seaweed. I imagined Hans beside me, eyes wide, drinking it all in, and felt a stab of missing him. He wouldn't get to see this magical spot; by the time he got back, we'd have moved again. He was still only in Stanley, probably leaving in an hour or so for the airport, and I felt the wrench again that I really could have—should have?—gone with him that far.

That evening after dinner I found Paul and Liz sitting with Helen, Finn, and Marcia in a cluster of chairs in the lounge, into a third liter of red wine. Paul called to me to grab a glass, which I did. I sat by Helen on the couch.

Marcia was draped over a chair across from us, head on one of its plush arms, legs over the other, a glass of wine held on her stomach. She'd returned that morning from Stanley and was telling of her observations of large groups of cruise ship passengers that were visiting Gypsy Cove, which contained some of the nearest penguin colonies to Stanley. She'd stayed an extra day to observe them and was now wrapping up what seemed to have been a lengthy rant about the insensitivity of tourists "standing around in their matching yellow windbreakers, with their stupid cameras, whining that the Magellanics wouldn't come out of their burrows."

As her audience shook their heads, she took a healthy swallow of wine and focused her gaze on me. "Heard from your boyfriend yet?"

"Nope. We're not going to keep in touch." I knew exactly where he was at that moment, of course; whiling away a four-hour layover at the Santiago airport.

"Huh," Marcia said, and drank again.

Helen said, "That's wise. It's so hard to communicate by email or phone calls when you're used to in-person. Besides, when you're waiting to hear from someone, it can become all you think about."

Good old Helen.

"I did get an interesting email, though." I told them about the Big Bend job. I had just learned that it went to someone else. "One of my best leads, I thought."

A chorus of sympathy went up from all but Marcia, who said, "I'm sure Hans'll take care of you if you don't get a job."

"What's that supposed to mean?" I asked, amazed at the woman's thinly disguised hostility.

Marcia sat up and put the glass down, wiped her mouth slowly with the back of her hand. "Oh, you know. The family business ... He's the only son. He's got to be getting something."

"I suppose. But it's only a small company ... And anyway, it has nothing to do with me."

Liz sat up on the edge of her chair. "He must be fairly well off, though, to be able to travel all the time the way he does."

"He lives at home and saves his money," I said.

Marcia drained her glass. "Well, I imagine he'll shoot you an email if he decides to stay in Zurich."

"He's not going to stay," I said. "He's coming back in a week."

Marcia shrugged. "He's probably in charge of the business now. You don't work those things out in a week."

What did *she* know about it? Hairs stood up on the back of my neck; a precursor to some kind of primal catfight no doubt. But I stayed civil. "He'll do what's needed now—the funeral mainly—and deal with the rest after we're done here." *I* know what Hans thinks; not you.

"I guess we'll see," said Marcia. She stood. "I'm off to bed. Didn't get much sleep last night." And with a smug little smile, she was gone.

The rest of us looked at each other. Finn said, "Whoa." Paul held up the carton of wine. Four glasses floated forward.

I went up to Hans's cabin after drinking one glass too many and got in bed with my novel. After a couple of minutes of reading the same sentence over and over without comprehension, I shut the book and lay thinking about Marcia. I seldom encountered people who didn't like me. And Marcia clearly didn't like me. Why? Did she really want Hans for herself? That was catty stuff, how she spit out "boyfriend" and "I'm sure he'll take care of you." And what was that about her suggesting Hans might be staying longer than a week? Making it sound like she had special knowledge.

It wasn't until then that the thought struck me: Maybe they'd run into each other in Stanley. Maybe Marcia even stayed an extra night for the very purpose of tracking him down. Maybe she got him to go out for a pint. He could have said something that led her to believe . . . And what was with the "I didn't get much sleep last night"? Did she ply him with liquor, listen earnestly with her big dark eyes . . . ? I stopped that line of thought before it went any further. There was no way Hans would have succumbed to Marcia's wiles. "Right?" I asked Pru.

Things kept adding up about Marcia: the data discrepancies, running off to Stanley at every opportunity, that guy at the Globe the first night who claimed to know her, Finn seeing her in town with likely that very same guy. And how did the GPS go missing? Now this venom. At me!

I got out of bed and put my clothes back on. Out on deck it was nearly dark. Not even a week past the solstice; the days couldn't be getting shorter already, could they? Stars were coming out in a mostly clear sky and I stopped to look for the Southern Cross. After three weeks in the Southern Hemisphere I still hadn't seen it. Was that it? High in the southern sky was a group of stars in a cross pattern. Bill would know.

A light was shining from his window. I knocked, and he let me in. He was wearing pajamas, but with lamps on and a laptop on the tossed-back bed covers I knew I hadn't woken him. I sat on the couch; Bill on the edge of the bed.

I got right to the point, lest he think this was a social call. "Who's going to be keeping an eye on Marcia while Hans is gone?"

I half expected he'd say he hadn't thought about it. But he was ready with a plan. "Audrey. She's flying out tomorrow evening and will stay all week. Replacing Hans, in essence. Why the interest?"

I told him how Marcia suggested that I was really after Hans for a kind of meal ticket, and how she'd implied that he might stay in Zurich.

"Sounds to me like two women fighting over the same man," Bill said. "And you want to strike the next blow by catching her at something."

I scowled. "You're the one who told me to keep an eye on her, that she could be the one who's up to something."

"Well," he said. "The data's been pretty consistent lately, since Ian spoke to her about including who gave her which numbers. I suspect she was just being sloppy at first."

"Well, fine. But how about this: Finn saw her in Stanley with a guy last week. A red-haired guy. And the first weekend when we were out dancing at the Globe, a red-haired guy—rather drunk— kept insisting he knew her. She insisted he didn't and got us to leave at that point."

"You never mentioned that."

"I guess I didn't think much of it until Finn said he'd seen her with probably the same guy."

"Please. Tell me all this stuff."

"Well, half the time you act like I'm just looking for dirt on Marcia because I don't like her."

He held up his hands. "I'll stop. Anything else you forgot to tell me?"

I thought a moment, shook my head. "I already told you how she and Bernard suddenly stopped that private conversation when I showed up."

He nodded. "All right. It's all interesting. But we'll have to find something more concrete than 'They looked guilty.'"

"I just don't trust her," I said, standing.

"You don't have to rush off," Bill said.

"I should. It's late." I went to the door and opened it. Feeling I was bordering on being rude, I stopped. "Do you know what the Southern Cross looks like?"

"Of course," he said. He pulled on his parka and followed me outside, where we stood at the rail. "That's the false cross," he said, pointing to my guess. "And just next to it, you see what looks like a crooked diamond?"

I nodded.

"That's it." And he pointed out the two faint stars that pointed south.

"Hm," I said. "Not much to it, is there?"

"Not as distinctive as the Big Dipper," he agreed.

But there was no Big Dipper here. A clear sign I was far from home.

Two days later I was eating an early supper before going back out to do a shift on the skua project when Ian sat down across from me, clipboard in hand.

"A reporter from *Penguin News* is coming out tomorrow for a story on what we're doing here. I want her to talk to a scientist, a volunteer, and one of the grad students. Thought you could be the grad student."

"Oh!" Ian had a way of springing things on people. But I was pleased. *Penguin News* is the Falklands' one newspaper, a weekly. "Sure. When?"

"I'll have her out in the field with Bill as soon as she gets here. You can come in around eleven o'clock and meet with her then. She'll talk to Yoshi and Liz at lunch, representatives of the volunteers."

He tucked his clipboard under his arm and strode off.

The reporter's name was Karen, and she asked astute questions about skuas and gentoos. She'd read some studies and seen skuas in action herself. It was her opinion that penguins are not bothered enough by tourists for it to make a difference. I said that as far as my study went, the jury was still out.

Karen was making some final notes when Finn walked into the lounge. He saw us and immediately turned on his heel saying a quick, "Sorry," and was gone.

Karen said, "Was that Finn Markovich?"

"Yes! He's my research partner. You know him?"

She laughed. "He spent his first afternoon in the Falklands with us."

At my blank look, she said, "A lot of us here wear more than one hat. On Saturdays I'm a customs agent. We had some questions for Mr. Markovich. He spent several hours with us."

"Ah. So he told me."

Karen paused in the act of putting the cap back on her pen. "Tell me; how do you use those bags?"

"Bags?"

"Yes. Mr. Markovich had six large rubber bags. He said they were for his research."

"Oh!" The only bags I knew of were the ones he brought out from Stanley, the bags he was keeping for his friend. The bags that were now locked in the room down on Deck Two. "Yes ... ," I said, "I'm not sure exactly. He has his own thing going. He's not the most forthcoming person. Hasn't shared the details with me." Why in the world was I covering for him?

"Interesting." Karen jotted something down in her book. "Perhaps we can find him and ask him." She capped her pen, put it and her notebook in her bag, and we went looking for Finn. We combed the ship, but he couldn't be found. Back in the dining room Carl was getting a cup of coffee and when asked if he'd seen Finn, said he had just taken him ashore.

I told Karen that Finn had stored some bags down on Two, and we got Carl to unlock the storage area. She confirmed that the bags were the very ones Finn had with him when he arrived.

As soon as I got in from the field that evening, I found Finn and asked him up to my "office" for a talk.

"So . . . I got interviewed by a gal from *Penguin News* today."

"That woman I saw you with? How'd it go?"

"Fine. It turns out you've met her."

"Yeah?"

"She's a customs agent . . . on Saturdays when the plane comes in." I waited, but evidently he needed more encouragement. "Turns out she had quite a lengthy talk with you the day you arrived."

Finn snapped his fingers. "*That's* where I saw her before."

"She asked me how we use those bags in our project."

He blinked.

"That you told me belong to your friend? Who was moving?"

Finn picked up a pen and started dropping it on its end on the desk, over and over.

"According to her, they were in your luggage when you arrived. And you told her they were for your research project." I waited again, but it seemed I needed to remind him. "But that wasn't your story when you brought them out from Stanley."

"What makes you think they're the same bags?"

"We went to look at them. She said they were." When he said nothing, I said, "Finn. What's going on?"

"What did you tell her?" Stalling.

"I said you had your own project going and hadn't shared the details."

"Why'd you say that?"

"Darned if I know."

"Well." He leaned forward in the chair, stopped fiddling with the pen. "Thank you."

"Look, Finn," I leaned forward, too. "You've been less than honest about a few things. You said going into town last week was a spur-of-the-moment thing. And yet Marcia said you seemed eager to get a ride. Then the bags. Keeping them for a friend. That sounded a bit odd at the time. And now it seems you've lied to customs as well. What's going on?"

He sat up straight. "Nothing's going on. You've got to trust me." His jaw was firm, but his eyes were pleading.

I was silent, wondering what to do. If anything.

Finn looked directly at me for the first time. "It's just . . . something that doesn't matter anymore."

As I got into bed that night, I realized I hadn't told Bill any of this. I didn't feel like telling him, either, not yet, though it definitely fell under the category of things he'd want to know. Was it because I wanted to nail Marcia? *Was* it part of fighting over the same man? I didn't want to think so. Perhaps instead it was that I was fond of Finn despite his quirks and prickliness. There was something about him, I realized, that reminded me of myself at that age.

If Hans had been there, I would have told him about the latest on Finn and his bags. He'd been gone almost five days, still three to go. I grabbed Pru, turned out the light, and hugged the fuzzy bundle to me.

SIXTEEN

Black Eye

*Lest you be tempted to consider skuas nasty, unwelcome additions
to the food chain, remember that their chicks are, like those of their
prey, small, irresistibly fluffy, and always hungry.*

—*Kevin Schafer,*
THE FALKLAND ISLANDS:
BETWEEN THE WIND & SEA

O N WEDNESDAY AFTERNOON we moved to the bay where
Hans would arrive on Saturday, brought out by Land
Rover from the airstrip, over a ridge and down the faint track
to the beach. The bay was teeming with Magellanics and rockhoppers, but most of the gentoos were in the next cove south. A
trip by Zodiac was considered too tricky due to the rocky coastline and strong westerlies, so Bill, Paul, Liz, Finn, and I volunteered to hike three miles up and over the south headland the
next day. We would spend the night, observing skua behavior
and counting every breeding pair of gentoos that afternoon and
the next morning.

I gathered Thursday morning with Paul, Liz, and Bill, along with tents, sleeping bags, and food enough for the overnight trip. But Finn was not among us.

"He woke up with a cold," Bill said. "He'll stay and work here."

"A cold or a hangover?" Paul said. The previous evening everyone had stayed up past midnight celebrating New Year's Eve and Josef's eightieth birthday.

We trudged up the slope of grass that had been cropped to the nub by a couple centuries of sheep grazing. Bill and I pulled ahead and moved into thickening tufts of grass and diddle-dee, the ubiquitous maroon-berried shrub. Though my pack was heavy, I felt strong after almost three weeks in the field and the workouts in the gym with Helen. Once on top of the ridge, the wind nearly flattened us, so we kept low as we moved down the other side until the gusts eased some. We stopped to catch our breath in the knee-deep scrub and sat down to wait for Paul and Liz.

I dug out my camera and took a few shots of the little cove below us.

"Did it seem to you like Finn really had a cold?" I said after a moment. "He's strong as a horse. And he wasn't drinking much last night."

"He actually looked pretty fit," Bill said. "But he said he didn't feel well and then made a great show of blowing his nose."

"Huh."

"I wonder what he's up to," Bill said. "He and Marcia . . ."

I looked at him. "You don't think they're working together?"

"It seems unlikely on the one hand. Different . . . worldview. But going to town together that time. And what you told me about the day she helped him with your project."

"Yes," I said. "That afternoon showed the highest skua success rate so far. It'll be interesting to see if they work together while we're away today and tomorrow."

I was about to tell Bill that Finn lied about the bags, when Paul and Liz came swishing through the scrub, exclaiming about the view. I postponed saying more.

We set up camp on the grass near the beach and put in a two-hour shift for my project before dinner and another after. The wind picked up, and during the evening shift I got nearly as cold as I had on the hypothermia day, so I called a halt a bit early, and we all hiked up the southern arm of the cove and back. Much revived, we huddled in Bill's and my tent—the larger of the two, as Finn was supposed to be there sharing it with us—and sipped hot chocolate and played Spades until Paul complained he couldn't sit cross-legged any longer, and we called it a night.

Before I had a chance to feel awkward about being alone in the tent with Bill, he offered to step outside while I got ready for bed, and asked if I was decent before he came back in.

We settled with a sleeping bag-sized distance between us. It was ten o'clock, with still plenty of light out. I thought about how to tell Bill about Finn and the bags, not quite understanding why I was hesitant.

I stalled a bit longer by asking him about WSR and his suspicions over the last count. "It seems odd they didn't take you more seriously," I said.

He shook his head. "They insisted they'd done what they could to look into it, and everything seemed in order. But I was sure something was fishy and I couldn't drop it. I only ended up making a pest of myself." He was lying on his back, hands clasped behind his head. "I finally let it go. All I accomplished was making enemies in the field. By the time I retired last year, people had come to see me as someone who had stayed too long." He hesitated before adding, "I was expecting to be offered the position of head scientist on the count this year. The position Ian has."

"Oh!" My heart went out to him. A disappointing way to wrap up a brilliant career! I'd certainly heard nothing negative about Bill and said, "Well, any tarnish on your reputation hasn't made it into academia."

"Not to the students, maybe."

"Nor to the faculty," I said. "They all spoke highly of you."

We were quiet for a few moments, listening to the wind on the tent. Then I brought him up to date on Finn. How the *Penguin News* reporter had recognized him, how when customs had detained him, he had rubber bags, and the reporter and I confirmed them as the ones Finn had stored in the equipment room. I told how I'd confronted Finn with all this, and he'd as good as admitted to lying about the bags, but asked me to trust him, that it was something that didn't matter anymore.

Bill listened with interest, more interest than when I brought him my reports on Marcia. Had he made up his mind that Finn was the culprit, Bernard's accomplice, while I'd decided it was Marcia? Not how good detectives would do it, making up our minds to the point of closing them to other possibilities. I shared this thought with Bill, and he agreed to try to be more open-minded if I'd do the same.

I plumped my fleece-covered bundle of clothing into the semblance of a pillow and pulled my sleeping bag up under my chin. It had grown dusky and was long past time to sleep. But the wind wasn't cooperating; just when I became lulled by a steady thrum on the tent, a gust would slap the walls, jerking me awake. I saw that Bill, too, was restless.

"This wind is never going to let us sleep," I said. "Did you get anything more from Audrey? I've seen you together a lot recently."

"She's been filling me in on the latest on oil exploration. They're on the point of expanding offshore searches, moving into deeper water. Water they decided twenty years ago was too expensive, and too dangerous, to work."

"Have we learned nothing from the Gulf?" I said. A recent explosion on a drilling platform, a fire, and months of oil spewing into the Gulf of Mexico were fresh in my mind. "And these waters are so much wilder. An accident here would be . . ." I shook my head. "They couldn't begin to fix it."

"Not much human population here to worry about," Bill said.

"Just the environment, just the wildlife." We were both silent until I said, "It's hard sometimes to not feel like you're fighting a losing battle."

After a moment, Bill said, "You know Bernard's a huge supporter of exploration and development of that industry. Audrey says he's invested a lot of his own money."

"I wonder what he's doing here, working with us."

"I asked her. She thinks his boss sent him to try to raise his awareness of conservation—you know he's got that part-time government post? Apparently this guy is much more conservation-minded than Bernard is, realizes if the penguins disappear, tourists will stop coming to the Falklands. And tourism is now the second-biggest industry. But from what Audrey tells me, Bernard would just as soon have the world leave the Falklands and him and his businesses alone."

I pondered this until I began to feel drowsy. But there was another slap of wind. This time Bill continued the conversation. "We've also been talking about us; me and her."

"Oh!" I wasn't entirely surprised by this, having noticed a closeness between the two of them.

"We had a bit of a thing ten years ago when I spent a month here. She was single at the time." He looked at the tent ceiling. "She's not very happy in her marriage. Thinking about leaving her husband."

"Oh!" I said again, and after a moment, "Wow."

"Yeah." Bill curled on his side, facing me. "I'm not holding my breath."

We lay silent with our thoughts then. I finally closed my eyes. After a time, the wind lessened, the gusts stopped, and I drifted to sleep, with only the occasional squawk of a Magellanic punctuating the swish of wind.

The next morning Bill and Paul made a count of all the penguins in the cove while Liz and I put in one more two-hour shift on the last gentoo colony. She and I had hardly spent any time alone together since the first night on Volunteer Beach when she lectured me about Hans and Bill. After we watched quietly for a few minutes, Liz said, "So . . . Hans comes back tomorrow."

I nodded, eyes still on the colony.

"Unless he decides to stay," Liz said.

"He's not going to stay. I don't know where Marcia got that."

Liz said nothing.

"I'm sure he's already on his way." In fact, according to my calculations, he was likely headed to the Zurich airport at that moment. "He would have contacted me if he'd changed his plans." I shook my head. "That Marcia."

Liz glanced at me. "I know she's not very friendly with you. But really, she's not a bad person."

"Hmm . . ." I put my binoculars up to my eyes again.

Liz smiled. "You should have seen her last week. There was one rockhopper with a giant gash across its chest. She thought it was from a seal attack. Poor little guy. We were watching several of them climb a steep path; he was definitely slower than the others. And then he stopped right in front of us. Not more than ten feet away, oblivious to our presence. He bent his head to clean his wound. Really, it brought tears to my eyes. I looked over at Marcia, and she was teary, too. She looked at me and said, 'You just wish you could do something.'"

I made an effort to picture Marcia as the caring conservationist, but I had trouble imagining her really caring about anyone, person or animal. Before Liz could say more, I changed the subject. "You and Pepa seem to be getting pretty chummy." I'd seen Liz with the red-haired cook talking earnestly over coffee a couple of times and once in the evening over glasses of wine.

"Poor girl." Liz sighed. "She's having a rough time."

"How so?" I knew her only as smiling and easygoing, an efficient and pleasant overseer of the galley.

"You know she and Javier have something going."

"Hard to miss. They make a nice couple, don't you think? Both from Spain, he's a doctor, she's planning to go to nursing school . . ."

She nodded. "But . . ." She glanced toward camp to check that we weren't overheard. "Did you know Pepa's married?"

"No!" I lowered my binoculars again.

"I shouldn't be telling you," she said, and looked out at the opening to the cove. It seemed she wouldn't say more, but after a moment, she turned. "Don't tell anyone. Javier doesn't know. She's afraid her husband will file for custody of their two boys if they separate. Especially if she has a lover." Liz's eyes were shining, as if the word *lover* were a foreign, and delicious, one on her tongue.

"Oh, boy. What did you tell her?"

She had a dreamy, unfocused look. "I told her to listen to her heart."

Huh, I thought; why isn't that your advice to me? But it was interesting news. The more I thought about it, though, the more I wished I didn't know. Javier had become a friend. How was I supposed to not say anything to him?

Liz interrupted these thoughts by saying, "Helen says you had a daughter who died."

A jolt passed through me, and I didn't answer right away. Helen and Hans were the only people I'd told. I'd assumed they wouldn't pass it on, although I hadn't asked them not to. I supposed that now Liz knew, the whole boat would know.

Liz said, "She only told me when I told her about Laurie. I guess she thought I knew."

"It's okay," I said. "It's not a secret. I've only told Helen—along with my whole life story for some reason—and Hans. I guess you wonder why I didn't tell you when you told me about your daughter."

"No. It's okay. I was being pretty pushy that night . . ."

Paul and Bill were walking toward us along the beach. "Two hours already?" I touched Liz's hand. "Let's talk more soon."

After lunch, we headed back to the ship. I brought up the rear, lagging behind, happy to be alone. Just over the crest of the last hill, the *Professor* came into view below, and I saw an inviting dip in the thick cushion of green before me. I called to the others to go on without me; I'd catch up. They waved and kept on down the hill, and I waded into the little nest in the scrub and sank to a cross-legged position in its lowest point. To my delight, I was completely protected from the battering wind. Below me was the green slope, the beach, the bay full of whitecaps, and the white *Professor* bobbing like a toy not far offshore.

What better place to sit and go over my data? Although it was a small sample, I was eager to see if there was any difference in skua success at this site, which had likely seen no human visitors in years. Finn and I had begun to see a pattern toward little difference in skua success between tourist and non-tourist sites, but this time the hours of observation in the remote little cove showed more skua success. A few minutes of perusing Bill and Paul's data showed the same.

I packed my notebook and pen away and lay back to watch heavy gray clouds scudding across the sky, reluctant to leave my shelter. My thoughts went back to the conversation with Liz. I wasn't eager to talk to her more about losing our daughters. Her wound was so fresh, mine an ancient scar. I felt Liz would want something from me, some kind of guidance, lessons on coping. I wasn't at all sure I was any kind of role model on coping. Stuff it away, don't think about it; that had been my method. And avoid future hurt by not loving again. Which led me to a question I'd had before; had I loved Bobby enough? He seemed to have turned out okay. Sure, he hadn't figured out a direction for his life yet, but that's not so unusual for a twenty-four-year-old, is it? And I shouldn't worry that he hasn't had a long-term relationship yet, should I?

Well. No point in thinking about it now. I stood, and as I was hoisting my pack, something caught my eye on the slope far below. A Range Rover, parked at the end of the faint track. And three people making their way up the slope toward it. I fished my binoculars out of my pocket and focused them on the slope below. It was indeed three people: two men I didn't recognize; the other was Finn. They each carried in their arms black bundles. I looked harder; the bundles could only be those black bags. Finn's friends with the bags. That either belonged to them or didn't. I watched as they reached the vehicle and tossed the bags into a pile on the ground. They stood around talking. Finn had his arms crossed.

I started downhill. My route took me below a rise and out of sight for a few minutes, and when I once again had the lower slope in view, the Rover was bumping up the faint track to the ridge, there was no pile of bags on the ground, and a lone figure was making its way back to the boat. And he was looking a bit dejected, if I dared speculate from this distance.

I kept an eye out for Finn during dinner prep duties—it was common to see nearly everyone passing by the galley at one point or the other, sniffing, lifting pot lids, inquiring about that evening's menu. That night was no exception, but no Finn. He didn't show up for dinner, either, and as soon as I finished eating, I went up and knocked on his door.

He answered on my second, louder, knock, opening the door halfway and standing back in the darkness of the room.

"Are you okay? I didn't see you at dinner."

He opened the door wider and retreated into the room.

"Dark in here," I said, stepping inside. The shade was drawn over the tiny window and let in only a dim light. When he turned, the light from the door showed his face. His right cheekbone was swollen and red, the hollow under his eye turning purple.

I shut the door, turned on the overhead light, and stood in front of him. I put a hand under his chin, reminding me of myself when Bobby was little, and turned his face up to the light. "You should put some ice on that."

He gestured to the bedside table and a wadded damp washcloth. I picked it up; inside was a tangled plastic bag dripping with mostly-melted ice.

"I'll get you some more." At the door I turned. "While you come up with a good story."

I got back a few minutes later, feeling I'd been a bit heartless, and after handing over the ice, examined him again. I touched his swollen cheekbone gently. "Does it hurt?"

He pulled back. "*Yes*, it hurts." He sat on the bed, leaning into the ice bag.

"Did you show Javier?"

He shook his head.

"Well, it might not be a bad idea." I sat in the only chair. "You can't hide in here forever, anyway."

He took a deep breath and let it out. When it looked like he wasn't going to volunteer anything, I said, "Before you try to tell me you walked into a doorframe or something, you should know I saw you with two guys and your mystery bags at a Range Rover this afternoon."

"Land Rover," he said, finally deciding to participate in the conversation. "Yeah," he added after a moment. "My friend came for his bags."

"His bags or your bags?"

"His, technically." It came out slowly; I assumed he was wondering how much to tell. "I brought them down from the States for him, then . . . he needed me to keep them for a while." He adjusted the ice pack. "And today he wanted them back."

"And you didn't want to give them back?"

He was silent for a moment, rewrapping the plastic bag. I waited.

"Look, Joanie," he finally said, "I just can't talk about it. No, I didn't want to give them back. So he hit me."

"But . . . why, if you didn't want to give them back, did you help carry them?"

"I changed my mind . . . During that walk. Let's just say it became clear my 'friend' didn't have the best of motives. That's all I'm going to say. And I'd appreciate it if you didn't go telling people about this."

I knew that if Finn didn't want to talk, he wouldn't. So I didn't bother asking what the bags were really for. Instead, I nodded toward his eye. "What are you going to tell the others about that?"

A faint smile. "I walked into a door?"

"Probably better that you slipped on a rock."

Up in my room, I sat on the bed with Pru on my knee, and we had a little talk about what to do. I had a lot more questions about Finn and his friends and those bags. Starting with what the heck were they for?

SEVENTEEN

One Last Drink

The relief of an incubating penguin by its mate is never a quiet affair. Penguins recognize each other by their voices, but sometimes, just the sight of a partner may be enough to start an intense greeting ceremony in which the birds bray and trumpet in unison.

—*Wayne Lynch,*
PENGUINS OF THE WORLD

I FOUND FINN DOWN in the dining room the next morning, at the center of a group, telling the story of slipping on a rock, complete with the details, when asked, of where it happened, the kind of super slippery algae on the rock, how he turned to answer a question from his Stanley friend when he slipped. Quite a convincing little storyteller.

Hans was due back late that afternoon. I spent the morning counting active Magellanic burrows, and found a moment to catch Bill alone and bring him up to speed on the real reason for Finn's black eye. I still felt protective of Finn, but two heads are better than one, and I wasn't figuring this out on my own.

After lunch I headed directly toward the computer room determined to spend a couple of hours filling out an application for one job and looking for others. After sending the application, I went to get a cup of coffee and came back to sip it and stare at the screen, too restless to do more than that. Having pretty much succeeded in putting thoughts of Hans aside all week, they now came tumbling back. I could barely wait to see him. I'd done so well all week, getting work done, staying on top of the job hunt. Could I keep that up once he was around again? Of course I could. I just needed to set boundaries, make lists, stick to them.

I drained the coffee. Right now what I needed was a little exercise and fresh air. I logged off and stood.

Out on deck a thin, side-slanting rain stung my cheek. Shore was a blur. Josef was at the rail, and I went to stand beside him.

"Care to join Helen and me for a hike, lass?"

I looked doubtfully at the shore, my resolve to go out in the elements fading. "When?"

"Now!" He pointed toward the saddle in the line of hills. "Word is there's a white sand beach two miles yonder."

When I hesitated, he winked and said, "Don't worry, we won't lose the view of your road."

I blushed. Josef, probably along with everyone else, knew that spotting the Land Rover bearing Hans was the focus of my afternoon.

We got back a bit past four thirty without seeing any sign of a vehicle. I positioned myself with a cup of tea and my field notes at a window in the dining room. By sitting up to my full length, I could see from the saddle all the way down to the beach. The notes were a ruse, I suppose; what with stretching my neck to look out every minute or so, I wasn't exactly working. When a Land Rover finally crested the hill at a quarter past five, I was up, closing my notebook, and shrugging into my raincoat in a single sweep. Carl had promised to take me ashore at a moment's notice, and downstairs I found him already lowering the Zodiac.

We slapped across the choppy bay, watching the approaching Rover bounce and zigzag down the slope, following its obscure path. It reached the beach before we did, and Hans was out the door. I was close enough to see his face was lit with a smile. Carl ran the boat up on the sand, and I stood before we stopped and ended up half falling, half jumping off the bow. Hans was there to catch me and we hugged, laughing. When we pulled apart to look at each other, his face was flushed, eyes bright. We kissed, aware of our audience: Carl and the driver, who had already unloaded Hans's bag and a heavy box onto the grass.

"Let's take a walk." Hans said.

We turned to Carl, who looked at his watch and said, "See you in an hour. I'll get the luggage."

As the Zodiac and Rover pulled away in opposite directions, we stood watching for a moment before turning to kiss again. I melted against his chest, tingled at the touch of his unshaven chin, breathed in the smell of him.

I had pictured myself showing a little more restraint, but couldn't pull it off. "I really missed you."

He looked down into my face and said, "Really? I missed you so much. Thinking of you was what got me through it."

"Really?" I said, not minding the echo.

He nodded. We started walking down the beach, arms around each other.

"How was it?" I said. "Tell me everything."

He shook his head. "Where to start . . . Tell me about your week first."

So I told him the short version; how we'd moved twice, the weather pretty mild until midweek, when I'd hiked across the mountain for the overnight. "It was pleasant enough. I was busy," I said in conclusion. I would save the Finn and Marcia stories for later.

We headed toward a bluff covered with a thick grove of towering grasses. "Let's go see if we can find sea lions. Yesterday they were sleeping among the tussock grass. I almost stumbled over one."

We climbed a steep muddy slope and came out on top of a sharp bank. "Never get between a sea lion and the sea," said Hans, quoting Ian as he looked around. We stepped carefully between the head-high clumps of tussock grass, and after a couple of minutes saw a round brown rump, a sleeping sea lion. We stood quietly, listening to the swish of the grass blades, wide as swords, around our ears. Hans took a deep breath, let it out, eyes closed. "It's good to be back."

We backed away from the beast without waking it and found a place to sit on the edge of the bank, backs to the grass and the sleeping sea lion, facing the bay, feet dangling over the edge. A king cormorant landed on an outcrop and looked about with its bright blue eyes.

Hans told me about the flight home—he'd traveled twenty-six hours with almost no sleep—then about seeing his sisters, about the funeral. "My father... I told you we didn't get on well... He didn't approve of me." He paused. "We read the will... He didn't leave me much."

"Oh! I'm sorry," I said.

"He had a special letter written to me. He said it wasn't that he didn't love me, it was *because* he loved me. He thought if I didn't have much money, it would make me try harder to make something of myself."

"Oh, Hans."

He laughed. "And it's stupid, really; it's only symbolic." We watched the cormorant lift its wings, catch a draft, and sail off. Hans glanced at me. "There's something I haven't told you."

"Yes?"

"You know Hotz Chocolates?"

"Yes ..." Who didn't? In any shop that sold high-end chocolates, there they'd be, little squares wrapped in their regal gold foil.

"That's my family." He waited, looking at the water. As I seemed to be missing the point, he looked at me. "They're rich. Very rich." Then he laughed a bitter laugh. "And I guess I was, too."

"Wow," was all I could say. We must be talking *very* rich. And suddenly a host of tiny hints clicked into place and I had a new thought: *Marcia knew.*

Hans was watching me, waiting for my reaction. I was nodding, considering, finally coming around to what bothered me most about this; he'd withheld this essential part of himself from me.

As if he'd read my mind, he said, "I'm sorry I didn't tell you." He put his hand on my knee. "It was so hard not to. I want to share everything with you. It felt like I was lying not to tell you."

"Why didn't you?"

"I never tell people when I'm traveling. It's my one chance to be free from that identity. At home I'm never sure if people like me for me or for my money."

I nodded, understanding a little.

He went on. "That world, it's incredibly shallow. It's all about things, possessions and more possessions, having the best of everything."

I did see how this could be a burden, sort of. And I found myself already seeing him in a different light. Which, I supposed, only proved his point.

"Well . . . ," I said, "How bad is it? I mean, how poor are you?"

"I have one million."

I raised my eyebrows.

"My sisters each got tens of millions, including stock options. And property."

I whistled.

He went on. "I can have more—*my* third—if when I am forty I have some acceptable career. My sister Astrid gets to be the judge of what's acceptable."

"Whoa . . . That's kind of demeaning."

"Yes."

"A million dollars. You're in pretty good shape anyway."

He nodded. "One million euro, actually. I can get by."

I laughed.

"And I have other money," he went on, "not too much, from my uncle, my mother's brother—it's her family that's Hotz." He shook his head. "So there's mostly the demeaning part."

We were silent for a few moments. Then I said, "It's hard to believe your father's dying wish was to humiliate you."

Hans picked a long stem of grass, put it in his mouth, and gazed out to sea.

"I don't believe it," I insisted.

"Maybe," he said finally. "But that's how it feels."

I laid my head on his shoulder and he put his arm around me. We sat that way as the wind swished around us, the giant grass blades carrying on their sword fight behind us.

Walking back along the beach I kept thinking about Marcia, and when we reached the place where Carl had left us, we sat on the sand. "You didn't happen to mention it to Marcia?" I asked. "About . . . your family?"

"No!" He frowned. "Why?"

I told him about the night he left, the group sitting around in the lounge, Marcia well into the wine. "She more or less accused me of liking you for your money. And I said something like, 'What money?' and then she looked sort of confused and tried to cover up saying, 'Well, with his father dying and all, he'll probably inherit something.' Which of course didn't make any sense because I was after you before your father died."

Hans grinned. "You were after me?"

"Liked you. You know what I mean. Are you getting my point? Don't you think it's odd?"

"Not really. She maybe researched me on the internet. It's not so hard." He pulled me close. "You see? That's what I mean. All my life women have been after me for my money." He kissed the top of my head. "Do you know I was the Most Eligible Bachelor in Zurich a few years ago?"

I looked up at him. His face looked so aggrieved that I burst out laughing.

"It's not funny," he said. But he was smiling.

As we watched the splash of the Zodiac launching from the *Professor*, I couldn't ignore the other thing about Marcia that had been nipping at the edge of my thoughts. I said, "Marcia also suggested you might not be coming back in a week . . . I wondered if she ran into you in Stanley last weekend."

"Oh, yeah. She came into the Upland Goose while I was eating dinner. She sat down and we talked for a while." He frowned. "But I didn't say anything about staying away longer."

It was hard to imagine Marcia passing up this opportunity of having Hans alone, and I was dying to know what happened next.

Just as I was trying not to ask, Hans said, "She asked me to go to the Globe with her, but I said I was going to bed. After she left, I went down to the Narrows Bar. I met some fishermen and stayed for a couple hours." He turned to me, eyes alight. "They told me how you can charter a boat to South Georgia Island. It takes five days to get there from here . . ."

As the Zodiac plowed onto the beach, he was still talking excitedly about the hundreds of thousands of king penguins to be seen on South Georgia.

Before Carl jumped out of the boat, Hans asked me not to tell people about his family connection or the will, and I promised I wouldn't.

I was reassured about Marcia. But now I had another question: what had Hans been drinking for those couple of hours at the Narrows Bar?

He had brought a case of good wine back with him, and at dinner he opened bottles and went around setting them on each table. He was welcomed back like a long-lost son, and he reveled in the role, pouring wine, drinking his share, telling stories that reminded us it was winter in the Northern Hemisphere. I lost touch with him at dinner, gave him up to the group. I was happy enough to do it, happy he was well loved, only a little worried about his drinking.

But as it grew late, Hans drank more and talked more. Around ten thirty I slipped away and went up to our cabin. I knew I wouldn't sleep until he came up, and sat in bed with my novel, thinking. Was that scotch with Ian before he left the start of a slide back into what he called "a problem"? Was this a whole new Hans now that he was drinking again?

Shortly after eleven o'clock, he came in, jovial and amorous. I wanted to talk first, regain the connection we'd had on shore before dinner. But he crept into bed from the foot, crawling slowly under the blankets, kissing my foot, my ankle, behind my knee. I went along, thinking I'd catch his fire. But I never did.

He fell asleep smiling, and immediately began to snore; it was the first time I'd known him to snore. I watched him for a while thinking, Is the honeymoon over? I gave him a little push; he mumbled, turned on his side, and the snoring stopped. I lay on my back, but didn't find sleep until long after I heard the last of the shipmates pass by on their way to bed.

Sunday morning I awoke early to more snoring, gentle this time. He had a little frown between his eyes. Probably a headache, I thought with a teeny bit of satisfaction. I got up, showered, and stood looking at him as I toweled my hair dry. He hadn't moved.

At breakfast I learned that Bill and a group were going in two Land Rovers to Hill Cove to see the only stand of real trees in all the Falklands. I hadn't seen a tree since leaving Seattle. There was room for me if I wanted to go.

Back in the cabin, I kissed Hans on the lips. He opened his eyes, smiled, pulled me to him and immediately resumed the soft snoring. I lay with him for a moment, thinking. And concluded that after his long trip, sleep was what he needed.

I kissed him on the forehead, got up, and wrote a quick note on a blue sticky note saying I'd be back after lunch. After a moment's hesitation, I signed it "love, Joanie," and stuck it on the bathroom mirror.

At five fifteen I pushed through the doors of the galley and plopped a flat of tomatoes down on the counter—part of the purpose for the trip had been to pick up a shipment of fresh produce that came in to the airstrip that morning. Hans was standing at the island in the center of the room chopping celery, a glass of wine next to the cutting board. He glanced up, then back to his task as others poured noisily into the galley with boxes of lettuce, onions, and apples.

I stood next to him, my arm touching his. "Did you get my note?"

"Mm-hmm," he said, not breaking his rhythm.

"I'm sorry I didn't wake you . . . you were sleeping so soundly. And I thought we'd be back a lot sooner. One of the Rovers got stuck in the mud and we couldn't get it out. We had to radio for another one to come from the settlement." I was breathless and happy from the adventure, sure he'd see the fun of it in a moment.

He pushed a pile of chopped celery aside, reached for the next bunch.

The galley was crammed full of people. I put my hand on his arm. "Hans. Come outside with me for a minute."

He nodded toward Liz, bent over the sink, and Javier, who was donning an apron. "Our shift started twenty minutes ago."

I looked around in frustration. He was right, of course, but I wasn't about to wait to talk to him until after dinner, after hours of drinking, a repeat of last night. Paul came into the galley and headed toward Liz. I intercepted him and asked if he'd swap half an hour with me. He agreed, and I went out into the dining room and made the same deal with the first person I saw, Helen.

Back in the galley I stood across the island from Hans. "Okay, we have half an hour." And when he didn't immediately respond, I said, "Hans. Please. It's important to me."

He laid down his knife and untied his apron, handed it to Helen. And picking up his glass, he followed me down the stairs to the alcove. We sat on the couch, side by side, facing the gray, agitated water.

"I *am* sorry, Hans. It was a snap decision. You were asleep. And I thought we'd be back hours ago. I didn't think you'd mind sleeping in a bit."

"Bill went, right?"

"Bill and six other people." When he didn't respond, I said, "Bill and I *are* getting to be friends, but it's nothing more. I would have gone with or without Bill."

"I don't see why, if you were so eager to see me, and this is our last day off for a week . . ."

"I see that now. Sorry. Just because I'm older doesn't mean I'm always going to be the mature one. I can be selfish, too."

After a moment, he said, "Have I been selfish?"

I didn't answer.

He set the glass down on the little table in front of us. "You're mad about last night."

I shrugged. "Not mad. I was disappointed." I hadn't considered until then that last night might have had something to do with my decision to go.

He was silent a moment, looking at the glass. He looked at me, connecting for the first time. "I'm sorry about last night."

"I know." I put my hand on his leg. We leaned back against the couch. "Hans."

He turned his head.

"We're a couple for the time we're here. And being a couple means something to me, even if it's for this short time. It means we're more than just fun and a roll in the hay. We're there for each other, we support each other. I know it doesn't seem that way today. I didn't think about how . . . about what you've been through in the past week. I thought you wouldn't care that much if I wasn't around today, for part of today. I misjudged." I turned my hand palm up on his knee.

He put his hand in mine and held it tight.

"Here's what I think," I said after a moment. "Because you've had a week of dealing with your family and thoughts about your dad who never treated you with respect, it got all those feelings stirred up and now you're looking to . . . now you're expecting that kind of treatment from me."

He glanced at me, the hint of a smile. "What are you, a psychiatrist?"

"I took a psych class in college."

And we were reconnected. I leaned back and he put his arms around me, kissed my forehead. I lay my arm across his chest. We stayed that way for a few minutes, looking out. A storm petrel glided by.

"Well, I only bought half an hour," I said, sitting up straight. I looked at my watch. "We've got about ten minutes." I took a sip of his wine, set it back down. "That's great wine, by the way. A nice change from that stuff we've been drinking."

He took it, rested it on his knee, sloshed it around. "I had a drinking problem until I was thirty, thirty-one," he said. "Two years ago I quit completely. That scotch I had with Ian was good.

I ordered a drink on the plane going home. And then another. And I drank every night when I was there, usually too much." He watched me, judging my reaction.

I hesitated, not wanting to sound like a shrink again. Or, God forbid, a mom. "Do you . . . want to quit?"

He shrugged. "Oh, you know . . . yes. And no."

I nodded. "I have an idea." I paused. "We quit drinking together."

"What?" He shook his head. "No. You don't have a problem."

"Maybe, maybe not. I do have a glass of wine or two practically every evening. It's definitely a habit." I paused. "I often think it wouldn't hurt to try to do without for a while. Now's a good time."

He was shaking his head. "You don't have to do it. I'll stop anyway."

"But I will, too. I want to." I kissed him and stood up. He stood too, and we looked down at the glass of wine on the table.

I said, "Do we drink to seal the deal?"

"That seems like the thing to do. On one hand."

I picked the glass up. "But probably more meaningful to give it to the sea."

We turned and leaned our elbows on the rail. I handed him the glass and he held it out over the water. A flash of sunlight glinted off the rim. He glanced at me.

I gave him one last out. "You sure?"

"Sure." And he poured it into the wind, a spray of silver gone in an instant.

When we arrived at the top of the stairs, Hans turned and said, "What am I going to do with those last bottles?"

"Give them away, I guess."

He looked pained. "They were expensive, too."

"Yeah, and you really have to start watching your pennies now that you've only got a million euro."

So I wasn't going to drink. I took the apron from Helen, saying, "I owe you."

Helen picked up her glass of red wine, winked, and said, "No, you don't."

Paul carried off a glass of beer, all cold and frothy, Liz had a glass of white going; people were enjoying alcohol everywhere I looked. I opened the fridge and pulled out two sparkling waters and gave one to Hans. We clinked bottles and got to work.

Pepa asked me to start pasta water boiling. The pots were enormous, so as I stood at the sink, water running into one, then another, I had time to think.

I really had been stabbed with remorse when I realized Hans had been hurt by my abandoning him that day. Remorse plus the thrill of realization that what I did mattered to him. That *I* mattered to him. I had told him I was sorry and given him all my reasons for going off that morning; even admitting to being miffed about last night. But I was left with a vague feeling that I hadn't been entirely honest, that I was withholding something important.

And about halfway through filling the second pot, it came to me. While everything I'd said was true, it probably didn't add up to even half of what the real reason was. That reason now bubbled up out of the rising water: I was afraid of how much I liked him. By going away today, I'd been asserting my independence, showing myself I was in control of my feelings.

"Nice try."

"What?" said Liz.

I snapped back from my thoughts to see Liz looking at me, spoon in hand, eyebrows raised.

"Oh." I shut off the water. "Just thinking out loud."

EIGHTEEN

Pru Advises

All visitors to penguin breeding sites need to understand that a common sign of fear is the cessation of activity even though the bird remains on the nest.

—*Pauline Reilly,*
PENGUINS OF THE WORLD

LATER THAT EVENING we were lying on the bed, fingers entwined, my leg draped over his. I'd missed talking to Hans, bouncing ideas off him, getting his level take on things. Now the recent developments spilled forth: the missing GPS showing back up again, the numbers discrepancy from the afternoon Finn and Marcia worked on the skua project, the reporter from *Penguin News* recognizing Finn and revealing that he'd brought the bags with him. I told about the overnight trip Finn was supposed to join us on until he bowed out at the last moment. I stopped there, remembering my promise to Finn not to tell anyone about how he got the black eye. Telling Bill had been enough.

Hans asked questions, and I answered them until I remembered I shouldn't be sharing the whole story I'd heard from Bill, especially Audrey's suspicions about funny business and Bernard and his probable accomplice on board. By honoring my promise to Bill, I was leaving out key information, and the talk was less than satisfying.

"You haven't told me much about your time at home," I said. "Other than they read your dad's will and you drank too much."

"Hmm . . . a lot of rain, some snow, traffic everywhere . . . opposite to here. It started to get dark at four thirty. We spent a lot of time in offices; a lot of arguing."

"Sounds nice." I curled toward him. "How are your sisters taking it?"

"All right . . ." He was running his fingers idly through my hair. "Freya asked me if I met anyone interesting here."

"Yes?"

"I said I met someone very interesting."

My heart gave an extra thump. "Yes?"

"Astrid came in then, and they both started asking me all kinds of questions; where is she from, what does she do, what does she look like . . ."

". . . how old is she . . . ," I finished.

"Yeah." A little smile touched a corner of his mouth.

"Hmm . . . I bet they were impressed."

"Very impressed. They said what am I doing? Looking for my mother?"

"Hm."

"That was Astrid. Freya said she thought it was cool."

I immediately liked Freya and was not so keen on Astrid. "And Astrid is . . ."

"My oldest sister, eight years older than me. So forty-one, I guess. But really, she's older than you. Her thinking, the way she looks, dresses . . ."

"She's the one that took over mothering you after your mom died."

"Yeah."

"She probably had to grow up fast, to take care of you and Freya."

"Yeah . . . she's all right. I love them both . . . but they try to control me."

"Well," I said. "It's your life. It's *still* your life, even if they do control the purse strings."

He looked at me.

"You'll be fine, you know." I touched his cheek. "Even if you never convince them you deserve a proper inheritance. The world doesn't need another chocolate executive, anyway. The world needs you. Even if you spend the rest of your life counting penguins and carving seabirds . . . that's enough."

We were silent for a few moments. I rested my hand on his cheek until he turned and took my face in both his hands. He kissed me.

Damn, I thought; I love this man. And I almost said it.

But across the room, Pru went, Ahem. And when she had my attention, said, What about your precious plan that you've clung to ever since you ditched that boyfriend? It wasn't supposed to include a new man. It was about being able to move around without the baggage of another person, making your own decisions, no more compromises. Focusing on your work.

I wanted her to stop, but she was on a tear: And the age difference makes it ridiculous. You're in your fifties, don't forget. You can't pretend to be young forever. Despite all your good diet and exercise and keeping yourself young with challenges, starting a new life and all, you can't hold back aging forever. You'll get old, and he'll still be in his prime. It was Pru's longest speech so far, and I didn't care for it.

But I had to agree. This thing was never meant to go beyond our time here. Hans wouldn't want it to, either, not if he thought about it. So. It was best not to talk about love.

"What are you thinking?" Hans ran a finger slowly over my mouth.

I smiled, ready. "I really like you." I rolled on top of him and kissed his neck, one side, then the other.

"I really like you, too," he said.

To stop either of us from saying more, I pushed his shirt up and started exploring the little forest of curly blond chest hair.

In the days that followed, the *Professor* moved often. Finn and I and our team worked harmoniously together, seeing a slight uptick in skua success at these seldom-visited colonies. On our time off there was always new territory to explore: tall cliffs dotted with albatross nests, windswept beaches, hidden coves. The air was alive with swooping birds and their calls, the land covered with rockhopper and gentoo colonies—and the slippery guano-mud mix surrounding them. The sea breathed penguins and seals and porpoises. Hans and I spent every free moment together, making up for the week apart. I didn't *want* to want him around so much, but couldn't help it. The rush of warmth I felt in his presence, from my eyes to my toes, my skin to my core, wasn't something I wanted to resist. I managed to keep my emotions more or less in check by telling myself to enjoy it for what it is, what we'd agreed to—a six-week fling.

Beneath it all, though, was a rising sense of unease. A voice inside me that I couldn't quiet kept saying: It's going to be really hard to say goodbye to this man in just over two weeks. You're going to end up with a broken heart, and probably he will, too.

A couple of nights after Hans's return, he and I were eating dinner at a table with Bill, Marcia, and Javier. Hans was telling about a gentoo coming up to him that day.

"It looked exactly into my eyes—I was sitting, so we were on the same level." Hans's eyes were alight, blond eyebrows high. "It was about five feet away, and moved its head from left to right . . ." He demonstrated. ". . . looking at me from different angles."

The audience was captivated, as whenever Hans told a story. He was untrained, but observant and easily delighted, and his stories from the field were a refreshing change from the numbers and data and scientific terms that were more often tossed about the dining room.

Marcia, sitting on my right, said to Bill, who was sitting across from her, "That sounds like last week when you and Joanie had that gentoo outside your tent—didn't it come right up to your door?"

I caught Bill's eye for a second before digging into my salad. Hans, sitting on my left, paused in his story. I hadn't mentioned to him the part of the overnight where Bill and I had shared a tent. There didn't seem to be any smooth way of telling him about it now in front of everybody without sounding defensive or guilty, so I kept munching away.

"Right," said Bill. "And when we opened the zipper, it only stepped back a little. Like it was making room for us to come out and join him."

I added, "And when we did go out, it stuck around for a while. Until Paul and Liz came out of their tent; then it left."

"Didn't like them as well," Bill finished.

We all laughed.

The conversation went on through the rest of the meal, from stories of more close encounters with penguins to tourism in general to the cruise ship that had unloaded numerous boatloads of people near the research site that afternoon. Hans contributed little more.

When everyone started getting up to clear their places, I put my hand on Hans's arm to stop him. Alone at the table, the room still half full of people, I said quietly, "You're probably wondering why I never mentioned that Bill and I stayed in the same tent on that trip."

"Yeah." He was looking at me.

"No special reason. We had so much else to talk about."

He nodded.

"Maybe I didn't mention it because . . . well, when it might have come up was the day I went off to see the trees. When I got back, you were upset. I didn't want to bring it up with everything else going on." I shrugged. "It just wasn't important."

"Okay, but was that a good idea, to share a tent with a guy who is interested in you, and you say you don't want to encourage him?"

I bristled at the "you say," but stayed calm. "It wasn't planned to happen that way. I told you how Finn was supposed to come with us, but he got sick at the last minute and didn't go."

And, motivated by a desire to connect with him, I went on to tell the story of how Finn really got his black eye, how I'd managed to get some information out of him and how I'd promised not to tell anyone.

"What are the bags for?" Hans asked.

"He wouldn't say." And I asked him to keep it to himself, adding, "I've only told Bill."

We fell silent until I said, "Anyway, it was a pretty big tent. And Bill was a perfect gentleman."

"Okay," he said, reaching to smooth down my bangs.

"He snores, though," I said. "I really did make the right choice with you."

"Hm." He smiled. "Let's not keep things from each other anymore. It feels . . . not right."

I agreed, of course. But I knew I was keeping something bigger than the story of Finn from him, bigger than Bill and me sharing a tent. I was still acting like all was light and fun between Hans and me, when in fact, I had fallen madly in love.

We took our plates to the galley window and went out to stand against the rail in a gentle breeze.

"I was thinking," he said.

"Yes?"

"We should go somewhere when this is finished. You know, a kind of vacation."

I watched an albatross sail by on the wind. "I don't know, Hans. I have to get a job."

"But if you don't. We said we were going to have a six-week fling, right?"

This made me smile.

"We missed—what? Eight, nine days of it? We have to get that back."

I laughed. "We'll see. It depends on how my job search is going."

We went upstairs, Hans talking about where we should go; Patagonia? Buenos Aires? South Georgia? At the first opportunity, I changed the subject.

The next evening Hans went ashore with Yoshi. He took a sketch pad and his carving tools, and Yoshi took his watercolors and an easel. I stood at the rail waving as they zipped away in the Zodiac. Of all the beautiful evenings to stay in. It was mild with very little wind. Ashore were rolling hills of green grass, lichen-covered rocks, and a "gentoo highway," as we called the path the gentoos had beaten to their rookery, more than a mile inland. I felt like a little kid who'd been grounded.

But I was determined to stay in. The job situation was becoming worrisome. I'd really imagined that by the time I left, I would have at least *one* interview lined up, if not in fact be waltzing off to my new job. Above all I expected to have heard from Parque Nacional Isla Magdalena. I was a perfect match for that job! My Spanish, the master's degree—a *fresh* master's, and now my fieldwork with penguins. But so far, nothing had come through. Had my faith that I'd get *that* job kept me from mounting a serious search for other jobs? I didn't really think so, but, in any case, it was time to ramp up the effort.

An hour spent searching my bookmarked sites for the National Park Service, the Audubon Society, Nature Conservancy, and others produced a few new leads. I spent another hour doing the online application for the most promising—resident ornithologist at Iguazú Falls in Argentina—and saved the others for the next night.

I was about to log off, when Marcia stuck her head in the room. "Back at your job search, eh?" I nodded. Marcia and I weren't in the habit of talking much, but I politely asked how her own job search was going. "Great!" she said, and asked if I knew where Hans was. When I told her he'd gone ashore with Yoshi, she left with a breezy "Thanks."

What was the woman up to now? I got thinking about Marcia and her ongoing interest in Hans. How easy would it have been for her, really, to find out from the internet that Hans was wealthy and that he was coming here to the Falklands to work on this study? I typed in his name and got over fifty hits. When I typed in "Switzerland," it narrowed to four. From there, it took only a few seconds to find that there were several references to one particular Hans Schaller, mostly in articles on Hotz Chocolates. I even found the exact year Hans had held the "Most Eligible Bachelor of Zurich" title, four years earlier.

But how would Marcia have known, assuming she had the name, which Hans Schaller would be the one coming here? I typed in words that might bring up something on the penguin count, but wasn't able to access anything that gave more information than the names of the lead scientists. And I knew that Ian hadn't sent out the names of the other researchers beforehand. The only reason *I* had a copy was because of my professor friend. I remembered the day Brenda had gone through the list and put a star by the names of Bill, Yvonne, and Ian, saying, "I'm not really supposed to give this out; better keep it to yourself."

I logged off and went looking for Bill. I was convinced now that Marcia had indeed had prior knowledge of Hans, and found out that he was from a wealthy family. But how did she get his name in the first place? There must be a way to ask Bill about all this without giving away Hans's secret about his family and their wealth.

Bill was in his room, the door open. A tripod was set up just inside the door and he was bent over the camera that was attached to it. I knocked on the doorframe, and he invited me in. The chair and couch were covered with a jumble of papers and camera gear and clothing, so I sat on the edge of the bed and watched him dust his camera with a little brush.

After a moment, he glanced at me and said, "What's up?"

"I was wondering—mind if I shut the door?" After I did, I said, "Was there a way for participants in this project to learn each other's names before the trip began?"

He stopped and squinted. "I got a list of the names from Ian. Yvonne would have, too." He flicked his rag across the camera a couple of times and began unscrewing it from the tripod. "But I don't think anyone else would have. Privacy and all. Why?"

"Oh . . . just wondering." I paused. "The Marcia mystery in general."

"Ah." He folded up the tripod with a click of legs.

"Do you remember what kind of information was on the list?" Maybe his list had more information than mine.

After a brief search through a pile of papers on his desk, he produced a sheet of paper and handed it to me.

I saw at a glance it was exactly like mine, giving no more information than names, countries, and whether the person was a scientist, student, or volunteer. I studied it for a minute or so, pretending I'd never seen it, then handed it back to him. "Even if someone had this, they couldn't really . . . use it for anything."

"Use it? What are you thinking?"

"I don't know . . . I'm just trying to think of everything, trying to figure out what Marcia's up to."

He tilted his head and peered at me for a moment, then, out of nowhere, said, "Is Hans wealthy?"

"What? No . . . no, not that I've heard." I wasn't actually lying. Hans didn't consider himself rich anymore. "Why do you ask?"

He sat next to me, hands on his knees. "You told me what Marcia said the other night, when she implied he might be. And Liz seems to think there's something to it."

"Really? What did Liz say?"

"Oh, she's got this hypothesis and three or four points to support it. Like why is he on Deck Five, for one. The captain, the scientists, and anyone who paid extra are up here."

I considered for a moment who was indeed up here: Ian and Caroline, Yvonne, and Bill; all the scientists. The captain and the first mate. Helen, who admitted paying extra for a nicer room. Hans, who said one of those first days that he didn't know why he was up on Five. Huh. And Marcia. Marcia? She was supposedly a struggling student. Why would she be up here?

Bill was going on. "I suppose if it were true, that Hans is rich, and Marcia knew about it ahead of time, that would be . . . interesting." He was watching me.

I was supposed to be helping him figure out what was going on with the count, and this could be relevant. Besides, he seemed to know, or at least suspect.

"Okay, listen, Bill." I turned to face him. "You can't tell anyone, because I promised Hans I wouldn't tell. But he is rich. Really rich." I told him I had just learned of the Hotz Chocolates connection. But I left out the part about the will. If Bill let something slip out, well. . . it wouldn't be the entire story. And this way I wasn't giving away Hans's whole secret, only the part people were starting to figure out anyway.

Bill whistled. "He must be inheriting quite a fortune."

"I suppose so." Another little truth evasion.

His shaggy eyebrows rose up above his glasses and he smiled. "Lucky you."

"What do you mean? We're having a little fling while we're here, that's all. I told you."

"I don't know," he said. "I think he really likes you."

I didn't want to talk about Hans with Bill. "Well, he's certainly not going to want to *marry* me." I got to my feet, ready to end the conversation. "And besides, it's not what *I* want. All I want is a biology job."

Bill stood up, too. "You're something, Joanie."

I didn't stick around to hear what he meant by that.

As I was leaving Bill's cabin, Marcia was entering hers two doors away. She said, "Hans was looking for you." She pointed to his cabin and slipped into hers.

Okay, not jealous. I'm not even going to ask him about Marcia.

But first I went past Hans's door to the little patio and sat in a lounge chair out of the wind to collect my thoughts. A pale crescent moon was floating high in the northern sky, and the wind rattled the stays and the flag overhead. Would I tell Hans that Bill had guessed he was rich? All these secrets I had agreed to keep; for Finn, for Bill, for Hans. I wasn't doing a very good job.

Hans was on the bed, propped up on one elbow reading Lonely Planet's guide to South America. I sat down by his knees and we kissed.

"How is your job search going?" he said.

"Pretty good, I got one application sent and two more I'll do tomorrow."

"Anything interesting?"

I told him about the one in Argentina.

"Maybe you'll get an interview there after we're finished, and I can go with you. We can make it part of our vacation."

I thought that wasn't such a good idea, to show up for a job interview with a young man not my husband in tow, but I said, "Yeah, maybe," and scooted up against the pillows alongside him. "Listen to this," I said.

He closed the book and gave me his full attention.

"While I was on the internet, I thought I'd see what I could find about you."

"Yes?"

"Easy as pie. There are others with your name, but only one rich chocolate heir."

"Former rich chocolate heir."

"The internet doesn't know that yet, not that I saw." I shook my head. "How did she get your name in the first place?"

"She could have done it after we got here."

"I don't think she did, though. Remember how she *was* the moment she met you? She was all over you, furious with me when she saw us getting together."

"You don't think it was my charm?"

"Well, possibly . . ." I kissed his forehead. "Probably. But let's just say she came here knowing you were rich and she wanted to get you for your money. One, how did she get your name, and two, how did she know that the Hans Schaller who was coming here was the rich guy?"

He tucked a curl behind my ear. "My little detective."

"Well, it's *interesting*. She's definitely up to something . . . So I went to see Bill. He had a list of everyone's names. He'd gotten it from Ian before the trip and he was pretty sure that no one but he, Ian, and Yvonne had a copy . . ."

There was a soft tapping on the door. Hans got up and opened it.

Yoshi was standing there, and gave a slight bow. "Sorry to disturb you." He bowed again and presented Hans with a small painting. "For you." He looked at me and pointed back and forth between us. "For both."

Hans took it and persuaded him to come in. I stood at Hans's side, and we admired the watercolor. Clearly painted from shore that evening, it was a small white ship with a red stripe alone in a vast sea. Immense white clouds billowed up behind it over the somber, roiling water.

"It's beautiful, Yoshi." I felt a prickling in my throat. He'd given it to Hans and me.

Hans thanked him and asked him to stay for a while, but he wouldn't.

When he was gone, Hans propped the painting on a little shelf next to two of his carved birds and considered it. "He's very good. He did this in half an hour." Hans sat back on the bed, reached for my hand. "You were telling me . . ."

I sat beside him. "Right. So all that's on the list are names, countries, and positions here on the project. No cities or occupations or ages; no other clues."

"Hm." He had begun to rub slow circles in the middle of my lower back.

"So how did Marcia find out you were rich?"

He got up and locked the door, came back, and sat beside me. He slowly pushed me back against the pillows and started unbuttoning my shirt.

"You're not taking me seriously," I protested.

He looked at me beneath lowered lids. "I take you very seriously."

NINETEEN

Bermuda Triangle of Love

[With gentoos] . . . some populations use same site annually while others progress inland selecting new sites each year, which may result in colonies up to 3 m (5km) inland from original landing area or at an elevation of some 430 feet.

—Ian Strange,
A FIELD GUIDE TO THE WILDLIFE OF THE
FALKLAND ISLANDS AND SOUTH GEORGIA

SATURDAY NIGHT WE were up on Five having cocktails with Helen and Josef, Hans's and mine being club soda over ice with a slice of lemon. I was getting the hang of not drinking. Hans seemed to be doing fine with it, too.

The four of us were huddling in a circle of chairs watching one albatross after another sail over our heads on the wind, when Josef said, "Hans, lad. Why didn't you tell us you were a Hotz?"

Hans glanced at me and back at Josef. "Ah . . . it's common knowledge now, is it?"

Helen said, "There's been a rumor going around, and then someone—was it Liz, sweetheart?—googled you and there you were."

Hans licked some spilled drink off his fingers, took a sip, and told them how he liked to keep quiet about that part of his life. "I didn't even tell Joanie until I got back."

They nodded and Josef said, "Excuse me for being nosy, but I imagine you're pretty well set up now?"

"Sweetheart . . . ," Helen said.

Hans smiled. "Yes, pretty well set up."

Back in the cabin before dinner, sitting side by side on the edge of the bed, I said, "Remember when I was talking to Bill the other night? I asked him about how Marcia might have found out about you?"

Hans nodded.

"He asked me if you were rich, said people were starting to wonder. I didn't deny it. But I told him you didn't want people knowing."

Hans lay back, hands crossed behind his head. "It doesn't matter."

I smiled. "And just like Josef, he imagined you were 'pretty well set up.' I said I imagined so."

He laughed without much humor. "So, by the time everyone thinks I'm rich, I'm not anymore."

"Yeah. Funny," I said. "Let's go eat."

I pulled him up and we stood holding each other for a moment, his chin resting on the top of my head. "The only thing that matters," he said, ". . . is that you liked me before you knew."

After breakfast Sunday I spent the morning completing two more job applications, sent them off, and went looking for Hans. Not finding him on the upper decks, I checked the alcove on Two. Sitting alone in the middle of the couch, elbows on his knees and hands clasped, was Bill.

"Oh, hi," I said. "I was looking for Hans."

He turned to look at me, then back out at the water. "Haven't seen him."

"Is something wrong?" I asked.

He leaned back against the couch, looking quite forlorn. I sat down beside him.

After a moment he glanced at me. "Audrey's back. She told me she's decided to stick with her husband."

"Ah, Bill . . ."

He shook his head. "Unlucky in love, that's me."

I hooked my arm through his, and we looked out over the thrashing sea. I felt we'd gotten to a point where I could do this and it would be taken in the proper spirit. I'd become fond of Bill and found myself wondering what would have happened if he hadn't come on so strong in the beginning. Perhaps I wouldn't have been thrown together with Hans, and who knows if things would have developed the way they did. Might I have gravitated to Bill instead? Ended up with a life partner, a man more or less my age, of my culture, someone to grow old with?

But no. If I'd been looking for a man, Bill would have been someone I might have. . . explored. But I *wasn't* looking. Hans, on the other hand, was someone I never would have considered. Which was partly why I'd let him in.

Bill interrupted these thoughts. "I must sabotage relationships somehow."

I shook my head. "Maybe. But that probably wasn't the case with Audrey. She is married, after all . . . and she seems like an honorable person, loyal to her family. She's got a couple of kids still at home, doesn't she?"

"One. And one at Oxford."

We sat a bit longer. I was on the point of taking my arm from his when I heard footsteps in the corridor.

Hans put his head around the corner. "Oh," he said. "There you are."

I unhooked my arm from Bill's and stood up. "I was looking for you."

Bill got up, too. "I was just leaving. You kids stay." He moved to the doorway, saying, "Thanks, Joanie." He nodded to Hans and passed down the hallway.

Hans raised his eyebrows. I pulled him down on the couch with me.

"He's upset about Audrey," I said.

"Audrey?"

"Yeah. You knew they were getting something going?"

"No."

"He thought she was on the point of leaving her husband . . . In fact, she told him she was going to talk to him when she was home last week. But then she told him she didn't do it. Wasn't going to do it."

"How am I supposed to know these things?"

"I told you. Maybe you weren't listening."

"I don't remember," he said, and after a moment, "But why is it *your* job to comfort Bill?"

I let out an exasperated breath. "Jeez, Hans. You're really getting to be the jealous type."

He looked out at the water for a moment, a stubborn thrust to his jaw, then back at me. "What are you doing?"

"What do you mean? I'm not doing anything. Bill's my friend, just like Helen, or Liz."

"I'm not talking about that," he said. "You're just . . . different lately."

"I'm the same. We're the same."

He was silent, rubbing at a black smudge on the knee of his pants with his thumb. "Do you want to go somewhere together when we are finished here, or not? Just say it if you don't."

I sighed. "Oh, Hans." I put my hand over his. "It's just hard for me to think about a trip right now. I'm getting worried about finding a job."

He didn't speak, turned his hand over and entwined his fingers with mine. "Okay," he said quietly, gave my fingers a squeeze, and started to pull away.

I held tight. "Hans."

He looked at me.

"We . . . we can't go on after this is over. A trip, maybe, if it works out." I shook my head. "But it just wouldn't work for long. Our age difference . . . everything."

"Right," he said. "That's always been the agreement." He took his hand back and got up.

I followed. "What are we going to do this afternoon?" I said. "I've done all I can as far as the job search."

He shrugged. "I don't know. Maybe read."

It was a brutal day out, with howling wind and slanting rain.

"Sounds good," I said, trying to inject some enthusiasm. "Let's go read."

We lay on the bed next to each other, reading our books. Hans picked up a novel in German, leaving the guide to South America he'd been poring over lately on the bedside table. I kept at my airport novel. We read for a while, arms touching, my leg leaned against his, sharing an occasional thought or tidbit.

But I couldn't concentrate. Things were unsettled between us. I wasn't being honest with him. Why not just tell him I'd fallen madly in love with him? Tell him I was afraid of the pain I'd feel when it was over. Did I think he'd try to convince me to stay with him? Or was I afraid he'd tell me he didn't feel the same? I sighed and put my book down. Two weeks left together.

He laid his book on his chest, a finger marking his spot, and put his hand on my thigh.

"You okay?"

"Yeah." I curled against him, laid my arm across his chest. He put his book aside and put both arms around me.

I said, "You?"

And he said, "Yeah."

We lay there, communicating no more than that. His chest rose and fell, and I drifted into sleep to the beat of his heart.

I awoke alone on the bed, a blanket pulled over me. Was it day or night? My watch said 12:35; the light outside told me it was lunchtime and not midnight. I remembered it was Sunday.

Hans wasn't in the dining room, and as I set my tray down at a table with Paul, Liz, and Javier, Liz said, "Hans just left to go ashore with Marcia and Yvonne. He asked me to tell you."

"Ah." Did the stab of disappointment I felt show on my face? I unloaded my tray and sat down, saying, "Thanks." Fair enough, I thought, remembering the previous Sunday. But he hadn't even left a note.

I dug into the Spanish tortilla, a dense omelet packed full of potatoes. "Mmm ... Pepa is such a good cook." I said it to Javier, as if he somehow shared the responsibility. It was then I noticed a subdued atmosphere at the table and stopped, a bite midway to my mouth. "What?"

Paul and Liz exchanged a look, and Liz said, "How are you and Hans getting along?"

"Fine. What, was he arm in arm with Marcia or something?"

"No, of course not."

"But ...," I encouraged.

Liz looked at Javier this time. "It's just that other romances seem to be hitting rocky spots. Bill and Audrey, for instance . . ."

I nodded. "Well, she *is* married."

Javier had had a bite of omelet impaled on his fork for some time, not eating it. "Pepa's married," he said, and thrust the bite in his mouth.

"Oh!" I looked around the table. "But separated, right?"

"Not exactly. Not as separated as she said," said Javier, chewing.

"Oh . . . and you just found out." I looked over at the galley window where Pepa was passing a plate of food to the captain.

"Does she . . ." I looked at Javier. ". . . not plan to leave her husband?"

"She doesn't know what she wants." He tore a piece of bread and mopped his plate with it. "We're taking a break."

"I'm sorry." I felt bad for him. More so than I did for Bill. I'd had the feeling that Javier and Pepa were in a love-of-a-lifetime relationship. Where Bill was just looking, always looking, for a mate.

We ate in silence for a few moments until Liz said, "Your turn to share."

Paul said, "Sweetheart . . ."

I laughed. Liz was so . . . consistent. Somehow I didn't mind the question, though. "Well, maybe we've hit kind of a rough patch. Inexplicably."

Paul said, "We've entered the Bermuda Triangle of Love."

Even Javier joined in the laughter.

"Has anyone checked on Helen and Josef?" I said to deflect any further questions.

Everyone thought they were fine.

"And you?" I asked Paul and Liz.

"Oh, fine as ever," said Paul, smiling. Liz beamed.

When lunch was over, rain was hammering the dining room windows, and going out didn't appeal, so Liz, Paul, and I got Javier to play Spades. After an hour of this, the sun came out, leaving the deck strewn with glistening drops. Paul and Liz went up to their cabin, and I suggested to Javier that we go ashore for a little exercise.

We walked along the flat, hard sand, battling into the wind, not saying much for the first few minutes. When the wind let up slightly, I said, "I'm sorry about you and Pepa . . . I like you both so much. I like you together."

"Yeah." He walked along, hands in his pockets.

"Maybe she just needs a little time," I said.

For a moment I didn't think he would talk, but then he said, "It's not that. It's me. When she told me she was still living with her husband, I was angry. She's been lying to me all this time. She said before that they were separated and getting a divorce soon. But it seems that's not true."

"So you told her . . ."

"I told her I didn't want to be with someone who couldn't be honest with me . . . Maybe she wanted to say more, but I wasn't listening."

We walked along in silence for a few moments, heads down, hair whipping around our ears.

"I wonder what she's thinking." I didn't realize I'd said it out loud, but Javier glanced at me. We stopped walking and turned our backs to the wind.

"I mean," I went on, "you don't know why she misrepresented the situation in the first place." I hugged my arms against myself for warmth. "People have their reasons . . . And then for some reason she decides to come clean. Maybe she sees the end of our time here is approaching and . . . wanted to talk openly with you."

He said, "And I shut her out."

I nodded. "She must be feeling bad also."

We walked on until the beach became narrower. When we came to a place where a cliff rose straight ahead of us and a treacherous-looking grassy slope hemmed us in on the left, we stopped and looked up.

I pointed to a faint path that angled up to a gentler slope, which started about twenty feet above. "Want to go up?"

It was slippery with mud, but we found footholds. At the top we stopped to catch our breath and looked down on the beach and the wind-whipped waves. After a moment, I said, "I'm not taking her side. I'm just trying to understand. I think she's a good person." I thought for a moment. "Sometimes you just tell a little lie, before you know someone very well, thinking it won't matter. And then you have to keep telling more lies to support that first lie . . . and before you know it, you realize you're being dishonest with this person you've become very close to." I looked at him and finished my little speech. "And so one day you get your courage and go to that person to set it right . . ."

"Okay, okay," he said. A wry smile touched his lips.

"I'm just saying," I said.

He turned and looked up the bright green slope, which disappeared into the low cloud cover. "See that rock?" He pointed to a large gray outcrop a couple hundred yards above us and just below the clouds.

"Let's go," I said.

We climbed, not speaking, careful not to step near Magellanic burrows that riddled the slope, though twice causing one of the penguins to scurry into its hole. We arrived at the immense square rock after ten minutes. By climbing onto it from the uphill side, we found a flat place to sit and dangle our legs off the front.

We drank some water and looked out over the slope down to the beach, the bay, and the little white ship with the red stripe holding on tight in the tossing water. Not a human was in sight, not another boat on the water, nor any kind of building. A group of four sheep grazing to our right along the hillside was the only sign civilization was somewhere not too far off.

When I looked back at the beach, three figures had appeared at the far end. Javier saw them, too. "Hans and friends?" he said.

A look through binoculars confirmed that this was so. The three were walking toward the red flag that marked where the radio had been left, apparently heading back to the ship. We lowered the binoculars.

His eyes still on the beach, Javier said, "Another person with a secret."

I looked at him, still not sure what everyone knew.

"That he's a Hotz," he said.

The three tiny figures arrived at the flag and stopped. "He kept it from me, too," I said. "Until he got back from Switzerland. It felt funny that he'd been keeping such an important part of himself from me . . . but I understood."

"It's not the same kind of secret, though, is it?" Javier said.

"No."

We were silent for a moment, then he said, "Things are not . . . going well with you?"

I shrugged. "Oh, I don't know . . . we're just . . . finding things to argue about lately."

He was silent.

So I added, "I think he'd like us to stay together after our time here is over." I twisted a piece of grass between my fingers. "And I . . . don't think it's such a good idea."

He looked at me. "Because for you it's just a . . . ?" He waved his hand.

"Oh . . .No." I shook my head. "I've never felt this way about anyone before in my life." I hadn't even put it quite that way to myself. Why was I telling Javier? Once I started, I couldn't stop. "But it will never work away from here. This is a fantasy world, our world on the boat. I'm fifty-one and he's thirty-three; it wouldn't work out in the real world. And besides, I've got to get a job, focus on that. I . . . it won't . . . it'd never work."

"What does he say about it?"

"We're not exactly talking about it." I watched Hans move closer to the rim of churning foam and run back, playfully dodging a wave. The two women stood watching him. "We're just doing things like going off for the day without telling each other, or even leaving a note." I hadn't meant to sound so aggrieved. "We should head back."

We climbed down off the rock and stood for a moment in its shelter.

"So," I said, trying to lighten the mood. "Any advice for the lovelorn?"

"Lovelorn?"

"You know, people having problems with love."

"Oh . . . No advice. But I do see two people who make each other happy. And what else is there?"

Back on board I found Hans in the lounge, telling a story, surrounded by a gaggle of listeners. He saw me and held out his arm. When I sat by him, he pulled me close and said, "You got my message, right?"

I nodded; we had an audience, after all. I smiled and said, "Thanks."

He continued his story. They'd hiked across a wide, low isthmus to a remote gentoo colony. "Then we followed their path toward the sea, it was maybe a mile away."

"At least a mile," Marcia said.

Hans said, "About halfway to the sea, we sat down to watch them, a couple meters off the path. We can see them coming from both directions, marching to the beach and back to the colony. We want to see if they will stop or go around or just walk past us." He took a drink from a can of diet cola.

"What happened?" Helen said.

"They stopped, maybe twenty or thirty meters away. They looked at us for a while. It looked like they were talking about it.

After maybe five minutes, one of them starts moving, takes a different, a wider, path around us. The rest soon followed."

"So they weren't all that bothered by you . . . ," Paul said.

"The point is," said Marcia, "we slowed them down. And especially at this time of year, when they're feeding their young, they can't afford to waste any time, any energy, at all."

Hans added, "And with their numbers decreasing all the time, when people bother them . . ."

"But," Helen said, "it's these areas where they hardly see anyone, isn't it? Where they're bothered more? In heavily visited areas, they get used to people."

Marcia said, "That's just propaganda from the tourist bureau."

I stayed out of it. Was Hans being swayed by Marcia and her agenda after spending the afternoon with her? I looked at my watch, got up, and interrupted the discussion, saying, "Five o'clock. Time to hit the galley."

As Hans and I started sautéing onions and garlic for soup, he tried to break through my businesslike shell and apologized for leaving without a word that afternoon.

"No problem," I said. "We don't own each other." It didn't come out sounding too gracious. He didn't comment.

I kept the corner of my eye on Pepa and Javier, forced to work in close proximity, probably for the first time since their breakup. At one point I came upon the two of them alone in a corner of the galley, Javier standing close and saying something to her. She nodded. He glanced up at me and winked. I smiled, picked up a stack of napkins, and went back out.

Later that night in Hans's cabin I couldn't keep myself from saying, "So, are you becoming a member of the tourism-is-bad camp, then?" We were sitting in bed reading.

"You have to agree there's something," he said.

"Of course there's something to it . . . it's just not something to go changing the numbers about."

He put down his book. "I don't think she's doing that. It maybe seemed like it at first, but lately . . ."

I didn't say anything.

"If you're mad about me going this afternoon . . ."

"I'm not mad."

"Good," he said, and kissed me.

We read a little longer, then turned off the light and spooned together. It was the first night we hadn't made love, and it loomed with significance.

TWENTY

The List

One of the oddest guests at the party, however, is not a true preda-
tor, but a bold and persistent scavenger. It is the Snowy Sheathbill,
a pure white bird—quite common in the icy landscape of coastal
Antarctica—that subsists almost entirely on bits of spilled food and
feces. Scampering in between crowded penguin nests, the sheathbill
is largely ignored: he poses no threat.

—Kevin Schafer,
THE FALKLAND ISLANDS:
BETWEEN THE WIND & SEA

ON MONDAY THE wind and rain battered me and my team as we observed gentoos and skuas on the beach. Despite Bill's parka and the pad I was sitting on, by lunchtime I felt like a block of ice. We were finishing tuna sandwiches and about to cut our lunch break short to get moving again, when Hans appeared over the hill. He was working at the other side of the spit in a bay often visited by cruise ships. It must have been a couple of miles away.

He sat down in the little circle, loosened his hood, and wiped the rain off his face. "I came to check on you." He said it to everyone, but no one was fooled; he meant me.

"We'll get back to work," said Javier, "so you can check on Joanie."

As the others walked away, we kissed.

"I was worried about you," he said. "It's so cold today."

For a moment, it felt like we were back to the way we were, before things started to get complicated.

The tenderness carried into the evening. We watched the movie together, along with ten or so other people, a romantic comedy that made me teary. We held hands throughout and went up early and made love as if we'd been apart for weeks.

But Monday night's tenderness was followed by squabbles. Tuesday Hans and his group worked the same bay; this time it was filled with a cruise ship's bright bulk, with boatloads of passengers coming ashore. That evening he told me he saw more skua kills of gentoo chicks than he ever had.

As Finn's and my work hadn't included cruise ship visits, I listened with interest.

But when Hans said, "Marcia thinks that cruise ships especially . . . ," my interest gave way to irritation and I said, "Oh, Marcia. What do *you* think?"

He put down his book. "Stop treating me like I can't think for myself."

It was the first time I'd seen him mad. "I'm sorry. It's just that I don't trust her. She's up to something and now she's trying to get you on her side."

"I'm capable of making my own conclusions."

"Yes, I know. Skuas don't seem to be the least bit afraid of people."

"One or two visitors is one thing, but so many people . . . ," he said, trailing off.

I agreed. And wondered aloud if my project should have included cruise ships. Hans reassured me that my study had value, that by showing visits by individuals or small groups had little impact, as our research was showing, we might influence policy.

We ended the exchange making peace with each other. But it felt fragile.

The next evening, Wednesday, I played Spades and didn't see Hans until I went up to bed. When I opened the door, he was sitting on the edge of the bed and silently watched me come in. At the look on his face I stopped.

He held out a single sheet of paper and said, "What's this?"

I took it from his hand and saw right away what it was. "This is the list of everyone on the boat, the one I was telling you about, with their country and position on the project. Where'd you get it?"

"Here." He gestured at the desk. "I was looking for my field notes from yesterday."

It was then that I noticed my name at the top; it was the copy of the email Brenda had given me. "It's mine," I said.

"You told me you didn't have one."

"No, I didn't." I looked up, frowning.

"You said only Bill, Ian, and Yvonne had them."

I looked again at the list, confused. The three names of the scientists were starred, just the way I remembered it. But there was something else; Hans's name had a heavy black line under it.

I sat down on the couch and looked at Hans, trying to understand what it meant. I shook my head. "I never said I didn't have one."

"You never said you *did*."

Was that true? I looked back at the list. "Why is your name underlined?"

"I thought you could tell *me*."

"Hans," I said, "It never was underlined before." Of this, at least, I was sure. "These three names with the stars—they're the scientists. My advisor gave me the list. She's an old friend of Ian's. She thought if I knew their names right away, it might help with making connections." I shook my head, looking hard at the list. "But your name was never underlined."

Hans was hunched over, elbows on knees, hands clasped, looking at me, saying nothing.

"Why?" I said. "What are you thinking?"

He didn't speak right away. Then he said, "I just wonder why you didn't tell me you had a copy."

I thought back to the night we'd been talking about it—probably about a week ago. "I don't know, I don't remember telling you. But if I didn't, it wasn't intentional." I thought hard. "It must have been the night I googled you . . . then I went to Bill to ask him about how Marcia might have known your name . . . then I told you about it . . ." I shook my head.

Hans wasn't letting it go. "It's not the first time you forgot to tell me something."

"What else?"

"You and Bill in the tent, for one. "

"That again! Well, that *was* intentional. I thought you'd react, so I didn't tell you. Also, it wasn't important."

"But this is important."

"Hans, the last time I saw that list, your name was *not* underlined." I watched him, slowly understanding what he must be thinking. "You think I knew about you before I got here? You think I've been after you for your money?" I let out a bark of a laugh. "That's too funny."

He looked at his hands, clasped on his knees.

"Oh!" I was really clicking along now. "And why am I pulling back from you lately, as you say I am?" I paused. "Because now you're not the rich guy you once were. Perfect! Who would want you without your money? It all fits!" I stood up. "And this list? I don't think it was even up here. I left most of my papers down in my room. You've been going through my stuff!" I didn't really think this; didn't know what I thought, but I'd whipped myself into a fury.

Hans stood up, too. "Joanie—"

I didn't give him a chance. "I'll sleep in my own room tonight." And I thrust his precious list at him, turned, and walked out the door, shutting it firmly behind me.

Once I was in my room, I remembered my toothbrush was in Hans's bathroom. So I marched back up, knocked on the door, the door I hadn't knocked on in weeks.

"I need some things." I swept into the room, went about as a whirlwind while he leaned against the dresser, arms folded. Toothbrush and towel out of the bathroom, book and journal from beside the bed, Pru, who was sitting on the couch. The only words I spoke were, "Excuse me," when I wanted in the dresser. He moved aside, and though I didn't look at him, I was aware of him watching me pull out handfuls of underwear, socks, and shirts.

Don't say a word, I kept thinking, not one word, or tears will be everywhere.

"Good night," I said when my arms were full of my belongings.

He said it, too, hardly more than a whisper, and closed the door behind me.

Tossing everything on the bed, I sat down to think. I really was almost a hundred percent sure I'd left the list in my cabin, had never taken it upstairs. I got up and opened the desk drawer. There was my handful of files. I easily found one with the label "Pretrip." As I plucked it out, I immediately had the thought that I shouldn't be handling it—what about fingerprints? But that was silly. I flipped quickly through the file—there were only nine or ten sheets of paper—and saw that my list of names was indeed missing. Was anything else gone? I glanced around the room, which seemed to be as I'd left it. A quick check through my desk showed all my files seemed to be where I'd left them.

I immediately suspected Marcia had something to do with this. I never locked my door when I was out and seldom locked the desk drawer. Had she come in here, looked through my stuff, found the list, underlined Hans's name, planted it in his cabin? But why? An attempt to break us up?

My mind was going at full speed. I wanted it to. I wanted to think about this stuff—the who, the why, the mystery. Otherwise, I'd be left facing the fact that Hans and I had fought and I'd be sleeping alone tonight. That this was *it*, the breakup I'd known was coming.

I stood up and paced back and forth, hugging my arms to my chest. The other puzzle was why I'd never told Hans I had a copy of the list. I was inclined to believe it was true that I hadn't—I certainly couldn't call up a memory of telling him. I sat again on the edge of the bed amid the chaos of my recently collected possessions, trying to think, but getting nowhere.

Maybe if I tidy up a bit, I thought. So I went about putting things away. As I was putting my underwear in the top drawer of the dresser, I saw the bottle of wine I'd bought in the Santiago airport sitting there, a tempranillo, that, if price meant anything, should be pretty good. I rummaged around in the desk drawer for my Swiss Army knife and got the glass from the bathroom. Moments later I was sitting on my single bed, propped against the two pillows, legs stretched out in front of me, shoes off, glass of wine in hand, telling myself that everything was fine.

Well, maybe it wasn't that good at the moment, but at least the urge to cry had passed. I sipped the wine, my first in something

FEET FIRST

like ten days. I looked down at Pru, leaned against the pillow beside me. "Why did I not tell Hans that I had a copy of the list?" I asked her, but Pru was silent.

I drank again, as if the answer could be found there. Gazing across the room, I came to focus on the carving that Hans had given me mere days after we'd met. He'd been so pleased that I'd recognized it as a black-browed albatross that he'd given it to me. I suddenly remembered Yoshi's watercolor: the white boat alone in the ocean and sky. He'd brought it to our cabin the night Hans and I had been talking about the list.

That was it! I sat up, swung my feet to the floor. When Yoshi left, Hans hadn't been interested in hearing more about my theories and suspicions, or any more about the list. So I'd never got to the part where I, too, had a copy of it.

I looked at the door, considering going upstairs to tell him. But I was holding on to my anger. How could he even think I'd been after him for his money? After all we'd been through, how well we'd come to know each other? And now that I'd realized why I hadn't told him about the list, I was able to feel righteous as well.

Maybe even righteous enough to go to sleep. I downed the last of my glass, brushed my teeth, changed into my pajamas, and curled up in bed with Pru and my book.

TWENTY-ONE

Back in the Burrow

[One reason penguins nest in discrete subcolonies, as opposed to one large colony as most seabirds do, is that] a flightless bird like a penguin must walk from the outside edge into its nest, running a gauntlet of pecks and harassment from irate neighbors each time it returns home.

—Lloyd Spencer Davis,
SMITHSONIAN Q & A: PENGUINS:
THE ULTIMATE QUESTION & ANSWER BOOK

AFTER LUNCH THE next day, I found Bill sitting cross-legged in a little dip in the grassy hillside, writing in his notebook. I sat down next to him.

He looked up. "Something about the Magellanics I hadn't noticed until today," he said. "The parents seem to be leaving the chicks alone while they both go out foraging."

"Interesting." It was. It could mean the chicks were getting big enough to take care of themselves. Or it could mean food was so scarce that it required both parents to bring enough for the chicks. But I had things other than penguins on my mind.

Bill finished making a note, closed his book. "Things going okay with you and Hans?"

"Hah! What makes you ask?"

He peered at me over the top of his glasses. "You were seen last night entering your own cabin with an armload of clothing. Another report was that you and Hans were avoiding eye contact at breakfast this morning."

I gave a hoot. The fluffy Magellanic chick that had just poked its head out of a nearby burrow disappeared.

"You've gotta love this little community of ours." I shook my head. "Well, no. Things are not going well with Hans and me. And it relates to what I want to talk to you about."

After explaining how I happened to have a copy of the list, I told him about Hans finding it with his name underlined. I told him how I'd neglected to mention that I had a copy of the list, and how this had led to his suspicions, my anger, our fight, and me storming out of his cabin. With the armload of clothing.

"What I suspect," I concluded, "is that Marcia found my list in my cabin, underlined Hans's name, and planted it where he would find it."

Bill frowned. "For what purpose?"

"I don't know! That's why I wanted to talk to you. To make it look like I was interested in him before I met him? To break us up because she still wants him and his fortune?" I had reminded myself before going to look for Bill that everyone on the boat now believed that Hans was fabulously wealthy, and didn't know the latest on his disinheritance.

Bill said, "Hmm . . ."

"Well." I put my hood up and tightened the string. It was time to get back to work. "I just thought you should know. Something to add to your dossier on Marcia."

I was having a glass of the wine in my room before dinner when there was a knock on the door.

"Who is it?" I called. People mustn't see me drinking alone in my room, I thought. When I heard "Bill," I put the glass on the bedside table, half-hidden behind the fat novel, and got up to let him in.

"You'll be interested in this," he said, standing in the doorway. "I was just talking to Ian. Michiyo's going home early—her father fell and broke a hip."

"Oh! That's too bad."

"Ian mentioned that he needed to get ahold of Bernard about Michiyo's visa." He waited for me to comment.

"Yeah . . . ?" I said, not yet seeing where this was going.

"I asked him what Bernard had to do with it. Turns out he was involved with all the arrangements from this end. Has been from the beginning . . . for all of us."

"Yes?" He had my attention now.

"He had access to all kinds of information about us, long before we arrived."

"Perhaps including financial information," I said.

"It's quite possible."

I thought. "And he could have told Marcia ahead of time that there was this one really rich guy, this eligible bachelor, who was going to be on board. If Bernard *knew* Marcia, that is."

"If he knew her," Bill agreed.

"It all fits!" Realizing I'd been loud, I pulled Bill in and shut the door. Whispering now, I said, "She's got to be Bernard's contact here on the ship. They're connected somehow."

Bill nodded. "It's possible. Well. I'm on dinner duty." He opened the door, paused, and nodded toward the nightstand. "Thought you weren't drinking."

"That was to support my boyfriend."

He nodded solemnly. If he was happy at the recent turn of events, it didn't show.

There was time before dinner to go get the rest of my things from Hans's cabin. I didn't feel mad anymore, not in the same way. Hurt, disappointed, sad. And I could kind of see, on the one hand, how it might have looked to Hans. He finds this list, clearly my list, dated months earlier, with his name underlined. He remembers me telling him about these lists and that only certain people had them. It looks like I intentionally withheld the fact that I had one. Put all that on top of the fact that he was already paranoid about women being after him for his money, and I could see why he might have reacted the way he did.

I considered telling him what I'd remembered about Yoshi interrupting our conversation that night. I could tell him again that I'd never underlined his name. And that I was pretty sure I'd never even brought the list up to his cabin. It hadn't even been out of its file for weeks—not since the first couple of days when I'd been learning everyone's name.

It hurt me to think Hans had lost his trust in me. It hurt me to think of *him* being hurt. The urge to go to him and make it all okay again was almost too much. To hold him, comfort him, make him not hurt. Make me not hurt. It would be easy enough, he'd soften, we'd say we were sorry. It would be sweet, tender.

But then what? Get back together just to say goodbye in a little over a week? It was going to have to end anyway, right? It was never meant to be anything long term. And with his idea of a trip . . . it would just prolong the pain, postpone the breakup.

No, I told myself. It's better to follow this through, make the break complete. That way, we'll both have time to get our bearings before going back to the world. I finished my wine, rinsed the glass, brushed my teeth, and blew into my cupped hand to check for wine breath.

Hans's door was open and I heard a familiar voice as I approached. Marcia. I steeled myself and knocked on the frame.

"I'd like to get the rest of my things at some point. Is now convenient?" I spoke to Hans, ignoring Marcia.

Marcia stood up from the chair she'd been sitting on. "I was just leaving—dinner duty," she said brightly. And she gave me a wink as she passed by.

"She's late," I said, striding across the room to get my duffel bag from the floor of the closet. Pushing aside the flash of memory of joyfully tossing it there a few weeks ago, I put it on the bed. "You can help me." I indicated the little shelf where three of my books were mingled with his five, and the desk that held some of my papers.

Hans hadn't spoken, but he slowly began filling a paper bag with things from the desk while I loaded the duffel with the rest of the clothes from the drawers, a few things hanging in the closet, slippers off the floor. I got my shampoo and conditioner, deodorant, shaver, a couple other things from the bathroom. There wasn't much—it all took less than five minutes.

I looked around. "Well. I think that's it. If you find anything more, you know where to find me."

He zipped the duffel bag shut and picked it and the other bag up.

"I can get them," I said, holding out my hands.

"I'm going down anyway."

We must have seen—and been seen by—at least five people on the short trip. Caroline just shutting the door to her cabin, Finn leaning on the rail with Liz in front of her open door, Helen and Josef coming down the stairs as I opened my door. Helen stopped and opened her mouth to say something, but Josef ushered her on downstairs.

Hans came into the room and set the bags on the bed.

A prickling was starting behind my eyes. Trying to ignore it, I started pulling at the bracelet he'd brought me from Switzerland. "I should give this back . . ."

He put his hand on my wrist to stop me. "No," he said. "It's yours." And he took back his hand.

I stuck my hands in my armpits. "Okay."

His eyes met mine for a moment.

What could he be thinking? I looked away, said, "See you at dinner."

He nodded and backed out the door.

TWENTY-TWO

Cousins

The chicks of most species of birds have evolved some way to stimulate their parents to feed them ... A penguin chick simply vibrates its beak against that of its parent, and when the adult bird gapes, the chick wedges its bill inside and gobbles up the slimy regurgitant directly.

—*Wayne Lynch,*
PENGUINS OF THE WORLD

I CLOSED AND LOCKED the door and flung myself onto the bed. Tears filled my eyes as I scooped my pillow and Pru into my arms and curled tight around them, sniffing and taking short, shallow breaths. "What have I done?" I whispered to Pru.

Cast aside the one true love of your life, she answered.

I pressed my wrist and its bracelet against my chest and sniffled some more.

After a few pillow-soaking minutes, I sat up. I blew my nose twice. When I was pretty sure I was done, I washed my face in cold water, fluffed up my hair, and kept checking the mirror until I determined that I looked more or less normal.

In the dining room I unloaded my tray onto a table occupied by Ian, Javier, and Bill, figuring the group of men would be less likely to say something sympathetic and get me going again. Sure enough, after a brief greeting, they went on talking about the best portable hard-drive devices for storing photos. I put the food methodically into my mouth, turned down Javier's offer of a glass of wine, and contributed nothing to the conversation.

Not talking gave me a chance to look around the room. The usual noisy chatter: Helen and Josef had their heads together, Finn and Alejandro and Hans were listening to Yvonne. My eyes eventually fell on Marcia and Bernard, sitting side by side at a table across from three others. My view of them was from the side, and Marcia, farther away, was sitting forward, leaning on one elbow. I could see both their profiles.

Marcia really was a striking woman. That ebony hair, long and shining, the heavy black eyebrows, her skin a smooth, even brown, nose straight and long. If anything took away from her beauty, it was the mouth, and even that just added interest. A small mouth, the thin lips made a sort of M shape, turning down at the corners.

Marcia smiled at something Caroline said, then turned to watch Bernard reply. I shifted my attention to him. Which was when I paid attention to his mouth for the first time. For a heavy man, so full everywhere else, they were thin lips. They curved in an M; up in the middle, with two little points, and down at the corners.

I fiddled with my email in the communications room and waited for everyone to settle down to their various evening activities. When the after-dinner movie started with both Bernard and Marcia safe inside, I got to work.

A few years back I'd dabbled in genealogy, so I knew my way around the databases. With my library card number, which popped easily into my head, I could get into Ancestry.com, the U.S. census, and other sites that provided a wealth of information on people and their ancestors. I knew Marcia's and Bernard's first and last names, but no middles, and I knew their approximate ages—Marcia had said she was twenty-seven, and I guessed Bernard to be about my age, maybe a little older. Using my best guess for birth years, I went from there.

I didn't get very far with such sketchy information on Marcia Brower. So I googled Bernard McConaghy, and, not surprisingly in a place like the Falklands with such a small population, he was one of two with that last name. And it wasn't hard to find a bio on him, complete with full name and date of birth—two years younger than me, I noted. With that, it was fairly easy to find he'd been born in the Falklands, that his father was originally from Scotland, and his mother came from a long line of Falklanders. He was a middle child; an older sister lived in England and a younger brother also lived in the Falklands.

I returned to Marcia, and was amazed again at how many people shared the same name; I found over fifteen people with her first and last name. But I didn't know where she was from. She'd mentioned graduating from Columbia University, but that was little help. To get any further, I needed an exact birthplace and date and a middle name.

The movie would be letting out at any moment, and I didn't want anyone showing up at my back and peering over my shoulder, so I logged off. When the moviegoers filed through the lounge in laughing groups, I was draped comfortably over one of the big leather chairs, engrossed in a crossword puzzle. Hans was walking next to Marcia, smiling down at her as she talked. That's good, I told myself, ignoring the knot in my stomach. I want him to be happy. I do. But *Marcia*.

When I saw Bill, I called him over, and once the room had emptied, I gave him a brief rundown on what I'd been up to. He was intrigued and agreed to get in Ian's files the next day and bring me as much information on Marcia and Bernard as he could find.

All Friday morning I worked observing gentoo colonies. The weather was turning again; rain slanting in, wind battering tightly tied hoods, cold stiffening even the best-gloved hands. A good day to hunch within, talk no more than necessary. When my mind wandered, it went to Marcia and Bernard. I felt sure they were somehow related, and I could barely wait to find out if I was right.

With my focus on skua behavior and Marcia and Bernard, I managed to avoid thinking about Hans. Only once, when I saw him standing at the rockhopper colony far along the slope, in his red raincoat, did the memory ambush me of the day I got hypothermia and we lay down together for the first time.

"S.G.!" It was Paul, noting a "search ground." I focused back on the colony and made the entry on my form.

I was set to spend all afternoon helping on the count. But at two thirty Josef, Caroline, and I, those prone to suffer from the cold, were sent back to the communications room to enter data. We each sat at a computer and Bill gave instructions on what to do. Then he went around to help each of us get started. He got to me last and at the same time he was showing me how to enter a batch of Magellanic numbers, he put down two papers and gave them a couple of taps with his finger. It was the information on Bernard and Marcia.

I finished my work on Magellanics in twenty minutes or so. A glance around convinced me the others were so engrossed in their work they wouldn't notice what I was doing.

I started by googling the Marcia Elizabeth Brower that had been born in Hartford, Connecticut, and went from there.

By four forty-five, just before the teams came back in, I had found some very interesting information. I was bursting to tell Bill. But he wasn't back yet, so I joined Helen in the gym.

"Any plans for the weekend?" said Helen. We were side by side on the stationary bikes, pedaling up a sweat.

I knew she'd eventually get me to talk about Hans, but I tried to deflect her. "Not really," I said. "I'll put in a couple of shifts on the project in the morning, then . . . just more job search, read . . . catch up on sleep." As soon as this last was out of my mouth, I realized it sounded like a reference to Hans and the breakup and all the time I could now spend sleeping.

Helen nodded, and we were silent for a moment. I gave my face its first mop with the towel. Without further preamble, Helen said, "What happened with you and Hans?"

I kept looking straight ahead. Where did this strong wall I was feeling come from, this aversion to talking about it, with practically my best friend here? I said, in a case-is-closed tone, "We broke up."

Helen got off her bike and went over to close the door. Once she was pedaling again, she said, "I can *see* that you broke up." She looked at me, waiting.

"There's really nothing more to say." I pedaled faster, but Helen kept her eyes on me, pedaling right along, so I added, "It ran its course; that's all." A small drop was making slow progress down my temple.

After a moment, Helen said, "Bullshit."

I burst into a laugh; such language coming from Helen! I said, "It was only ever meant to be a six-week fling. It just ended a little early. Of course, I'm sad . . ."

Helen was shaking her head. "You're brokenhearted. You both are. It's obvious."

I mopped my face again. Hans and Helen were pretty good friends. Had they talked? What did he say? What was he feeling? Damn it, I didn't want to get started. "I really don't want to talk about this now."

Helen apologized for pushing, and after a moment, said, "Josef and I are going to Audrey's tomorrow afternoon. She invited us to spend the night at the lodge. Her island is only a fifteen-minute flight from here. She has another room available, a single, and we couldn't think of anyone at the time she asked, but that was when you were . . ."

"Part of a couple," I finished. I stopped pedaling and climbed off the bike. "It's nice of you to ask, Helen. Are you sure? Maybe Hans wants to go. Instead of me."

"I'm asking you."

I went over my latest list in my mind: talk to Bill, meet with Finn, do laundry, more job search. Nothing that couldn't be done tonight or wait until Sunday afternoon. "Okay. I'll go. It sounds nice. I'd love to get out of here."

"Great. I'll call FIGAS and see if there's room for you on the flights." Helen hopped off the bike and gave me a quick side hug, saying, "And I won't make you talk if you don't want to."

Back in my cabin, I was splashing cold water on my face when Liz came knocking. If I hadn't wanted to talk to Helen about Hans, I certainly didn't want to talk to Liz. But I offered her the chair and perched on the edge of the bed. She twisted a handkerchief in her lap and looked down intently. I waited.

"I'm sorry about you and Hans," she finally said, looking up.

"Really? Well, you're perfectly welcome to say 'I told you so.'"

She shook her head. "No, I've . . . you were so happy together, so good together. I . . . I guess I got used to it."

Tears, always lurking, jumped into my eyes.

"Oh, I'm sorry." Liz grabbed a tissue from the box by the chair and held it out to me. "I know I butted in at first, and it was none of my business." She sat back, holding the tissue box. "But I was just . . ." She looked around, searching for words. "It was too . . . strange for me, him being so much younger. And I really liked you from the start. I admired you for going back to school and all at your age. I wanted to be part of it, somehow . . . to help." Noticing my need of another tissue, she held out the box. "I felt you were making a big mistake, going with Hans. Appearing not serious to people who could make a difference in your career . . . Throwing away opportunities."

"So you never really were advocating me sleeping with Bill . . ."

"No, of course not." After a silent moment, she said, "You know, when I was your age, maybe a little older, I tried for a new job. I had all this experience nursing, but I wanted to get into something less strenuous physically. And emotionally. There were all kinds of things; semi-administrative, IT . . . but it was amazing how difficult it was. After a while I came to the conclusion there was a certain amount of ageism going on."

"Did you ever get anything?" I dabbed at my nose.

"Yes. I finally got a good supervisory position. At the same hospital where I'd always been. I worked there for nine more years."

We were silent for a moment. I gave what I hoped was a final honk into my tissue.

Liz smiled. "I also admired you for not listening to me. For following your heart."

This got me going again. Liz set the whole box in my lap, patted my knee, and left.

After dinner, Bill and I went to the alcove on Deck Two. I had with me copies of census data, immigration records and the like.

"Here's the deal," I said once we were seated on the couch. "Bernard's father came from Scotland to the Falklands in the 1940s. He had three sisters, two of whom stayed in Scotland. The youngest married an American, a John Brower, and moved to the states in the early 1950s. They had five children. A son named Philip married and then fathered three children." I looked at Bill. "One of them is our Marcia. Marcia's grandmother is Bernard's aunt." I put down my papers and sat back, arms folded.

Bill squinted. "So that makes them . . ."

"First cousins once removed. Marcia's father and Bernard are first cousins."

Bill raised his eyebrows. "Good job." He looked out at the whitecaps. "The fact that they've kept their relationship secret has got to mean they're up to something . . ."

"And probably that Bernard told Marcia ahead of time about the wealthy heir that would be here."

"Yes," Bill said. "And Marcia must be Bernard's helper in . . . whatever he's up to."

I said, "She's pretty eager to blame tourism for population declines. And Bernard does have the interest in oil drilling . . ."

We were silent, looking across the water toward the dim shore.

I finally said, "What are we going to do? We've got one week before the count is over and we all scatter to the winds."

"I'm getting some hard proof on what Marcia's been doing. Finn's been sticking to her pretty close, pretending he's being swayed by her. Hans, too."

"Hans, too?"

"Hans is reporting to me, too." He looked at me. "I thought you knew that."

"I thought that pretty much ended when he went to Switzerland."

"True, for a while. But I asked him about a week ago if he'd keep an eye on her." He smiled. "Finn's a bit too prickly to be very effective."

That was true; Finn being rabidly anti-oil, anti-fishing, and not shy about sharing those views with anyone and everyone. "I thought you didn't believe me at all about Marcia!"

"Just trying to be open-minded, as you suggested . . . I also asked Marcia to keep an eye on Finn."

"Oh!" I paused. "Clever."

He shrugged.

"And Hans," I said. "Why didn't you tell me you had him watching Marcia for you? I thought he really was becoming convinced that tourism was the bugaboo . . . he told me so, he gave me examples, observations." I thought back. "The other day I accused him of not thinking for himself, of being swayed by Marcia . . . He got mad."

"I imagine so," Bill said.

"Well . . . did he find anything?"

"He came to me with examples of cruise ship passengers being a distraction to penguins, so the skuas and other predators could make their kill. And the numbers are off again, but no one can seem to catch Marcia at it. Nothing new."

I slumped back against the couch. The wind was sneaking into the alcove, lifting the corner of one of my papers. I picked them up and folded them into quarters, leaned back again. Focused on my breathing, watched the occasional albatross shoot by on the wind.

Bill leaned back next to me, his shoulder touching mine. He turned his head toward me. "So what did happen with you and Hans?"

I kept looking out at the water through the frame made by the walls and railing. I wasn't any more eager to give Bill the details than I had been with Helen and Liz. "I guess it just wasn't meant to be."

"Hmm . . ." Bill looked out, too, nodding slightly. "Well. I'm sorry," he said. "It looked like you were getting along fine."

I didn't say anything at first, and finally couldn't hold it in. "We were getting along great . . . I'm not too happy about it." Tears filled my lower lids and I tried not to blink them onto my cheeks.

He lifted his arm and put it around my shoulders. We sat that way for a while and in the midst of this reverie, I had the crazy thought that if I looked into Bill's eyes, we would kiss, and that easily, I'd have myself a nice boyfriend, a decent man I could share my life with. I wouldn't even have to get a job . . . No one seems to want me anyway. What have I been thinking? That I'm thirty-one, not fifty-one? That I can find a job in this field, compete against young people? That I can have a love affair with a thirty-three-year-old man?

Here was Bill, a perfectly decent man. I could move to Colorado with him, we'd travel; we could write books! He'd take the pictures, I'd write the text; books about birds. It wouldn't be a bad life. A good life, in fact.

Bill began rubbing his knuckles a little, up and down my upper arm. Another albatross zoomed by just then, close to the ship.

It glanced over at us as if to check on our behavior. I sat up away from him and picked up the papers that threatened to jump off the table despite their fold. "Looks like I'm going to Audrey's tomorrow. With Helen and Josef."

"Ah."

"If FIGAS can take me. Helen's checking. We'll spend the night."

"How nice," he said.

I heard the edge in his voice and said, "Yeah . . . I guess nothing ever . . . you and Audrey . . ."

"Nah." He sat up straight, arched his back, rolled his head to the right and the left. "I haven't talked to her lately."

"I'm sorry," I said. I looked at the papers in my hand. "Well. I should probably check with Helen, then pack. You want these?"

He stuffed them in the pocket of his coat and we left the alcove.

Moments after I was back in my room, there was a knock on the door. Who now? I couldn't take one more of these intimate talks. But I opened the door, and Finn was standing in the twilight. "Can I come in for a minute?"

I let him in and we sat down, he on the chair, one arm on the little desk, me on the bed.

"I haven't been entirely honest with you," he began.

"Really." I heard sarcasm in my voice, and something flickered over Finn's face. Afraid he'd shut down, I said, "Sorry. I suppose you had your reasons."

He picked up a pen from the desk and began fiddling with it.

I encouraged him. "You've seemed kind of subdued ever since your friend came for the bags . . . What's going on, Finn? Maybe I can help."

He put the pen down, glanced at me then away. "They're planning an oil spill. My friends."

I sat very still, as if I'd spotted a rare bird and the slightest movement would make it vanish.

"Just a small one," he said. "This weekend. Needless to say I'm no longer in the loop. Monday a meeting starts in Stanley; oil companies, Falkland Islands government, British government officials. They're going to review applications to drill for oil under the sea west of the Falklands. Issue permits." He glanced at me. "You probably know this."

I nodded. The weekly *Penguin News,* which eventually caught up with us on the *Professor,* was full of stories on the matter.

Finn went on. "You probably *don't* know that the environmental impact process has been abbreviated so they can get started right away." He cleared his throat. "My friends . . . actually, *we* thought a carefully-timed spill would make them slow down and do that step properly. And gain us some time to figure out ways to get them to give up the idea entirely. Do you know how deep it is there? Over seven thousand feet."

I nodded slowly. "So, the bags are . . . for the spill?"

He nodded. "They're special bags, not available here. They degrade in salt water. Within eight or ten hours there will be no trace of them." He picked up the pen again. "Back in Missoula it made sense, the idea of sacrificing a few penguins for the long-term good of all." He shook his head, still not looking at me. "But I stopped thinking it was such a great idea. Since I got here . . . I can't stand to see even one penguin hurt. Or albatross . . . or duck or goose, even . . ." He looked at me directly. "Crazy, huh?"

"No." I knew what he meant. Once a Magellanic peers at you from its burrow, a rockhopper hops up a rocky path without a glance in your direction, bent on getting its meal to its chicks, or a gentoo with its round white chest cocks its orange beak your way, you connect with them. You'd just as soon hurt one of your own children.

I said, "Why are you telling me now, Finn?"

"A couple days after they took the bags, they got ahold of me and apologized. Said I was right, and they were calling it off. So I thought that was the end of it. But two days ago I found out they lied. The spill is still on."

I took this in, then said, "But why are you telling *me*?"

His eyes on my face, he said, "I need you to help me stop them."

TWENTY-THREE

Marcia Gets Lost

The homosapien is perhaps the most successful species on the planet. While many other species have become threatened with extinction, the human population has risen from one billion in 1804 to two billion in 1927 to three billion in 1961 and is now over seven billion.

—*Wikipedia, 2010*

FINN HAD HEARD about me going to Audrey's the next day. He wanted me to tell her about the planned oil spill. She, in turn, could call the authorities.

I was shaking my head before he was finished. "You have to call someone tonight."

He looked sheepish. "I kind of thought I could keep my name out of it. I'd be seen as an ecoterrorist. Doesn't look so good on the résumé."

"You'd be seen as the man who stopped the ecoterrorists."

"I don't think so."

"But the sooner we get someone on this the better our chances of stopping it. Use the sat-phone to call the police."

"It's too late. No one will be there. And Audrey will be in bed. You'll be there first thing in the morning and if you talk to her right away—"

"I won't," I interrupted. "If you recall, we're working in the morning. I'm going to Audrey's in the afternoon."

Finn looked bleak. I pressed. Finn argued. I finally agreed nothing could be done tonight, but he had to promise to get Ian's sat-phone first thing in the morning and call Audrey.

"I'll check with her when I get there," I said. "If you haven't called, I'll tell Ian everything."

I didn't let Finn go until he told me more. Where was the spill supposed to take place? He didn't know exactly, but somewhere in the western part of the islands. And when? Sometime this weekend was all he knew, before Monday. It wasn't much information.

We talked long past the time I'd planned to be in bed, Finn filling me in on the whole story. He'd first connected with a Falklands guy over the internet, and things evolved until they were planning this action. With the degradable bags he brought down, the source of the spill would remain a mystery. But the discovery of an oil spill would be enough, they hoped, to slow the issuing of drilling permits. The reason he rushed into Stanley at the end of the first week, he said when I asked, was because his friend had called and said the heat was on and he needed Finn to keep the bags on the ship for a while.

"The heat was on?" I repeated.

"Yeah, he's been in trouble before, drugs I guess. Apparently, the cops kind of watch him." Finn, elbows on knees and hands clasped in front of him, stared into the corner of the room. "By the time he came for the bags, I was thinking I'd tell him I didn't want anything more to do with it. I was going to tell him I didn't think it was such a hot idea and try to talk him out of it . . ."

"So why didn't you just toss the bags in the ocean?"

Finn shrugged. "I guess I hadn't quite decided at that point . . . But then we're walking along, me and my friend and this other guy I'd never seen before, me thinking about how to convince him, and this gentoo waddles by about ten meters away, all by itself, headed for the beach. It has this stunted, twisted wing. And my friend goes, 'Look at that little fucker,' and laughs. They both laugh. I saw everything then. What kind of people they were. I stopped and threw down the bags. Gave 'em my whole speech. They just laughed, and we argued, and pretty soon they weren't laughing." Finn sat up straight. "I got a black eye and they got the bags."

Once Finn was gone, I got into my pajamas, my thoughts churning. An oil spill! An intentional oil spill. Finn, what an idiot. Would he really call Audrey in the morning? Was I doing the right thing in not trying to call someone tonight? Surely there was a 9-1-1-type number here, right? Ian would know. But he was in the habit of turning in at nine o'clock. I ended up convincing myself that nothing could be done until morning.

My thoughts moved to Marcia and Bernard, the secret cousins. What were they up to? The numbers, all those mysterious absences of Marcia's—to see Bernard, it now seemed. And what did the red-haired guy have to do with it, if anything?

And Hans. Despite the half dozen times my thoughts drifted to him and I yanked them away, I finally gave in. The talk with Helen: "You're both brokenhearted, it's obvious." And both Liz and Bill, who'd been against me and Hans being together from the start for their separate reasons, now saying it's too bad, what a great thing it was, I'm sorry.

What were people doing? And what was I doing even listening to them? It was *my* business, it had been all along, and I'd ignored them just fine when I jumped into the relationship. I needed to ignore them now. I knew what I was doing.

I looked over at Pru and said, "Don't I?"

The penguin looked at me with its beady black eyes and said, What about Hans?

"What *about* Hans?" I said.

He'll be scarred for life.

Pru had been getting pretty melodramatic lately. But she did have a point. Hans already had issues with trust, that woman who'd more or less left him at the altar. By me letting him go on thinking I had deceived him, his belief that people wanted him only for his money would be reinforced.

Yes, Pru was right. I should talk to Hans as soon as I could. As part of an it's-best-to-end-it-now speech.

I got in bed and turned out the light. And thrashed these thoughts around endlessly, finally getting up, packing an overnight bag for Audrey's, crossing that item off the list and replacing it with "pack toothbrush, slippers, pjs." Back in bed I focused on my breathing and eventually slept.

On Sunday afternoon I waited with Helen, Josef, and Audrey in the wind-rocked Land Rover for the plane to come and return us to the *Professor*. The flat grass air strip, undulating hills, and a sky filled with scudding clouds surrounded us, not one sign of civilization in the emptiness but for an orange wind sock snapping on its pole and the white wooden shed with the emergency equipment that's required at every such airstrip throughout the islands.

Getting away for the night had brought me back into alignment. I felt calm and clear and ready to talk to Hans. I had some new thoughts on Marcia and Bernard, which I planned to share with Bill. And most importantly, I'd found a moment alone with Audrey and learned that Finn had indeed called her, and she in turn had called the police. I smiled at the memory of her report: "Guess what the police said?" Here Audrey had paused dramatically: "It's that Finn Markovich chap, isn't it? We haven't stopped wondering about those bags."

So much for keeping his name out of it.

Presently, a dot appeared in the sky, followed by a hum, and the little red Britten-Norman Islander was landing and whirring to a stop before us. We piled out of the Rover into the wind, handed up our luggage, hugged Audrey goodbye, and climbed aboard. Once we were tucked in, Helen next to the pilot in front, and me next to Josef, a familiar voice greeted us from the seat behind; Bernard.

"I thought you were skipping Watkins Island," I said, "busy preparing for the dignitaries." The oil and government officials would have arrived on Saturday's flight for meetings on Monday.

"The dignitaries can get along fine without me," Bernard said, his usual jovial self. But I wondered why he was here.

We were back on the *Professor* at two thirty. The plan had been to pull anchor immediately, cross twenty miles of open ocean to the Falklands' westernmost island, and spend two days sheltered in its lee. But it turned out we weren't the last ones back after all. Marcia hadn't returned from a late-morning hike. After some discussion-filled waiting, two search parties were sent out. But by that evening's dinner prep Marcia and the search parties had still not returned.

Shifts in the galley were the only time Hans and I had spent any time around each other since the breakup. That night we were polite, speaking only of rice, onions, silverware, and the like. Just as I started sautéing a batch of onions, we got word that Marcia had been found, walking in the wrong direction on the shore of one of the long fingers that riddled that part of the coast.

"That's strange," said Hans. "She has a very good sense of direction."

Marcia and the searchers were back on board in time for dinner. By then, however, the already short time planned for Watkins Island had been cut. By leaving a good four hours later than planned, we would arrive too late to get any work done that evening. Ian rapped on his glass once we were gathered for dinner and presented the possibility of skipping Watkins entirely.

But his suggestion met a wave of protest. The island was a unique environment, far from the rest of the archipelago. Due in part to its steep shoreline and lack of sheltering bays, humans had never lived on the island, cruise ships didn't stop, and it was only rarely visited by small teams of scientists. Finn and I had felt that observations of skua-gentoo interaction there would complete the picture we were forming. The meeting was over in under five minutes, and we dug into lamb stew as the *Professor* set out westward, into the swell.

I was at a table with Yoshi, Liz, and Paul, and learned that plans had been made while I was away for two people to go around to the windward side of Watkins in the small Zodiac. Yoshi was going, and he told me about the plans. Liz and Paul added details. A couple of small colonies of rockhoppers were perched on cliffs on the far side of the island. Taking the *Professor* around was out of the question, as there was no place to shelter a boat of that size. Hiking up and over Watkins's rugged spine had been suggested, but the way was long and difficult. The Zodiac would go the following morning, spend the night, and come back Tuesday by noon. The other person making the trip was Hans.

After dinner I stood by the rail outside the dining room with a group, watching a pod of dolphins leap and dive alongside the boat. West Falkland had long since disappeared behind us, and Watkins Island was a dim gray band on the horizon. It was the first time we'd been so far from land, and though the swells were constant, most of us now had our sea legs. The dolphins carried on for some time and as they moved farther and farther away, the watchers began to disperse. Helen and Josef left for their cleanup shift in the galley, leaving only me and Hans.

We were leaning on the rail, a good five feet apart, the first time we'd been alone together since I went for my clothes on Thursday afternoon. My body clenched against the desire to slide over until my arm touched his.

Snap out of it, I told myself. But I needed to talk to him. I said, "Quiet evening."

"Yes," he said. "Quiet before the storm."

"Really?"

"A storm is predicted for Tuesday afternoon."

"Oh . . . You'll be back before then?"

"Yes. We'll be back Tuesday morning." He glanced at me and back out at the sea. He said, stating the fact as if it surprised him, "I missed you this weekend."

I glanced at him. "I missed you, too." I did my best to say it lightly.

Neither of us spoke for a moment, then he said, "How was Audrey's?"

"Really nice." I was relieved to have something to talk about. "She has a great place, very fancy. We got to ride horses . . . ate a gourmet meal, five courses, met a group from Australia that was staying there. One of them actually knew Helen's niece; their kids are in the same daycare. They were full of questions about our work. We stayed up late, amazing them with all our stories." Drinking, I remembered, a bit too much; in fact, I was still nursing a wee headache. "And you? How was your weekend?"

"Fine, quiet . . ." He pointed to the dolphins that were bouncing back toward us. After a moment, he said, "The secret is out now, about my un-inheritance, did you hear?"

"Oh! No, I didn't."

He nodded and we looked back toward the dolphins.

I said. "I wonder how people found out."

"I maybe told a couple of people," he said.

I glanced at him and saw a little smile. We were silent for a moment, until I gathered my courage and said, "I figured out why I never told you about my copy of the list. It was the night Yoshi brought the painting . . ."

"Yes. I figured it out, too."

The dolphins were cavorting right below us, shiny backs arching, breaking the water's surface with sprays of white. Still watching them, I spoke again. "I just want you to know, I never underlined your name, I never heard of you until I got here, I never wanted anything from you . . ." My heart was thumping as I looked at him.

"I know."

His eyes had just met mine when Ian strode up saying, "Hans! Have you got a minute? I want to go over some things about tomorrow." He came to rest between us at the rail.

This was so Ian. All business. Every other person on the ship would know to leave Hans and me alone.

Ian turned to me, as if vaguely sensing something. "How was your weekend—had a nice time, did you?"

I told him I had, and he commented on the dolphins, which were moving away again. After chatting a moment longer, it became clear Ian wasn't going to leave, and I excused myself to go check my email. Hans and I nodded to each other as I passed behind him.

Good, I told myself, we're not mad at each other anymore, we can be friends. Maybe we don't need to say more. Maybe he realizes, too, that it would be crazy to go on with the relationship.

At the computer, I found that Iguazú Falls National Park in Argentina had written asking me to come for an interview. My first interview! At last. After all this looking, all this angst. So why wasn't I more excited? Sure, it wasn't my dream job, but I'd recently come around to thinking that I really might have to accept something less. And the Argentina job was good enough; conducting a bird study, housing provided, benefits, a pretty good salary. I wrote back suggesting any time in the week after the twenty-fourth and clicked "Send." But my hand felt as heavy as the elephant seal I'd seen slumbering on Audrey's island that morning.

I was back on deck in time to watch our arrival and anchoring at Watkins Island. Its looming green slope was topped with a jagged spine. With nothing here but the uneven coastline to shelter behind, the *Professor* pulled close enough to feel some protection from the westerlies.

I looked at my watch; ten thirty, certainly late enough to go to my cabin and get in bed with my book. But I was too restless for that.

The lounge was full of about a dozen people, buzzing with activity for this time of night. I announced my impending interview to a little group sitting around the settee. Helen got me a glass of wine and gave a toast. I took one sip to be a good sport. Paul dragged me into a game of Ping-Pong, which I easily lost, and feigning chagrin, I surrendered my paddle to Josef.

In the dining room I sat for a while with Bill, who was looking over a mountain of papers spread across the table. We hadn't talked since Friday night when I'd told him about Marcia and Bernard being cousins, and he'd comforted me about Hans. Our talk was necessarily in snatches what with Hans, Yoshi, and Ian passing through to get food for their trip and consulting with Carl over charts. Bill managed to convey that he was suspicious about Marcia getting lost, and Bernard showing up unexpectedly. This was when I should have mentioned Finn and what he'd told me. I almost did, but decided nothing was to be gained by it for the moment, so I honored my promise to Finn. At a bit past eleven, I took myself up to my cabin.

It was a lonely place. I picked up my book. Finally after five weeks I was almost done with it; maybe I could finish it tonight. But after two minutes reading, I put it down. I looked at the bottle of wine in its little alcove on the dresser. There was about a glass left. I should finish it, I thought; I should finish something. But I didn't want it. I touched the carved albatross Hans had given me so long ago, admiring the color of the wood, the detail, its smooth body.

I put it down, sighed, and looked at Pru. "I guess I'm waiting for Hans to come knocking." I looked at the door. "We sort of cleared the air tonight. Started to, anyway." I sat down on the bed. I knew he wouldn't come to me. It would be up to me to climb the stairs, knock on his door, cross the gulf between us—the gulf I'd created, or at least maintained.

I picked up Pru. "I could get him back if I wanted. He could come to Argentina with me. He could follow me around for a while, until he gets tired of me." I stopped. "Is that it? Is that what I think will happen—he'll get tired of me? That he'll end up breaking my heart?"

Pru had no comment.

Monday morning came just as I was sinking into the first good sleep of the night. I had breakfast at the same table with Hans, Ian sitting between us, showing Hans and Yoshi how to work the radio they'd be using to stay in contact. The storm that was due late the next day was now predicted to arrive a bit sooner. They were to call Ian first thing the next morning and get the latest forecast. It would be decided then whether they should stay and work that morning or come straight back.

After breakfast there was much hoopla about Yoshi and Hans and their trip in the Zodiac. The loading, the charts, the advice. You'd think they were going seven hundred miles to the Antarctic Peninsula instead of the seven-mile trip to the other side of the island. I joined the throngs down on Two and watched the final loading and departure. Slipping past several people, I stood next to Hans. He didn't notice me at first, but just before he moved to step into the boat, I touched his arm, and he turned.

"Be careful," I said.

He stood next to me for a moment as if unsure what to say or do. Someone spoke to him from his other side, and he said, "I will," before turning away.

They got in the boat, Yoshi started the motor, and they roared away, amid cheers and applause from the crowd staying behind. I stood, hugging myself, watching the Zodiac with its frothy white wake disappear around the side of the *Professor*. It would take them half an hour to round the northern tip of the island and get to their cove on the west side.

TWENTY-FOUR

Storm

Penguins . . . are not quiet creatures. Gather them together by the thousands and they can be deafening—perhaps the loudest, most persistent, chorus in the animal kingdom.

—*Kevin Schafer,*
THE FALKLAND ISLANDS:
BETWEEN THE WIND & SEA

WAS IT A premonition? I tried to convince myself it wasn't. The nudge of worry was little different from the skipped heartbeat I felt each time I saw or even thought about Hans lately. So I pushed it aside and got down to work, organizing my team to watch skua and gentoo interaction on this, one of the last days of fieldwork for my thesis.

We'd be observing two gentoo colonies, one spread along the little beach and the other tucked several hundred yards inland on the only flat ground along the whole east shore of the island. Finn was silent, brooding, letting me handle everything. The sky was a high gray blanket, the temperature mild. The wind, at ten knots most of the day, seemed a gentle breeze compared to the norm.

I retired to my cabin after dinner and went over the day's data until the numbers started to dance before my eyes. I fell into bed early and slept long.

Tuesday morning's sky was blue, Watkins Island's sharp ridge green, the *Professor* gently rocking in its lee. But in the direction of West Falkland, beyond the protection of our island, the water was bright with whitecaps. The wind was back. Ian announced at breakfast that Hans had called. They'd agreed that if he and Yoshi could finish up and head back before ten o'clock, they should be fine. The storm was still predicted for afternoon.

As Paul, Javier, Josef, and I sat by the colony busy observing a higher than average skua success rate, I kept one eye on the ocean. The whitecaps were advancing on the *Professor*, wind gusts becoming more frequent. A whisper of worry blew in on a gust. Shouldn't Hans and Yoshi head back, skip the last colony? I tried to limit my worried glances north along the coast to once every five minutes.

By the time we headed back to the *Professor* at eleven, the sky was filled with roiling dark clouds, and the sea of whitecaps had almost reached the *Professor*. So much for the storm arriving in the afternoon. I saw as soon as we approached that the little Zodiac wasn't in its spot on the landing, hadn't slipped by me unnoticed.

"It's probably taking them longer in this weather," Javier said, reading my mind.

He went with me up to Five, and we found Ian at the rail, peering north along the coast through binoculars. Javier and I stood on either side of him. Ian lowered the binoculars and looked at his watch. "They called at nine forty-five and said they were on their way. I haven't heard from them since."

I looked at my own watch: 11:13. My heart lurched.

Javier said, "It took them half an hour to get there yesterday, yes?"

"Yes."

We all stared north, silent but for the wind whipping our rain gear, clanking the stays.

Ian said, "Maybe they couldn't make it around the point . . . and went back to the shelter of a cove."

"But why haven't they called?" I spoke for the first time.

No one answered.

"And you've tried to call them . . ."

Ian gave a curt nod. "No answer." He raised his binoculars again. I got mine out and scanned up along the coast as far as I could see, which wasn't all that far—giant lashing raindrops were beginning to pelt us, blurring the air. The folds of hill faded into mists the farther from the ship I looked. We even looked to the south, a longer and more challenging way to go.

"Well." Ian lowered his binoculars. "We'll give them another half hour."

I looked at him. "And then what?" I was aware of sounding a bit shrill, and took it down a notch. "Then what?"

He looked at me for the first time. "Then we'll decide what to do." He left me and Javier standing at the rail.

"Can you believe him?" I said, staring after Ian.

Javier put his arm around me and pulled me against his side. "Calmate, chica. Chances are good they're going back to their cove, or some cove."

"Then why haven't they called?"

"Any reason . . . they're busy with the boat, the batteries have gone dead. Maybe they have lost the radio." He looked at me. "Don't think the worst."

Javier went downstairs, and I stayed at the rail for a few minutes more, watching through the binoculars. Then without binoculars. Then with them again. But I couldn't coax the little Zodiac out of the gray.

I ran down the stairs to my cabin and threw a small pile of supplies together: my rain gear, the parka, a water bottle filled from the sink. I stood and thought for a moment and then ran upstairs to Hans's cabin. I pulled a couple of turtlenecks, a sweater, and a pair of long underwear out of a drawer. Clothes flew, dropped on the floor. I went to Yoshi's cabin next and pawed through his drawers until I found long underwear. Seeing socks, I grabbed a handful of them; they'd need dry socks.

I dumped everything on my bed, pulled the door shut, and went down to Three.

The wind was tearing at the stays, rattling them in a frantic staccato; rain pounded the deck, and the shore had faded to a grayish blur. It was 11:35. I went to the communications room. Everyone was there. Ian was putting down the radio mike, having failed once more to make contact.

"We've got to go after them," I said.

There were murmurs of agreement.

"I can't send anyone out into this storm." Ian gestured out the window. "Look at it. A boat is out of the question . . ."

"We can go up and over the island," Finn and I said at the same time.

Everyone was talking at once, several voices saying, "but you can barely stand up . . . ," and, "you can't see five feet in front of you."

Ian stood his ground. "It's not safe. We're probably in the worst of it right now. In a couple of hours it should be better . . ."

"A couple of hours!" I interrupted. "What if the Zodiac has capsized, or crashed onto the rocks? What if they're soaking wet? We need to find them as soon as possible."

"It'll take hours to cross the island on foot," Caroline said, supporting her husband.

"All the more reason to get started now." Me.

"We don't need more people lost in the storm." Ian.

Opinions flew like gulls in a storm. "They're probably fine, hunkered down somewhere . . . But why don't they call? . . . Something probably happened to the radio . . . Chances are they're sheltering in a safe cove . . . But what if they're not?"

I left the room, saying to Bill who was standing near the door, "I'm going. Are you coming with me?"

"Joanie," he said. "Ian's got a point."

"And I've got a point."

Javier joined us as we passed into the dining room and I asked him, too. "Come on. We'll get supplies, a tent and everything. We'll get Carl to take us ashore."

I pushed out onto the deck and a blast of wind hit me, shoving me back against Bill.

"It's pretty bad." Javier had to shout to be heard. We stepped back inside. "Let's get ready," he said, "and see what the weather does."

Bill organized us. "Javier, you and I'll go downstairs to get tents and backpacks and all that. We'll also get Carl lined up . . . Joanie, why don't you see if you can recruit a couple more people, maybe Finn and somebody. Get some food together. We'll meet down on Two."

Finn and Alejandro—I went for the strong young guys—agreed immediately. I didn't say, "if the weather improves."

Ten minutes later we gathered at the Zodiac with our pile of gear. Carl was ready to take us, but Bill and Javier wanted to wait.

"Let's just *go*," I said. "We'll stay on this side of the ridge as long as we can; it'll be more sheltered than here."

Bill said, "It'd be wiser to wait a bit, and we may even gain by doing that. Visibility is so poor right now we won't be able to find the cove they were in, or see them from above. We could waste time following dead ends."

It was reasonable, but I wasn't listening to reason. "Just take me, then, Carl." I began picking up equipment, in the grip of something beyond me.

"I'm with you, Joanie," said Finn, and he bent to help. Alejandro joined us after a glance at Bill.

We'd informed Ian of our plans as we hurried to and fro, hauling food out of the galley. He appeared now at the foot of the stairs, followed by practically everyone. "I'll say it one more time: I don't recommend this course of action. You're putting your lives at risk."

"Thank you, Ian," I said. "We'll keep in touch." I handed gear to Finn. He and Alejandro stowed it in the boat.

Ian made one last effort to assert his authority. "*You* stay, at least, Joanie. Let the men go. It's going to be rough out there."

Javier bent to pick up the largest pack. "You know she'll jump in and swim ashore unless you put her in chains."

He and Bill were zipping their raincoats and picking up the last of the gear. As the little boat lowered into the water, Pepa pushed through the crowd and thrust a bag of sandwiches at us. "Lunch," she said. "Eat it now."

She and Javier kissed and she said, "Cuidado, amor." We all piled into the Zodiac, which was straining at its rope as if eager to be off. As the final passenger, Bill, squeezed into the lurching boat, Helen scurried up and reported she'd taken one last look from Five and hadn't seen them. The motor roared to life and we were off across the heaving water. I hung on tight during the thirty-second crossing, thinking, If it's this rough here, what does the west side like?

Watkins Island is about eight miles long and a mile or so wide. On the far side is a series of small coves, any of them large enough for the Zodiac to shelter in, though many, being hemmed by steep cliffs, are likely inaccessible from land. The cove where Hans and Yoshi would have camped was almost two miles north and across the island from our starting point.

Bill said, "We can be almost certain they didn't make it around the northern point; if they had, there'd be nothing to keep them from getting back to the ship."

So, huddling over the charts and bolting sandwiches, we formed a plan to head north for almost two miles, sheltering on this side from the worst of the wind, then cross over to the windward side and drop down to the cove where they'd camped. From there we'd make our way north, checking coves until we found them.

We hoisted packs and started up along the slope, climbing gradually to get above the cliffs that rose out of the water. The rain plastered hair to heads and fogged glasses. Though the wind was milder here than on the boat, at times a gust caught at one of the packs and caused the wearer to stumble; a taste of what was to come. I was fourth in line and could see I wasn't the only one this was happening to.

Now that we were moving, decisions made, pushing forward with a firm plan, I allowed myself to think about Hans and what might have happened. But such thoughts put a knife in my heart and jelly in my knees, so I forced myself to concentrate, putting one foot in front of the other, watching for slippery spots, bracing for those surprise gusts.

We slogged northward along the hillside, climbing only slightly, until nearly two o'clock, when we determined with the help of the GPS that we were almost directly across the island from the cove we were aiming for. It was time to go up and over.

Fifteen minutes of climbing brought us near the top of the hill and into a zone of stronger wind. We stopped, sweating and breathless. I felt the storm crouching on the other side of the ridge, winding itself into a fury, ready to beat us back. For the first time I questioned the wisdom of what we were doing. Bill had been right about visibility; the little swatch of green we were hiking through faded to gray mists a few steps away. We cinched straps, pulled hoods tighter, and set off upward, to where the hill met the sky.

A few minutes later we neared the summit, which was hammered by wind so strong that Finn, first in line, was yanked sideways and lost his footing. He fell to his knees and struggled out of his pack. The rest of us dropped to the ground and wriggled out of ours as well. We moved on in a kind of crouch behind the packs on the ground, heaving them forward a few feet, moving crab-like up to them, and repeat. This went on forever; heave the pack, take two steps forward, heave again. Over the top and down the other side, we followed our packs down the slope. The rain was fiercer, too, stinging faces, tearing up eyes, soaking gloved hands. It felt as if we were going into a hell that would never let us rest again; this was our lot: to cling to this hillside, clawing our way down, not able to see more than ten feet ahead, wind tearing our breath from us.

But eventually it let up a notch. My pack bumped into Finn, who had stopped to put his on again. The rest of us did the same. We got to our feet and kept moving diagonally downhill until the wind was not as strong as on top. The rain, too, had lessened. After a few minutes we were able to see below us for the first time, a view of crashing, churning water enclosed by rocky arms. Bill checked our position again and confirmed; it was the cove where Hans and Yoshi would have spent the night. The first place we would look.

Finn and Alejandro took one radio and set off down the slope. I fought the desire to follow them, the need I felt to check each cove personally. I told myself they were, in fact, more likely in a cove further north. Bill, Javier, and I watched our companions fade into the mist below. The view of what we now called Cove One closed off again.

I glanced at Bill. "How're we going to find Cove Two in this soup?"

"That's what a GPS is for." He looked at his watch. "Two thirty-three; it's about half a mile. We'll walk fifteen minutes along the slope and then stop and check our position. It should be about right."

After fifteen minutes of steady travel, we stopped, and Bill pulled out the GPS. "Just right," he proclaimed. The rain was still holding off, and while we couldn't see all the way to the beach, we could see enough to pick out a possible way down. The mist swirled below, moving over the green slope, opening even as we watched to reveal a beckoning V shape. We followed it down, and the little valley narrowed until the grass gave way to broken rocks and the slope became steeper. Ahead rocks formed an edge; beyond was the white of fog.

A few more steps brought us to the edge of an impassable cliff that fell below us. We looked right and left, but were in a narrow funnel-shaped draw, with no way out but back the way we'd come. As we looked around, the mist began to part, and we stood watching a beach emerge to the north, a hundred or so feet down, a small inlet, waves tossing white foam relentlessly over the rocky shore.

Javier saw it first. "Look," he said, pointing to a patch of gray, lighter than the rocks, on the left flank of the cove.

It had to be the Zodiac. We scrambled to dig out binoculars. The Zodiac was pushed up on the rocks at an angle, the nose bent, oars gone. As we watched, a wave rushed in and sucked it away into the water. When I located it again, it was buckling unnaturally, half-full of water, racing toward the rocks, then away again.

Bill radioed Finn with the news.

"All right," came his voice. "There's nothing on this beach. We're headed your way."

Bill described where we were and where we planned to go. He signed off after checking that Ian had copied.

I was already headed back up the slope, allowing myself to think only of finding a way down; nothing else. Trying not to think the worst. Javier followed, then Bill. Five minutes back up, almost to where we'd started down, then onward following the northern arm of the cove. In a few more minutes I stopped and waited for them. "What about here? It's another V."

This time we were successful; after following the funnel to the top of a steep rocky slope, we were able to pick our way down. At first we saw only across to the rugged shore where the Zodiac was again slung over black shiny rocks, but when we rounded a craggy outcrop, below and to our right was a sandy white arc. From this point the descent was gentle. We hurried down, pushing against tearing wind until at last we were on the beach with a view of the entire cove. The white sand stretched in a curve beneath a steep green slope, out a long point toward the open ocean. A hundred yards along this stretch was a rock as tall as a person. At its base was a patch of bright red—Hans's raincoat.

I saw them first and cried out, started running, as best I could, churning through the sand, into the wind. Halfway there, I shrugged off my pack and let it drop. Javier and Bill caught up with me. We were all three running, calling their names. When I got closer, I saw it was both of them, curled together, Hans's coat covering them. The rock had sheltered them from the worst of the wind, but not the rain.

I dropped to my knees, put a hand on each of them. Javier had a hand inside Yoshi's collar, feeling for his pulse, and ordered Bill to get the thermometer and stethoscope out of his pack. Hans's eyes opened, only slits, but he didn't seem to see us. His face was drained of color. Yoshi's lips moved; his eyes stayed closed.

Javier took the raincoat off them, and Hans struggled to sit up. I took his hands, kissed them. They were limp, icy. I began to rub.

"Don't rub," Javier said. "You and Bill go set up the tent and get a couple sleeping bags zipped together." He looked over his shoulder. "As close as possible, up on the grass there."

Bill finished a call to update Finn and Ian. I could barely tear myself from Hans, but I knew Javier was right; the sooner we got them out of the wind and began to dry and warm them, the better.

Setting the tent up was a wild, frustrating affair; the wind yanked the fabric out of our hands just as we got a pole lined up to thread into the sleeve. The ground cloth went tearing across the grass with Bill running after it at top speed.

I looked over toward the rock and saw that Javier had them both sitting up. Bill brought me back to our task, yelling, "Get inside with the packs, Joanie. Open the sleeping bags. I'll stake it down."

He held the tent to keep it from tumbling away as I tossed in my pack, then his, and piled in after, zipping the door shut behind me. As I pulled the sleeping bags out, a voice inside me kept saying, Don't let them die, until interrupted by Bill shouting orders. "Put a pack near the door. Hold down this corner." I made myself focus, silenced the voice. Finally, as I got four bags zipped together into a giant multi-person cocoon, the tent became more stable, and the furious flapping changed to a taut rattle. I dug around for dry clothing and towels. Bill called me to come out and help him with the rain fly.

Over at the rock, Javier was helping Yoshi to his feet. I took one corner of the rain fly from Bill and managed to subdue its wild flapping. When we at last got it clipped on, I stole another look toward the rock. Yoshi was sagging against Javier as they started toward the tent.

"Bill!" I yelled. "Go help Javier. I'll finish here." He bounded off and I clicked the last corner into place and went around tightening the lines that staked it to the ground. I tied the door to the vestibule open and pulled the packs out of the tent and into the space where they'd be under the protection of the fly. Five people in a four-person tent would leave room for little else.

I stood up as the three of them reached the tent, Yoshi on a chair made by Bill and Javier's locked hands, his arms around their shoulders, his head a dead weight against Bill. They lowered him gently into the tent.

"Start getting his clothes off, Joanie, all of them. Dry him off. Gently."

They went back for Hans as I started unzipping Yoshi's wet fleece jacket, unlaced his shoes. He made a feeble reach for his left shoe, but his hands weren't following orders.

I looked out the door as I got his second shoe off. The three of them, Hans supported between Bill and Javier, were walking slowly toward the tent, Hans's feet barely lifting from the ground.

TWENTY-FIVE

Hot Flash or No

When I visited the penguins on January 4, five days after the storm,
nearly half of the chicks were dead. Island resident David Gray told
me that the young birds had been too big for the parents to brood
and had gotten soaked and probably perished from hypothermia.

—*Wayne Lynch,*
PENGUINS OF THE WORLD

S LOGGING UP AND over the island in the gale had been tough,
but the next hours were even tougher. At least for me; lying
there, doing nothing, praying that Hans wouldn't die.

Of course, we weren't doing *nothing.* We got Hans's and Yoshi's
wet clothes off, dried them with towels, and put on the dry long
underwear and socks I'd brought. After peeling down to our own
long underwear, we stuffed ourselves in with them. The Javier I'd
gotten to know as a mild, sleepy-eyed man who'd rather not be
bothered by medical emergencies was locked into his doctor role,
giving orders. He had Bill lie at one end next to Hans, me in the
middle, Yoshi next, then himself. We all lay on our right sides first,

nestled together like spoons in a drawer. After fifteen minutes, he ordered us to turn to our left sides, saying we shouldn't let our two patients fall asleep yet.

Not long after I wedged myself between Hans and Yoshi, I had my first hot flash. It swept over me in a wave, my thighs, chest, neck, head prickling with heat. My eyes darted about, everywhere meeting tent walls, a mere three feet overhead. Panic rising, I loosened the sleeping bag from around my neck, just a little, to let some cool air in. But I worried that this tiny selfish gesture could also put cool air on Hans and Yoshi and tip the scales. I pulled it down tight again and to keep from going crazy, said, "Javier, is it possible to die of a hot flash?"

He didn't immediately answer, and repeated, "Hot flash."

"Oh, what do you call it in Spanish? You know, when a woman of a . . . of *my* age . . . gets really hot. Suddenly."

"Ah! Sofocos. No. Not possible."

"How about claustrophobia?"

"Not possible."

"I'm trying to believe you," I said. "But it's all I can do to keep from throwing off this damn sleeping bag and clawing my way out of here."

"Well, don't," he said. "These guys need all the heat they can get."

By the time this conversation was over, the hot flash was subsiding and so was my panic. And during the other two episodes I had over the next few hours, I focused on this one thought: I'm helping to save their lives.

They were both emptied of color, limp and listless, unable to speak more than grunts. I was focused on every sound, every movement, every ragged breath, looking and hoping for signs of recovery, fearing their decline. Yoshi was worse off, breathing shallowly, barely moving. Hans, having more body fat, seemed to have fared better.

Alejandro and Finn had arrived while we were getting settled, and I now listened to them set up their tent, an easier job than Bill and I had had as the wind had subsided considerably. It was comforting to be aware of them moving about outside, doing what they could to help, handing in another sleeping bag, tightening tent lines, calling Ian with an update.

At some point the guys outside made a meal, ate their share, and traded places with Bill and me. After we ate, Bill went back in to spell Javier. I wanted to go back in and take up my post as soon as I'd eaten, but Javier ordered me to stay outside and move around a bit. I paced around the beach, not straying far, trying to appreciate the beautiful evening the storm had left, but thinking only of getting back in next to Hans, as if only I could save him.

When I finally resumed my position between them, Hans was shivering. Alarmed, I called outside to Javier to ask what it meant. He assured me it was a positive development.

And indeed, they were both breathing more strongly. Their skin was pinker and they seemed warmer. Javier took their temperatures and found them both moving toward normal.

Before long, another wave of heat swept over me, prickling, worse than ever, leaving me sweating. Hans turned over and said, eyes still closed, "You're hot." His voice was strong, sounding exactly like it did the first time he was in bed with me and one of my hot flashes. I sat up out of that damn hot bag, whooping and laughing, along with Alejandro and Finn, who'd been lying at either end. Hans opened his eyes, startled. We'd awakened Yoshi, too, who said, "What happened?"

Those were the first full sentences either of them had spoken since they'd been found. The crisis had passed.

As we helped Hans and Yoshi put on dry clothes, they gave a bare sketch of what had happened. They'd gone over, and Hans had twisted his ankle climbing out of the water. The radio attached to Yoshi's belt snagged on a rock and was ripped away. They decided to hunker down out of the wind and wait for rescue.

"What about the other radio?" said Bill.

"Dead batteries," said Yoshi.

"What about the survival suits?" said Alejandro.

"We couldn't find them," said Hans.

Javier wouldn't allow any more questions until they'd had something to eat.

They drank tea, ate some Top Ramen. Javier took their vital signs again and looked at Hans's ankle, swollen with a gash on the outside, and proclaimed it a bad sprain but probably not broken. He doctored the cut and wrapped the ankle, told him to stay off it as much as possible.

The rain had stopped, and we took turns walking about, draping clothes over the tents and guylines to dry, straightening the bedding, cleaning the pots, making more tea. The cove still churned with waves, and the wind was steady. Alejandro and Finn made an attempt to rescue the Zodiac, which was tossing about at the base of the cliff, but waves were still smashing on the rocks, shooting spray into the air.

When the setting sun emerged from beneath a heavy bank of clouds and spread a honey glow across the cove and its grassy slopes, we stood watching until it set. Bill called Ian one last time and told him all was well. Ian would call in the morning and send a boat as soon as the seas had calmed. Then, as if we all agreed it was time, we gathered to hear the whole story. Hans, Yoshi, and I sat inside the tent in a half circle: Yoshi in the middle, Hans across from me, bad leg extended. I rested my hand on his foot; it felt cold, so I peeled off the sock and held his foot between my hands. We held each other's gaze for a moment and he smiled, not taking his eyes from my face until Bill passed him a cup of tea from his spot in the vestibule and said, "Let's hear the whole story."

Hans and Yoshi looked at each other, and Hans began. "We got up this morning; it was very windy, I mean, more than usual. We talked to Ian and decided we could still count the last colony and get back before it got too bad. So we did that and I called him when we were leaving." He shifted to get more comfortable, leaving his foot in contact with my hands. "We looked for the survival suits everywhere. The wind was very strong by then, but we weren't very worried. We got out of the cove and there were waves as tall as me, spray everywhere. But it was okay. We started north, stayed far out from the rocks. We went maybe ten minutes, around that point . . . and before we got around the next point, the engine stopped." He looked at a nodding Yoshi. "We tried to start it again, but we couldn't. We came closer and closer to the rocks . . . we used oars, but we couldn't keep out of the big waves near the shore . . ."

Yoshi took over, words tumbling one over the other. "We went over. Everything come out of boat, went in water. Me, Hans, tent, penguin, everything . . ."

"You had a *penguin?*" said Bill.

"Yes, dead penguin . . ."

"We'll tell you about that . . . ," Hans said.

Yoshi continued. "Rock is very . . ." He grasped at the air.

"Slippery," said Hans. "Steep. We came over this way to some lower rocks and got out. We were in the water maybe two, three minutes."

"Boat is gone," said Yoshi. "Everything gone."

Bill said, "How did the engine die? What did it sound like?"

Hans frowned. "We were just going through the water, up and down in the waves. Then, suddenly, like a . . . a cough. It stopped."

Javier said, "Sounds like it ran out of gas."

"I thought that," said Hans. "We didn't smell fuel, and we didn't have time to check the level . . . but I thought it was a full tank when we left. That should be good for four or five hours. We used maybe half an hour, forty-five minutes getting here. And a little more to get to the other cove."

Bill said, "I filled it myself."

"When?" I asked.

"After breakfast. Maybe seven, seven fifteen."

"You left around nine, right?" I asked. In fact I knew exactly when they'd left, 8:50; I'd checked the time as I watched them plow across the water.

"That leaves almost two hours," Bill said, "when someone could have siphoned some of the gas. And left you enough to get out here, but not back."

No one said anything for a moment, then Javier said, "But who would want to do that?" He paused. "And why?"

The faces around the circle looked at each other. Someone on the ship, one of our little family. I, of course, thought immediately of Marcia and Bernard, the people who'd been hiding something. I was thinking about all the possible *whys* when Hans spoke again. "Maybe it was something about the oil."

After a stunned silence, Bill said, "Oil?"

Hans pulled his leg in to sit cross-legged, wincing, and leaned forward. "This morning we went to the rockhopper colony that was one cove south. When we got there, we found oil. Oil on the beach, oiled birds: penguins, cormorants, one albatross. Some alive, some dead. We bagged a dead rockhopper."

Oil. Everyone looked at each other. I stole a glance at Finn. His eyes were locked on Hans's face, his expression unreadable.

"They must have known . . . ," Bill said slowly.

". . . and siphoned the gas so you couldn't get back and report it?" Alejandro sounded skeptical. "But who is 'they'?"

Javier said, "And whoever 'they' is would know someone would come looking for you. And see the oil then."

"Maybe," I said, "they figured the storm would get rid of the evidence . . ."

"But who?" said Javier again.

Bill and I looked at each other. Bill said, "Our best candidate would be Marcia. Marcia and Bernard." He nodded to me. "Joanie?"

I took a breath. "Marcia and Bernard are cousins, it turns out, actually first cousins once removed."

After a moment for that to sink in, Javier said. "They sure kept that quiet."

Bill said, "I've suspected since the last count that the numbers were off. That penguin populations were made to look healthier than they really are. Bernard owns a fleet of fishing boats. I suspect he wants to make it look like fishing is having minimal impact on penguin populations. And he had access to the numbers from the WSR count of five years ago plus the local one last year, so I've been keeping an eye on him. Audrey suggested he'd likely be at it again. She thought this time he'd have someone helping from within, one of us. And from week one Marcia's been turning in skewed numbers." He looked at Hans. "You were the first one to notice it."

Hans was shaking his head. "And then I started thinking I was wrong. She's so passionate to save penguins . . ."

I ignored a little bristle of irritation and said, "After I found out they were related to each other, Bill and I looked into Bernard's dealings. On top of his fishing interests, he's also deeply invested in Ridgecrest Petroleum, a company that's currently negotiating rights to drill for oil offshore."

Bill added, "We figured they were doing one of two things. Either skewing the count numbers to make it look like penguin populations are recovering, which would make it look like current fishing practices weren't having a negative effect. Or they may have been trying to make the tourist-visited sites have a lower chick survival rate."

"What would be the point in that?" said Javier.

Bill shrugged. "Blame the tourists instead of the fishing? Or take the attention away from oil exploration? I'm just speculating."

We were quiet for a moment. The wind whistled around the tent.

"There's one thing that doesn't fit," I said. "I assumed Marcia was after you and your money, Hans. We figured Bernard told her about you before she ever got here—he had access to all kinds of information about all of us . . . So why would she . . . put your life at risk? If she thought she had a chance with you?"

Hans smiled. "I told her a few days ago that my inheritance is very small. It was a sort of test. Whenever I saw her after that, she only said hello and kept walking."

Rain began a gentle patter on the tent, and Alejandro and Finn, sitting outside, scrunched into the vestibule. My watch said ten fifteen. Fearing the meeting was about to break up, I said, "We need to make a plan."

They all looked at me.

"We don't have any proof, for one thing," I said. "Only suspicions."

Alejandro nodded. "But attempted murder. If they realize we know, they could . . . Who knows what they will do."

Bill said, "I agree. The first thing we need to do is get that fuel tank and see if it really is empty. Then we'll decide what information to share and who to share it with. About everything—what you found, the oil . . . We need to tell Ian."

Finn spoke for the first time. "I don't trust Ian. He's on Marcia's side . . . And why didn't he want us to come out here today? Have you thought of that?"

I shook my head. "He was just being Ian."

Bill said, "He's honest, he's a scientist first and above all."

The others agreed. When Ian arrived, we'd tell him everything: Bill's suspicions about Marcia's statistics, Bernard and Marcia's relationship, Marcia likely knowing Hans was rich from the beginning, the oiled birds, our suspicion about the gas, the radio, the missing survival suits.

Hans asked Bill, "But doesn't Ian know already about Marcia and the numbers? We talked about it in the first week."

"He never took it seriously." Bill looked out at the rain and back. "Ian thinks I'm a bit obsessive . . . ever since I started complaining about the numbers from the last count. So I stopped sharing with him."

There was a silence. I reached over and squeezed his arm. "Well, he's about to stop doubting you."

The rain began to fall harder; the light was fading. As Bill and two sleeping bags moved from our tent to Finn and Alejandro's and the group otherwise prepared for bed, I followed Finn out to the clump of tall grass designated as "men's." I grabbed his elbow and hustled him up the slope, Finn saying, "Jeez, Joanie, people are going to wonder . . ."

"They're going to *know* when I tell them in the morning."

"I called Audrey..."

"Not soon enough, apparently."

Out of earshot, we stopped and I dropped his arm.

Thrusting his hands in his pockets, Finn said, "Please don't tell everyone. I'll tell Ian as soon as I get a chance."

"You'll tell Ian as soon as he gets here, while we're telling him the whole story."

"Ah, Joanie. Everyone doesn't need to know."

I felt a moment's pang for Finn, and hesitated, looking down at the camp, where Bill was helping Hans hobble back to the tent.

"All right. Tell him privately. But before we get back to the ship."

I was last to crawl in the tent. After peeling down to my long underwear, I slid in between Hans and the wall. Javier was on the far side, and Yoshi was lying next to Hans. Yoshi made a great show of complaining that it was better before, when I was in the middle. "Joanie is very hot." Whether he was aware of the nuances of that expression or not, everyone found it highly amusing and tossed about similar banter before finally settling down.

It was nearly dark, the wind a whisper, the rain a light patter on the tent. Hans curled around my back, held me against his chest. I was exhausted and fully expected to drift right into sleep. But now that the danger to Hans and Yoshi had passed, I couldn't help being aware of Hans lying next to me.

Scenes from the long day still coursed through me; the stab of fear when Hans and Yoshi went missing, the frantic trip preparations, the endless struggle through the gale, not knowing if they were alive or dead, and the long hours of lying in the tent, praying they'd survive. And now here was Hans, pressed tight against me with all his warmth. It felt like home, where I belonged.

But we'd broken up! We'd be parting ways in a few days. And now with today's worry, my racing out into the storm with no other thought than to save him . . .

This line of thinking wasn't leading toward sleep, so I made myself think instead about the oil spill, the dead penguins, and Finn. This had to have been the work of Finn's friends. Too much of a coincidence if not. But why would they do the spill way out here, where it could easily have been missed? And Marcia and Bernard. They must have found out about it—but how? And were they really so mercenary as to not care if someone died in their efforts to keep the spill quiet?

Hans turned to his other side and I turned with him, curling around his solid body. My breasts against him, his buttocks firm in my lap, I was swept with the desire to be alone with him. He'd almost died; how crazy with worry I'd been about losing this person who'd brought me such joy. This person I thought I'd so neatly pushed away. Here he was again. And here I was, wanting him, wanting to be back the way we were.

I must have made some kind of sound, because Hans turned onto his back and looked at me in the dusky light. He curled toward me and brushed a tear from my cheek with his fingers. He whispered, "It's okay. Everything's okay."

I was sure he didn't know what I was crying about—I hardly knew myself.

I closed my eyes, took in a deep breath, let it out, and lay listening to the patter of rain, the rhythmic slosh of waves on the sand, Bill's snores from the other tent. With Hans's hand on my cheek, and breathing his warm breath, I fell asleep.

TWENTY-SIX

It Was You

Penguins teach us that we only live once, that life isn't easy, and that human existence should make a positive difference to the other creatures with whom we share the planet.

— *edited by Pablo Garcia Borboroglu and P. Dee Boersma*
PENGUINS: NATURAL HISTORY AND CONSERVATION

"IAN TO BILL, Ian to Bill." I bolted up as if poked with a cattle prod and grabbed the radio lying two inches from where my head had been.

I keyed the talk button. "This is Joanie."

"How is everyone?"

"Just a minute." I looked down at Hans next to me, stretching and rubbing his eyes. He gave a thumbs-up. Yoshi grinned and did the same. Javier had one hand clamped to his eyes and waved with the other.

I called, "Bill? Alejandro? Finn? You all okay over there?"

There was a chorus of more or less affirmative grunts.

I keyed the mike. "Javier's grumpy, but otherwise we're all fine."

"That's good news." Was there a little waver in Ian's voice? "Carl and I are coming in the big Zodiac. We should be there in about an hour."

"What time is it?"

"Four fifteen."

"Yikes! I don't think we got our eight hours yet." Javier had opened the tent door, and I followed him out, radio in hand. The sea was a pale-blue gently heaving sheet. The air still and quiet. "The water's like glass," I told Ian. "You should have a lovely trip."

He didn't respond immediately, and I wondered if he'd thought I was referring to how unsupportive he'd been the day before.

He came back on. "Anyone need anything?"

Finn, kneeling in the door of his tent, running a hand over his frizzy hair, said, "Coffee!"

I got on the radio again. "One decaf latte, two double mochas, a grande macchiato, and three Americanos." I wasn't sure if there was such thing as a grande macchiato, but who would notice?

After another little pause, Ian said, "I'll see what I can do."

"Seriously," I said. "Yoshi and Hans could use some more dry clothes . . . windbreakers at least . . ." I thought about the half-hour trip back in the open boat. "Hats, gloves . . . I'll get back to you in a minute."

Bill said, Water, and Javier, Yeah, lots of clothes for Hans and Yoshi, shoes, everything.

I relayed the message and signed off.

I'd never seen such activity at four thirty in the morning. Finn, Alejandro, and Javier went off to retrieve the Zodiac, which was still bumping against the low rock shelf beneath the cliff. If the gas tank was still attached, they'd try to determine whether it had been tampered with. Yoshi and I made tea and dug out some granola. When Hans stood, he winced, so he sat back down and, whistling a little tune, began stowing the sleeping bags that we passed him. Yoshi, popping tent stakes out of the ground, burst into "Morning has broken . . . ," and most of us joined in with "like the first morning." No one but Yoshi and me knew the words from there, and we went on robustly, "Blackbird has spoken . . ." That glad-to-be-alive feeling times ten.

I was sitting on a pack passing a cup of tea back and forth with Hans when Alejandro came wading toward us in ankle-deep water, pants rolled to his knees, dragging the little Zodiac behind him with a rope, the hunter coming in with the kill. When he came even with the camp, Javier and Finn, who'd been following on the shore, helped pull it up onto the sand.

The Zodiac was clearly beyond salvage. One pontoon was ripped open and lay flat on the sand, water spilling out of it. The motor was gone, sunk to the bottom of the cove. Caught in a jumble of ropes and bungee cords against the one good pontoon was the red gas tank. Finn and Bill untangled it and set it on the sand. It was battered and dented, but had no obvious holes. Bill picked it up and shook it. "Empty," he said. A little liquid spilled off it. He sniffed his fingers, and said, "Water."

Alejandro, at Bill's suggestion, took the gas tank and waded out into the water, beyond the breaking waves, where he bent and held it underwater. He stared at the water's surface for a long moment, the rest of us watching him. At last, he shook his head. "No bubbles," he shouted across the breaking surf as he started back. "No leaks."

When he set it back on the sand, Bill unscrewed the lid and sniffed the opening, stuck a finger inside and ran it under the rim. "Just gas, it doesn't seem to be mixed with any water." He set it down again. "You must have set out with a fairly empty tank. You ran out of gas."

With everything packed and everyone fed a handful of granola, there was nothing left to do but wait for Ian to come get us. I wandered along the hard sand in the direction of the point. The sun had just spilled onto the beach and was warm on my back. A light breeze ruffled the tufts of grass growing at the edge of the sand, and a couple of little tussock birds flitted about over the carpet of green beyond. The cove was a luminous blue wedge.

Halfway to the point, a flat-topped rock sat in the water, about ten feet out and just big enough for a person to sit on. I watched the waves splash at it for a moment; none came close to washing over it. I took off my shoes and socks, put them on the sand, and rolled up my pants above the knee. The water was frigid, but in a few long strides, I climbed up onto the rock and settled myself, legs crossed, facing the bay. I looked out over the endless rolling blue ocean for a few moments, taking it all in. Then turned my head to the left and looked across the curve of beach and gently breaking waves to the little camp. Yoshi and Alejandro were playing with a long kelp whip, twirling it like a jump rope.

Their laughter reached me across the water. Finn was seated off by himself, hunched over clasped hands. Javier was rewrapping Hans's foot. Bill was sitting next to them.

I looked away, took a deep breath, and let it out. Wednesday morning. By Friday evening we'd be back in Stanley and our work would be done. I wasn't ready to think about that yet, that these people who had been my friends over the past six weeks would soon disperse to the far corners of the world. So I thought instead about the arrival of Ian, what we'd have to tell him, convince him of, in a short window of time. Would Ian be open to what we'd found out about Bernard and Marcia? Would he believe our suspicions that someone siphoned the gas, maybe replaced good radio batteries with bad, removed the survival suits? We hoped to persuade him to take a quick jaunt two coves south of us before we went back. Would we still find evidence of oil, almost twenty-four hours after Hans and Yoshi were there? More dead penguins? I thought about everything I could. Anything to avoid thinking about me and Hans.

I took another deep breath and concentrated on my surroundings. It was the most exquisite morning of the whole time I'd been in the Falklands; the folds of the island in shades of green, the ocean a shimmering blue, the pale sky laced with high white clouds. And only the lightest breeze. These stark islands that millions of birds called home, this fragile haven, hardly part of the world; I'd miss it, too.

A giant petrel sailed overhead, from out at sea, down the cove toward camp. It never once flapped a wing, but turned its head left and right, scanning the land and water below and the men at the head of the cove.

And the one making limping progress down the beach toward me. Hans.

He saw the petrel, too, and stopped to watch it glide over his head and swoop up the valley away from the water. Then he looked toward me, leaned on his stick—Bill's hiking stick— and stepped gingerly into motion.

Shaking my head, I thought; you should go to him. Clearly he's headed this way, and he shouldn't be putting weight on his foot. But I stayed on my rock, the waves slapping at its sides. Hans kept on, stopping now and then to rest and look around.

When he at last arrived at the pile of my shoes and socks, I shifted to face him, watched as he lowered himself to the sand. "You shouldn't have done that," I said across the ten feet of water.

"Well, I did." He was grinning.

He looked around for a moment, drinking in the scene, his face serene. "Beautiful morning," he said.

"Yes."

After a glance at camp, he looked back at me, beaming like a kid bursting with a secret. He said, "I asked Bill why you came with them, out in the storm like that."

"Oh yes?" I couldn't hide a little smile, remembering my frantic organizing.

"Yes, and he said, 'Hey, Javier, Hans wants to know why we let Joanie come.'" Hans paused, his eyes as blue as the shimmering bay. "Javier laughed, they all laughed." He laid the stick on the sand and looked at me. "They said you were like a crazy woman; no one would listen to you, but you kept saying, 'We have to go *now*, I'm going even if I have to go alone.' They said you were going to jump in the water and swim to shore."

"Yeah, well . . ."

His face was still then, his eyes holding mine, and he said, "Javier said if you got here much later, it . . . wouldn't be good."

I swallowed, unable to speak. My eyes began to prickle.

Hans said, "You're doing it again."

Though I knew what he meant, I said, "What? "

He tapped the corner of his eye, not breaking his gaze from mine. I took a swipe under each eye with the back of my hand. "Oh, it's just . . . everything. It's gotten so complicated. The oil spill, seabirds dying . . . people up to . . . who knows what."

"Yes," he said. "But I don't think that's why you're crying."

I waited, not encouraging him to go on.

But he did. "Remember when I got back from Switzerland and you told me why I was feeling like I did? When I didn't really know, myself?"

Of course I did. I remembered every minute of this affair. I couldn't help a little smile. "You said, 'What are you, a psychiatrist?'"

He nodded. "Now it's my turn. Do you want to know why you're crying?"

No! I thought, but said nothing.

He said, "It's because you love me."

I stopped breathing.

"All this about you being too old and me being too young? It's bullshit."

"Did you learn that word from Helen?" I said, a feeble attempt to keep it light.

He ignored me. "Also? About you wanting to be independent and free? It's only partly true." He kept his eyes on me. "You love me, but you're afraid of love. When you thought I might die, it touched something in you . . ." A wave broke against my rock with a slap, spraying a few drops against my back. "The person you loved most in the world was your daughter," he said, "and you lost her." He waited.

My throat was tight, tears piling up in my eyes.

He said, "You're afraid of hurting like that again."

I blinked and a tear squeezed onto my cheek. I pressed my hands together in front of my mouth, shut my eyes.

When I opened them again, he was holding out his hand. "Come here," he said. And when I didn't move, "Please."

I wiped my eyes with my sleeve. To wade across that water seemed an irrevocable act—admitting that all he was saying was true.

"Please," he said again, his face somber now, his hand still outstretched.

I swallowed and looked at the sky. A petrel, the same petrel, I was sure, had appeared over the hill behind Hans's back and swept toward the cove. It flew low over our heads, beating its wings this time, against the breeze, and out to sea. I looked at Hans; he was watching it. When it banked over the ocean, he met my eyes and smiled.

I gave my pant legs a tug to secure them above the knees and slid off my rock into the water. I waded carefully to shore, ignoring the icy stabs. When I dropped to the sand by his side, his arms came around me, pulling me in. I pressed my face into his shoulder, tears coming full force now. We sat that way, the occasional wave reaching our feet, the breeze ruffling our hair, until my breathing slowed and I became aware of his cheek against the top of my head. I took a long breath and let it out, which was sort of hard with him holding me so tightly.

He whispered into my hair, "Don't ever leave me again."

I wasn't sure what I'd heard, and I pulled away to look at him. A blond curl was batting at the corner of his eye, and as I smoothed it back, wondering what to say, I became aware of a distant hum, growing louder. We looked together toward the mouth of the cove as the big Zodiac arced around the point and swept toward us.

Relieved at the diversion, I picked up my shoes and said, "Come on, we don't have much time to tell Ian everything." I got to my feet and helped him up as the Zodiac zoomed past us, cut its engine, and glided toward camp.

We took a few steps and he stopped. "Unless it was Yoshi," he said.

I looked at him. "Yoshi what?"

"Who made you act so crazy."

I allowed a smile. "It was you." I put my arm around his waist and gave a little tug. "Come on." And we hobbled down the beach.

TWENTY-SEVEN

A Sad Little Lump

Oil is poisonous when ingested by penguins, it also clogs their feathers, destroying the waterproofing and insulating properties, turning their feather survival suits into mucky black cloaks of death.

—*Lloyd Spencer Davis,*
SMITHSONIAN Q & A: *PENGUINS:*
THE ULTIMATE QUESTION AND ANSWER BOOK

AN AND JAVIER had set up two big thermoses of coffee, a carton of milk, sugar, cups, and even chocolate syrup on a little folding table on the grass. As Ian opened a cloth-wrapped bundle of muffins made by Pepa that morning, Javier and I filled coffee orders. Then we sat in a circle and got to our story.

Hans told about the engine dying, about being dashed on the rocks, about the oiled beach, and oiled birds. Alejandro showed the gas can and explained how we figured there was no way gas could have leaked out, and that since Bill himself had filled it before the trip, our only conclusion was that someone had siphoned it. Bill brought up our suspicions about Marcia and Bernard, and I finished with my discovery that the two were cousins.

Ian nodded slowly, watching a large beetle walk across the bare sand in the middle of the circle. When we finished, he straightened and surprised us by saying, "It all falls together, doesn't it? I'd begun to wonder about Marcia and Bernard myself."

"Yes?" said Bill.

"I've been keeping an eye on her since you and Hans pointed out the statistics discrepancy in the first week. I haven't noticed anything concrete, just bits and pieces. And she and Bernard; there seemed to be . . . something between them; pretending the other one wasn't there when they were in a group, then quiet words when they thought they were alone."

A pensive moment followed, then Ian said, "But an oil spill. Here. Where do you suppose it came from?" We all turned our heads out to sea, looking for the answer, until Finn went, "Um..."

And he told his story. In front of everyone after all. About the friends, the plan, the bags, changing his mind, not succeeding in changing theirs, calling Audrey on Saturday morning to have her report the planned spill to the police. He didn't include the part that I already knew all this.

He finished with something I didn't know. "And the spill is here—now—because they wanted it to come from the west, where the proposed new fields are, and, well . . ." His face reddened for the first time. "Back in the beginning, when I was still down with the plan, I gave them our itinerary. They knew we'd be on Watkins Sunday afternoon through Tuesday and that a party was going around to the west side, so someone would be sure to find it."

People were staring at the sand, taking it all in, until Bill said, "Remember how Marcia got lost Sunday afternoon? How that delayed our departure, how we almost didn't come out here at all?"

Ian said, "You're saying Marcia and Bernard knew about the spill, and when they couldn't stop us from coming out here, they did all this?" He gestured toward the wrecked Zodiac. "To keep anyone from reporting it?"

Another question came from Javier. "But how did Marcia and Bernard learn about the spill?"

Finn shook his head, since Javier was looking at him.

Bill said, "Who knows? This whole archipelago is a fishbowl."

Carl, the boat driver who'd been silent until now, said, "Bernard knows a lot of fishermen; maybe one of them spotted it."

We got to our feet, and Ian said to Finn, "We'll discuss your involvement later."

As we loaded the Zodiac, Ian came and stood by me and cleared his throat. "I just want to say . . ." He studied the growing pile of packs and bags in the boat. "I'm sorry. If something had happened to Hans and Yoshi . . ."

He was speaking quietly to me, but everyone slowed what they were doing to listen.

Ian realized we weren't going to have a private conversation and said, "I thank you all. Especially you, Joanie, for your courage and . . . well, for persevering; you were right." He faltered again, so I helped him out.

"Well, I just as easily could've been *not* right. It was risky and crazy . . . I was . . . out of my head." I felt my face getting warm.

Wasn't I just admitting to the world what I'd barely admitted to myself?

Yoshi whispered loudly to Hans, "I think she mean you." Everyone heard it and laughed. Alejandro pulled Yoshi close to his side and said, "I came for Yoshi." And we went on like that, joking and roughhousing like a litter of puppies, as we finished loading the Zodiac and launching into the surf.

Before we even landed at "Oil Cove"—just south of "Yoshi Hans Cove"—we saw a sad little lump on the beach, sand piled up on one side; a tiny dune. Carl landed the Zodiac and everyone piled out. Finn and Javier helped pull the boat up on the beach, while Hans, limping along with Bill's stick, and Yoshi led a group to the dead penguin. It was a gentoo. Yoshi picked it up by its feet and gently brushed the sand off. Its feathers were matted with a black gooey slime, its eye dull. There was a moment of silence.

Ian broke the mood by snapping a garbage bag open. As Yoshi lowered the carcass in, Hans said, "The one we got was a rockhopper."

Ian gave orders. "We can't spend more than a few minutes here, so let's get cracking. Let's get a rockhopper, a couple other birds if you can find them, and any other evidence of oil."

We fanned out, and in the next ten minutes Hans and Javier bagged a dead rockhopper and some kind of duck, and Carl, who'd been getting more interested in our project as time went on, found an albatross. Finn, Bill, and Ian photographed pockets of oil, found half under rocks and up against the grassy fringe where it met the beach. Alejandro and I scooped up handfuls of oily sand and kelp and put them in plastic sandwich bags. We gathered back at the boat for a final briefing.

"I'll call in the spill as soon as we get back to the ship," Ian said. "Then Bill and I will meet and go over the evidence. If it looks like we have enough for a case against Marcia and Bernard, we'll call and have a constable waiting at Port Stephens this evening." He looked around the circle of nine. "We'll get that gas can into a storage unit along with everything else, and lock it. Other than that," he continued, "you can talk to anyone about anything, the oil, how you crashed, anything *except* that we have suspicions about the gas running out or any suspicions at all about Marcia and Bernard." His gaze landed on Yoshi, the one of the group with the shakiest English.

Yoshi gave a thumbs-up and said, "I got it. We don't talk about suspicion."

"All right. Let's get back, then, before *they* get suspicious."

By seven forty-five we were seated in the dining room over scrambled eggs, toast, sausage, fruit, juice, and coffee as the *Professor* made its way over the swell back toward West Falkland. The seven rescued and rescuers—Bill, Javier, Finn, Alejandro, Yoshi, Hans, and I—were squeezed around one table, with everyone else on board, crew and researchers alike, pressing tight around us, bombarding us with questions. Ian finally said, "Give them some air."

Everyone stepped back a bit, but the questions didn't let up. Hans was in his element, telling his best story so far, eggs getting cold on his plate. The arrival of his saviors out of the blurry mist, he and Yoshi not having the strength to give the cheer they'd felt in their hearts. He told how five of us had squeezed into one giant sleeping bag. The audience loved that and wanted to know all the details. Javier took over and told how those first few hours were touch and go, how good it was that we'd gotten there when we did.

Exhausted from my adventures and something like four hours of sleep, my thoughts drifted. I looked around the table at my friends, these people I'd gotten so close to in the past five and a half weeks. Especially these men sitting at the table; we'd bonded through our adventures of the past twenty-four hours. I couldn't believe I might never see them again. And if I did . . . maybe a trip to Spain sometime in the future; Javier would take an afternoon off work to show me the market or the local castle, maybe married to Pepa. Or Bill in Denver; we'd go bird-watching and hiking in the Rockies. Yoshi and Michiyo in Japan, in their world, their improved English fading back into rustiness. But it wouldn't be the same. Nothing would ever be like this.

And standing front row in the crowd around our table were my women friends—Helen, who'd encouraged me to go for it with Hans. I'd admired her so from the beginning for her cool, measured approach to life, her adventurous spirit. And Liz. She'd been so meddlesome and exasperating at first. But I'd gotten to know her, her big heart, still mending, still figuring out how to go on after her huge loss. I pictured visiting her and Paul, right next door in Idaho, and saw a comfortable, happy time, a relationship that would grow. I thought about everybody. But I still wasn't ready to think about Hans.

I came back to the present, to the dining room on the *Professor*. Ian was speaking, thanking the rescuers. And not a person had failed to notice my frenzied, hysterical trip preparations. Josef proposed a toast to me—"to our Joan of Arc." I blinked, saw everyone raise a coffee cup amid cheers and shouts of "Hear! Hear!" I was swept with a wave of exhaustion and didn't have the strength to protest, just smiled and raised my juice glass along with everyone else.

The *Professor* would be underway for four hours or so; once we hit West Falkland, we'd follow the coast south and pull into the tiny settlement of Port Stephens around noon. There we'd count our last colonies of Magellanics, and Finn and I would observe one more time the interaction of gentoos and skuas. During lunch the next day we'd start the long trip across Falkland Sound to East Falkland and up the east coast to Stanley, arriving in the evening. Friday we'd do the final organizing of data, the debriefing, have some free time, and in the evening, a going-away party. Saturday morning most of us would head to the airport for the weekly flight to the mainland.

I gathered my dishes and stood up. Hans paused in his story of finding the first dead rockhopper and looked at me.

"I'm going to take a shower," I said. All heads swiveled toward me. I smiled, not caring what people thought, and looking directly at Hans, said, "Then I'll be up."

Cheers filled the dining room.

After showering in my cabin, I climbed the stairs to Deck Five. Hans and Helen were leaning on the rail outside his cabin, facing out over the water and the approaching cliffs of the main island. A white towel was bunched in Hans's hands, his blond hair was damp and curling. He turned and smiled, and somehow I got my suddenly weak knees to carry me across the deck to stand beside him.

"Helen was telling me more interesting stories about your trip preparing yesterday," he said.

"Uh-huh . . ." I leaned forward to squint around him at Helen.

Helen winked. "I'll leave you two to your nap," she said, and floated off down the deck, humming to herself.

We stood for a moment, gazing across the water to the sharp angles of black rock with their patterns of yellow and orange lichen and white guano frosting the cliff tops. Hundreds of birds filled the air, gliding to and fro, mostly black-browed albatross visiting their high nests.

"Boy, you hate to go inside with all these wonders unfolding," I said. When I glanced up at Hans, he was giving me a look that made me laugh.

"Then again," I said, "There'd probably be wonders unfolding inside the cabin, too."

"Now you've got it." He linked his arm through mine. We stood a bit longer, taking it all in. He pointed out a patch of black and white high on a grassy slope, a rockhopper colony. As I began to feel his heat against my shoulder, in the crook of my arm, on my hip, I stopped paying attention to the scenery. "About those wonders in the cabin . . . ," I said.

He turned and kissed me on the mouth, the first real kiss since the breakup. Once we were inside his cabin, he locked the door and took my hands. "Joanie, I'm sorry I doubted you . . ."

I stopped him with a kiss. "I know. I'm sorry, too. But we can talk about that later." I kissed him again. I'd been wanting to get him alone since last night in the tent. Through all the drama of the oil spill and dead penguins and worry. I didn't know what was going to happen with us, didn't want to talk about it now. I pulled him toward the bed. He followed, and we fell on each other, laughing at first, then swept with hunger.

Just as I fell into sleep, I started awake at the memory of his words I'd only half heard this morning on the beach; "Don't ever leave me again." Did he really say that? Yes, we needed to talk. First chance we got.

TWENTY-EIGHT

When I'm Eighty-One

Penguins paddle, porpoise and flipper through the water, rocket and surf to reach the shore, then waddle, run, hop, leap and tobog-gan over land. The penguin seems to have a greater range of ways to move than any other bird. Its versatility in the water and on land is perhaps a way to compensate for its flightlessness.

—*Wayne Lynch,*
PENGUINS OF THE WORLD

A KNOCKING ON THE door woke us; Javier wanted to check Hans's ankle. As he unwrapped it and poked it and said the swelling was already going down, he told us we'd arrived in Port Stephens, everyone had gone ashore to work, and we could still get lunch, since he had an in with the cook. Oh, and Ian was waiting to talk to us.

So it was all bustle. Hans leaned on railings as we made our way down to the dining room. Ian was alone and beckoned us over to his table which was set for two, each place with a sand-wich wrapped in plastic and a bowl of soup.

He brought us up to date. Bill had called for the constable, who would fly to the settlement after dinner and come aboard to interview Bernard and Marcia. And what exactly was their relationship again?

I explained it, and when Ian was done making a note, I asked, "And Finn?"

Ian capped his pen. "We're seeing the Finn matter as separate. It seems he's learned his lesson, so I don't see a reason to bring his name into it."

I felt a moment's relief until I remembered. "It may be too late for that." And I told how the police had guessed he was connected to the oil spill when Audrey called.

Hans and I didn't have to go work if we weren't up to it, Ian said. But there were gentoos and skuas out there, waiting for my observations.

Port Stephens is a long, narrow bay, and due to a bend, we couldn't even see the open ocean from the ship. A cluster of seven or eight white cottages huddled on one shore. Carl took Hans and me ashore, where we separated: Hans joining the group counting Magellanics, me off to the gentoo colony, a half mile or so along the beach.

Finn was the first person I saw, sitting alone on a rock watching a small group of gentoos. I stopped to watch the penguins. How quickly it had happened; in mid-December the parents were taking turns sitting on their nests with their one or two eggs. Before a couple of weeks had passed, fluffy gray feathers and tiny orange beaks were poking out. Now the chicks were standing half as tall as their parents, taking a few tentative steps away from the nest. I regretted I wouldn't be here for the crèche phase, when groups of these youngsters would hang out together on the beach; teenagers full of bluster, not quite ready to take to the seas on their own.

I made my way to Finn, sat down beside him, and got out my binoculars. We spent the first couple of minutes talking about skua activity here—not much—and Finn telling me the where-abouts of the rest of the team.

We were silent for a few moments, watching the colony. Not a skua was in sight.

"A constable's coming this evening," I said.

"To talk to Bernard and Marcia?"

"As far as I know just Bernard and Marcia. But seeing as they've already guessed at your involvement in the spill, they may have a question or two for you."

Finn groaned. "I'm screwed, aren't I?"

I shrugged. "Ian's on your side, you know."

A squawking below got our attention. A skua was at the very edge of the colony, tugging with its beak at the tail of a young gentoo. The parent was fighting back, lunging at the bird with its beak. We watched, pencils poised, until the chick wrenched itself free and the skua let go, flew up into the air, and landed a few meters away.

"That's a new one," I said.

Finn put a note on his card. "It's always changing," he said, his voice reverent. "They're almost big enough to take care of themselves."

I looked at him, saw a dedicated scientist who loved animals. And who, in the last six weeks, had revised his thoughts on the best ways to help protect them. I gave his knee a little pat and settled down to silent watching of the colony.

Despite efforts to keep it under wraps, word got out that there was a constable aboard. As dinner ended, Ian discretely asked Marcia and Bernard if he and Bill could talk to them down on Two. Those left in the dining room were bursting with curiosity, and the seven of us who knew what it was about soon buckled under the onslaught of questions.

Javier said, "What difference does it make at this point? Everyone will know everything in a few minutes anyway."

True enough. We moved to the lounge, and settled with drinks before us. Javier invited me to do the telling. As succinctly as possible, I told how Bill had been watching Marcia all along, we'd discovered she and Bernard were cousins, and that we suspected they had siphoned gas in an effort to keep the information of the oil spill quiet. The room buzzed with questions.

After a few minutes, Paul stuck his head in the lounge and reported that the Zodiac was heading to shore with the constable. Marcia and Bernard, who he was pretty sure were handcuffed, were with him. Everyone jumped up and stampeded out to the rail. I swear the *Professor* listed toward shore.

The Zodiac was almost at the beach. Marcia had her back to the ship, but Bernard was facing us. He raised his hands, together, and gave a can-you-believe-this shrug.

"They *are* handcuffed!" said Liz.

The two got awkwardly out of the boat and onto the beach. The constable took Marcia by the elbow; she jerked away and walked on her own to the Rover, wrenched open the door, and got in without a look toward the ship.

As the Rover pulled away, Paul said, "I haven't seen so many of us on one rail since that orca was tossing the seal in the air."

That got everyone talking again. We realized Bill and Ian had joined us only when Ian said, "Do you want to keep making up stories or hear about it inside?"

We piled back into the dining room, and Ian gave a summary of what we'd pieced together.

"They didn't deny being cousins, though Marcia tried at first, and neither could give a good reason for keeping it secret. We interviewed them separately, and their stories didn't always agree. Marcia got mad and as good as admitted they knew about the oil spill, and that one of them had siphoned the gas and taken the survival suits and switched out the batteries. When the constable charged them with attempted murder, she said, 'No one was supposed to die.'"

Bill added, "Bernard just kept saying it was all a misunderstanding."

"We'll check in with the constable when we get back to Stanley." Ian shook his head. "It almost seemed that Marcia truly believed what she was doing was justified. She was saving the penguins."

It was almost nine o'clock, and I was exhausted. I'd had scant sleep in recent days and all I wanted was to crawl under the covers and sleep for ten hours. But, I reminded myself, I was back in Hans's room. And we wouldn't just sleep. It was time to talk, no more putting it off. Hans was at my side, a hand at the small of my back. "Ready to go up?" he said. And we climbed up to Five in the rays of the setting sun, me saying, "Wow, Marcia and Bernard arrested . . . ," and whatever else I could come up with.

Once in his cabin, we sat on the couch, legs touching. I kept chatting away, saying, "It's been quite the day, hasn't it?"

"Yes," he said, "But it's over. They will question Marcia and Bernard more and find out what they were doing. And maybe they'll even find that Bill was right about the count five years ago and he'll be . . . what?"

"Exonerated?"

"Yes."

I nodded. It was out of our hands. I leaned back against the couch and he put his arm across my shoulders.

I took a breath and jumped in. "I'm scared."

"I'm scared, too."

I shook my head. "Not like me."

"What are you scared of?" he said. "Tell me."

"I don't know . . . you'll stop loving me . . . this . . . here, this life on the ship, it's a fantasy world. Can we keep it going out there in the real world? I mean, our age difference and all?"

"We're just two people who fell in love," he said. "Who happen to be different ages."

"But it's huge. It's not nothing. I'm fifty-one today and you're thirty-three, both . . . adults. But in ten years I'll be sixty-one and you'll be forty-three. I'll be feeling creaky and looking, well, older, and you'll still be young." I was gathering steam. "Then I'll be seventy-one and you fifty-three, in your prime; people will *really* start to think you're hanging out with your mother, if they haven't already . . ."

Hans was shaking his head with that amused smile as he watched me, waited for me to come to my grand conclusion.

" . . . Then when I'm eighty-one and you're sixty-three and you're pushing me around the grocery store in my wheelchair, you'll, you'll . . ."

"I'll what?"

"You'll catch the eye of some cute young checker, and . . . and push me into the deep freeze and run off with her."

After a pause, we both started laughing. He pulled me closer.

"What are *you* afraid of?" I said after a moment.

"Oh, just . . . yeah. That it won't work out, it won't be the same out there, you'll stop loving me." He was stroking my hair. "But not the age thing. Don't you think if we last that long— you covered the next thirty years, you know—we'll be doing pretty good? We have as good a chance as any couple starting out today . . . A better chance, because we love each other more. Speaking for myself, anyway."

I pulled away and looked at him. "I don't believe you've actually officially said you love me yet."

"I haven't?" He looked across the room, frowning, and back at me. "That's because I've trained myself not to. I would have been saying it since . . ." He shrugged. " . . . the first week. And if I said it then, you would have run away."

I smiled. "True." And kissed him.

It was his turn to pull away and look at me. "You haven't officially said you love me."

"Oh, Hans . . ." I shook my head, feeling tears prick my eyes. "I never thought I would ever love anyone the way I love you."

And we talked no more that night.

The *Professor* left Port Stephens the next day during lunch. As we rounded Cape Meredith and headed across the thirty-five miles of open ocean to East Falkland, the researchers staked out various corners of the common areas to finish up paperwork and debrief during the long voyage back to Stanley. Yvonne, Helen, and Hans, at one table in the dining room, were charged with the task of organizing the data from Marcia's project and deciding what to do with it. Finn, Bill, and I had a table next to a portside window, where we were poised to watch the coast of East Falkland go by.

As we organized and analyzed our three hundred hours of observations from the six weeks, it became clear that what we'd suspected all along was confirmed; visits by small numbers of tourists to gentoo colonies had little effect on the success of skuas, though slightly more at remote sites where penguins were unused to human visitors. We agreed that Finn would write up the overall report, and I would prepare a proposal for future study.

As the islands off East Falkland came into view, I found myself alone at the table; Bill had suggested a fifteen-minute break and left the room, and Finn went off to check his email. I got a fresh cup of coffee and sat looking out the window and thinking about Hans. So I was in love, madly, wildly in love. And he with me. But what would happen beyond the flight to Santiago we'd both be on in two days' time? Our discussion hadn't really gotten that far.

Finn came back, his step jaunty, and said, "Where's Bill?"

"Gone to his room for something; he'll be right back."

He sat down and slid a sheet of paper across to me. "I've got a job interview; I need a couple of references from my current project. I thought you and Bill . . ."

"Oh, sure," I said. "I'm happy to."

Finn looked relieved. "Thank you . . . I mean, I know I'm asking a lot . . ."

"You mean I could say you're an ecoterrorist or something?"

He nodded, then smiled. "But I think you won't."

"You're right. I won't. I actually think you're rather brilliant and a hard worker and . . . compassionate. You've learned a lesson."

Bill slid in next to me; Finn asked him as well, then bounced off to tell Alejandro of his good luck.

I picked up the piece of paper and read the heading.

Stunned, I looked up at Bill. "Parque Nacional Isla Magdalena. He's got an interview with Parque Nacional Isla Magdalena."

Bill glanced down at his copy. "Go see if you've got one."

Somehow I wasn't surprised that my email was of the thanks-for-your-application-however kind. I told Bill with a tight-lipped "Oh, well," and went to the gym for my five thirty date with Helen.

She was already sweating away on one of the stationary bikes, looking exactly like she had on the day I'd met her.

As I got on the other bike, Helen said, "Why so blue?"

"Oh, nothing … only that my dream job has fizzled, and I don't have any good leads on others. Just an interview for a job I'm only lukewarm about." I told her how Finn had gotten an interview with Parque Nacional and I didn't.

"That's absurd!" she said. "Finn doesn't even speak Spanish!"

"I guess that's why he and Alejandro have been practicing," I said.

We pedaled silently for a bit. When I heard a little snort from Helen, I looked over and saw that she was smiling.

"What?"

She looked back and said, "It really is rather amusing, isn't it? How Finn, that little rabble-rouser, may get the job you've wanted for so long. When you could have gotten him in big trouble and perhaps even taken him out of the running."

"I still could, I suppose." And I told her about the recommendation he'd asked for.

She laughed out loud at this.

And I began to see the humor in it, too. We both knew I would write Finn a glowing recommendation.

After more silent pedaling, I said, "Hans might come with me to my Argentina interview."

She nodded. "And then?"

"I suppose it would depend on what happens there."

"I'd think you'd be happier about it."

"Oh, I'm happy with Hans, really happy ... It's just ... I wonder; was it a trade-off? Have I failed to get a job because I was so busy falling in love?"

"Don't be ridiculous. From what you've told me, that application was already sent off before you ever met Hans. You've hardly failed."

"Yes, but I have no good leads." And as I said it, I knew that any lack of effort in my job search was due more to my belief in getting my one dream job than anything to do with Hans. I changed the subject. "How about you and Josef?"

"Josef and I have enjoyed each other's company. He's a fine man. But we didn't have that special connection. So we're going back to our lives, our kids, our grandkids."

Two crew members came into the gym then, greeted us, and set about lifting weights, and the conversation with Helen ended.

Everyone stayed on in the dining room and lounge long after dinner was finished, watching the coast glide by. Hans was often by my side, but we were never alone together. Bleaker Island came into view, and Liz called us to look. With me, Hans, Bill, and Yoshi gathered around, she told the story of how she'd rescued the penguin chick and insisted on a funeral. She shook her head. "I should have thrown it back to the predators, shouldn't I?"

Bill put an arm around her. "You were a greenhorn then."

"Green *horn*?" said Hans and Yoshi in unison.

By ten that evening, the *Professor* rounded Cape Pembroke and steamed into Stanley Harbour. It was ten thirty before we'd moored, and though it was getting past the bedtime most of us had grown used to over the past six weeks, everyone went ashore. A cruise ship was in town, so shops were still open, and though it was nearly dark, the streets were full of people. We stood in an uncertain clump where the pier met the shore, feeling a bit like country bumpkins in the big city. Hans took my hand, and whispered, "Care for a look at the shipwrecks?"

I was worried about him walking so far, but at his assurance that he'd only go as far as he was comfortable with, we set out.

It was the same route we'd taken that first morning. I'd known him less than a day, and I'd already felt an irresistible pull toward him. Now here we were almost six weeks later. Who'd have guessed then that we'd have a fling? That we'd fall in love? It had been an early morning walk then, the start of a new day. And now the sun had set, leaving a peach-colored band in the western sky.

We walked along, hand in hand, Hans limping slightly, the wind at our back, pushing us forward. I was cold and Hans put his arm around me and pulled me into the lee of the visitor center to shelter there for a moment.

Without thinking, I said, "You know that day you found the list?" He nodded, and I said, "Did you ever really think I was after you for your money?"

He stared down the harbor, hands in his pockets, uncomfortable.

I said, "It's okay, babe, if you did. I understand. It looked . . . pretty fishy."

He spoke. "That afternoon I did. When I found that paper, the list . . . I didn't see what else it could mean. You said my name wasn't underlined, but. . ."

"You didn't believe me." I thought back to my sarcastic laughter, my anger.

"No . . . ," he said. "And you got mad. I saw as soon as you left, I was wrong."

I looked at him; he was looking so mournful, so contrite.

I touched his face. "It's okay, Hans. It takes a long time to really trust someone . . . to know how they'll behave in a certain situation . . ." I smiled. "We'll get there."

His face transformed. He repeated, "'We'll get there' . . . This is the first time I've thought you might really want to stay with me."

"Of course I do. It's just . . ."

We were standing facing each other, a finger of wind curling into our shelter and lifting our hair. Hans took both my hands in his and looked at me. "Joanie," he said. "I want to marry you."

"Oh, Hans." I wasn't ready for this.

"'Oh, Hans,'" he repeated. "'Oh, Hans' what?"

I swallowed. "I don't think . . . I don't think we should be making those kinds of decisions yet . . ."

He waited. Out over the harbor a flock of gulls squabbled noisily in the air. It was all going so fast, my plan I'd held so dear for so long—to be alone in the cabin on the Chilean coast—gone. I should have protested more, right? But instead what came out of my mouth was this: "Let's see if we still feel this way a year from now. And if we do, we can get married then."

We looked at each other for a moment.

"Yes?" A slow smile spread across his face. He said, "Let's get married one year from the day we met, December thirteen. If we still feel like it."

This was six weeks less than a year, I was quite aware. I shook my head. "You don't give up, do you?"

"Okay?" he persisted.

Feeling ridiculously happy about losing this battle, I said, "Okay."

He picked me up off my feet, held me close, twirled me around.

"Hans, your ankle," I said, laughing.

He let me down and we kissed. He pulled back and looked at me again. "One more thing. Tomorrow? I want to buy you an engagement ring."

"Oh, Hans."

"'Oh, Hans' again. Why not? What is an engagement ring, anyway? It shows an intention to marry. We have that, right?"

I could only shake my head. "You're the most romantic person I've ever met, man or woman. I give up. Okay, an engagement ring. But not a diamond. One of those pretty Falkland Islands stones."

We stepped into the wind and continued toward the shipwrecks.

But he still wasn't done, stopped. "And we can announce it at the party Friday night."

To keep myself from saying 'Oh, Hans' again, I just shook my head.

He said, reasonably, I had to admit, "We'll want them to come to the wedding, won't we?"

I squinted up at him. "I suppose we could tell them to write the date in pencil."

How, in mere minutes, had waiting to talk about the *possibility* of getting married a year from now morphed into announcing our engagement the next evening?

We turned around then and walked back to the ship, arm in arm, against the wind, crazy grins on both our faces.

Friday morning we finished our work by eleven, mostly a summing up by Ian of what we'd done on the main count and what it meant. He and Bill had determined that despite Marcia's tweaking of the numbers, we had enough sound data to make a reliable report. It would take more compiling before we clearly knew which penguin populations were declining and if any had grown. "But it looks," Ian said, "like the gentoos are the healthiest, possibly doing better than five years ago. The kings are stable, and the Magellanics and rockhoppers are still declining, especially the rockies. There's work to be done on all fronts. You'll all be getting my final report in a few weeks." Finn and I and Alejandro all gave brief reports on our projects.

After the meeting we streamed off the boat. Hans and I went directly to pick out a ring, and we found a lovely local pebble set in a silver band. I was swept along on this wave of romantic feelings, while at the same time wondering what in the world I was going to do if I didn't get—or didn't want—the Iguazú Falls job. As we left the jewelry shop, I heard my name called. It was Audrey. We hadn't seen each other since the night on her island, and we all hugged. "I've been looking for you," she said. "There's someone in the visitor center who wants to talk to you."

I must have looked surprised, because Audrey added, "The visitor center? Where Falklands Conservation is housed?"

"Oh!" I said. "I guess I'd better go see what they want."

I arranged to meet Hans for lunch at one o'clock and went off with Audrey.

Just before one, I skipped down the street to the Brasserie. Hans was standing on the sidewalk in his red raincoat. "You look happy," he said.

"I am happy." I took his hand and we walked up the steps to the door of the restaurant. "Of course I'm happy, I'm engaged to marry the man I love." I was really getting into this.

"And?" he said.

I made us wait until we were seated. Then I leaned forward. "You like it here, don't you?"

"Where? The Brasserie?"

"The Brasserie . . . yes. You wouldn't get tired of it being your go-to restaurant for, say, a year?"

His face lit up. "They offered you a job?"

I nodded. "I'll start work on the February follow-up count, then move into helping update the best practices brochure on visiting wildlife. It will be especially for cruise ship operators and passengers. It's a temporary job, for a year. Then we'll see if it can be more."

"And you told them . . . ?"

"I said yes . . . I said I was going to run it by my fiancé, but I was ninety-nine percent sure he'd love the idea."

"Fiancé," he said.

"Yup. It rolled right off my tongue."

He stood up and leaned across the table and kissed me. The server arrived just then, and we ordered.

Once the server was gone, Hans said, "Your fiancé loves the idea. When do you start?"

"Right away! So I can get some work done while the penguins are still here. When they've all left and it starts getting into fall, I can take a couple of weeks off then."

"But where did this job come from? You never heard about it until now."

"It was supposed to be Marcia's job. I guess Bernard worked things so they didn't have to advertise it. But now ..." I shrugged, not exactly proud of this aspect of the job offer.

But Hans just nodded, and after a moment said, "We have to ... you have to, make new plans ... Do you still want to go to that interview in Argentina?" he said.

I thought about that for maybe two seconds. "I don't think so. I never was very excited about that job. It feels right to stay here."

⁀⁀⁀

Back on board the *Professor* in the late afternoon, everyone was packing. The party would start with dinner; Pepa was making paella again, and I'd be helping.

After stowing everything still left in my cabin into my duffel bag, I hauled it and my backpack up to Hans's cabin. Somehow in the last two days a lot of my clothes had migrated back up there.

He wasn't in the room, and I spent a few minutes emptying the drawers and closet of my stuff.

As I was closing the zipper on the duffel bag, Hans came in and sat down next to my pack. "Ian's got Marcia's things packed up and wants me to take them to her," he said.

"Oh!" I wondered for a moment why it had to be Hans, but said, "Maybe you can find out something about her motives."

"That's what I thought."

I kissed him. "And maybe she'll apologize for trying to kill you."

TWENTY-NINE

A Falklands Pebble

Tourism does, however, hold the prospect of one indirect but huge benefit for penguins: it is impossible to look at penguins without developing an empathy for them. Every enamored tourist becomes a potential ambassador for penguins, an advocate on their behalf in the fight for their conservation.

—*Lloyd Spencer Davis,*
SMITHSONIAN Q & A: *PENGUINS:*
THE ULTIMATE QUESTION AND ANSWER BOOK

W HEN HE WAS gone, I went downstairs to find Liz. She and Paul were in their cabin packing. Liz made space for me to sit on a chair, saying, "All done?"

"Not quite, but I just wanted to see you, to say goodbye properly."

Liz put down a stack of neatly folded shirts on the bed and sat next to them. "It's sad, isn't it? To be leaving."

Paul put a handful of socks in a suitcase on the dresser and said, "Shall I step out?"

"If you don't want to see a couple of women cry," I said.

He considered a moment, and said he thought he'd go pay a visit to Josef.

When he was gone, I said, "I was just thinking about everyone and how we'll all sort of stay in touch, and maybe visit each other when we go on trips and all, and how . . . well, it'll never be the same. What we had together, we had here, and . . . that chapter is closed . . . with most people. But you . . . somehow I feel that . . ." I shrugged. "I don't know, we've come through some stuff, together. I think that . . ." I looked at Liz. "That there's another chapter there. That we've become real friends."

This got Liz all teary. She said, "Oh, Joanie . . ."

We stood and hugged each other, and laughed, and talked about how Seattle wasn't that far from Boise, although of course I didn't know how much I was going to be in the Northwest for a while. I told her about the job I'd been offered just that day, here in the Falklands.

When Liz was done congratulating me, she said, "And Hans?"

"Hans is going to stay with me." It was all I could do to keep the engagement thing to myself, but I'd promised Hans we'd save it for that evening.

Liz made it hard. "Have you talked about marriage?"

I hesitated and could feel my face getting warm.

Liz jumped up and down and squealed.

So I showed her the ring. "I didn't say anything, okay? But stay tuned for an announcement tonight. Try to keep it quiet in the meantime, will you?"

Liz zipped her lips. "I won't even tell Paul."

I'd planned to visit Helen as well, but decided to catch her later. The secret was in danger of getting all over the ship if I told one more person, and Helen was a pro at getting things out of me.

I decided instead to go up and say goodbye to Bill. Even if I did end up telling him about the engagement, I figured he could be trusted to keep it to himself. His door was open; he was sitting on the edge of his bed next to two huge black pieces of luggage. When I saw them, I remembered. "Oh, the parka!"

He was writing on his clipboard and looked up. "Keep it. I don't have room. Well . . . maybe you don't have room . . ."

I sat down across from him on the chair and said, "Well, if you really don't want it, it can stay here with me . . ."

He raised his eyebrows.

"And my job."

He put his notebook aside. "Well, well, well . . ."

I gave him the details, and he congratulated me. "Falklands Conservation is an excellent organization."

"I wanted to say goodbye properly," I went on. "I've been so wrapped up in . . . everything, but there are people that have come to mean a lot to me. I just wanted to say, you know, more than just 'It's been great, see you around.'"

He nodded.

I didn't know how to go on and laughed. "It's funny . . . I just said goodbye to Liz; we gushed, we cried, laughed, hugged each other . . . but I feel shy now."

He looked at me over the top of his glasses. "Must be the boy-girl thing."

"Must be. Probably there's a biological basis for it."

He nodded. "Tell me what you told Liz."

I smiled. "I told her how much she meant to me. How with most people on the ship I feel we'll stay in touch, but it's pretty much . . . over. Except for with her, I feel different, like I've made a friend for life . . . that we'll see each other again, our friendship will grow . . . that there are other chapters out there."

The light from the open door glinted off his glasses. "So, you're saying ditto for me?"

"Yes, ditto."

Bill gave a brief nod and said, "Helen's going to come to the states in May and look me up. I'll take her around the Southwest, taking photographs."

"No Josef?"

"Just Helen."

I nodded. "I guess they really did manage to contain their romance to the ship, just like she always said." I looked down at my hands, saw the ring. On impulse, I held out my hand. "Hans got me an engagement ring today." I rushed on so he'd have time to absorb the information before he had to respond. "We weren't going to tell anyone until tonight, so mum's the word. It's tentative, we'll live together and get married in a year if it seems right."

He smiled. "Congratulations. You guys are great together."

"Thank you," I said, and I stood up to go. "Liz and I cried and then we hugged."

"I don't know about the crying part . . . ," Bill said, but he stood up and we hugged, tight and quick. I started to get a little teary, so I kissed him on the cheek and got out of there.

I was chopping chorizo in the galley when Hans found me. He gave me a wink as he walked over to Pepa and said something in her ear, then came back to me, and started untying my apron. "Come on. The boss says you can go." I protested and looked at Pepa, who said, "Javier is coming, he can take your job."

We found the alcove empty and settled on the couch.

"You were gone awhile," I said. "Did she talk, then?"

"She didn't stop talking. She's still mad. She can't believe people don't understand her. I think she was desperate to explain to someone. She believed she was doing a good thing. I think she really did. Bernard—she calls him 'Uncle Bern'—started the whole thing. He knew about the count and he knew she was about to graduate, so he asked her to apply. He told her about his plans to mess up the numbers and how he needed her to help. She resisted at first, according to her. Then he told her about the job here *and* about this rich guy coming; single, not so bad-looking, and she made up her mind."

"He must have seen that Most Eligible Bachelor list."

"Probably. She always hated being poor. She really does love wildlife, seabirds, penguins. She came here once, she was thirteen, and she lived here a year. There were more birds then and almost no tourists, no cruise ships at all. She fell in love with the Falklands. That's when she decided to become a biologist."

I thought he was sounding a bit too sympathetic, but I kept a neutral face, and said, "She must have met that red-haired guy from the Globe then."

"I guess so. Bernard found out about the oil spill on Sunday from his fisherman friend. They knew by then that Yoshi and I were going out there. Monday morning Bernard siphoned the gas while Marcia stood guard."

"What about the radio?" I said. "Didn't they think you might call when you saw the oil?"

He nodded. "They did. They found a radio in the gear and changed the batteries in it for bad ones. They didn't know we had another radio with us."

"The one you lost."

"The one we lost."

"Didn't they think . . ." I didn't know what.

"They were in a hurry. She admitted it wasn't a very good plan." He smiled at me. "That's when she came close to apologizing; she said they were only trying to delay our return a day or so, and then the contracts would be signed and a little oil spill wouldn't matter. She said they didn't know about the storm."

"Huh. That's hard to believe." We sat for a moment watching a fishing boat chug past on its way to a nearby dock. Mostly to prolong the moment, I said, "So, her going after you for your money . . . wasn't really related to the rest of it."

"No. That was her own thing. She got Bernard to put her and me in cabins near each other on Five. She thought she'd have no trouble seducing me. She couldn't believe it when I preferred," he grinned, "'that old bag.' I think those were her words." And with a look of feigned innocence, he said, "What does that mean?"

I gave his arm a little punch.

He laughed and put his arm around me. "And she never gave up. She just kept watching us, waiting. She felt sure we wouldn't last long. And when she saw us . . . having problems, she made some of her own."

"Like the list."

"Yeah, that was her. She got it out of your cabin, underlined my name, put it in my cabin, just like you thought."

I put my head on his shoulder. "That nearly got us."

After dining on another superb paella, everyone retired to the lounge. Hans gave a short version of his visit to Marcia; how she claimed Bernard was behind all the mischief and persuaded her to help. An avalanche of questions and speculation followed.

Helen asked, "What will happen to her? And Bernard."

"They've got lawyers," Ian said and looked to Audrey, the only Falklands resident in our midst.

"There'll be a trial," she said. "Word around town is the prosecution is taking it very seriously. They're going for attempted murder, among other charges. It's anybody's guess what will come of it. Such events are extremely rare here." She shook her head. "And involving a foreigner . . . I can't think of anything remotely like it ever happening."

I looked around the room. People were shaking their heads, commenting to their neighbors. But, as far as I could tell, not a tear was shed for Marcia. I found myself feeling a bit sorry for her. Who had her friends been? Maybe Yvonne, maybe Liz, but they didn't seem any more broken up than the rest of us. Marcia had been so busy scheming about getting Hans, plotting with her cousin Bernard . . .

After a few minutes of chatter, Ian called everyone back together. The next day almost all of us were leaving the Falklands, most never to return. Liz had collected everyone's contact information and was distributing copies of the list she'd made. Ian suggested that we go around and say what was next in our lives.

He and Caroline were going to visit her parents in Scotland for a couple of weeks; he'd do the project wrap-up there. Finn had the job interview in Chile. Josef was heading back to Switzerland to a late eightieth birthday celebration with his kids, grandkids, and great-grandkids. Helen told about her upcoming trip to the United States. When it was my turn, I told about finally getting a job and staying in the Falklands for the next year.

Josef called from a far table, "What about your boyfriend?"

I glanced at Hans, who was sitting beside me.

He stood. "I've asked Joanie to marry me . . ."

After the cheers and ruckus died down, he said, ". . . and she said no."

Groans of disappointment.

"So we are going to live together, here. I'll do my carvings, learn to cook, take care of the house, see about starting some kind of foundation to help with penguin conservation. She says she'll marry me after one year if we still feel like it." He had to pause again for the applause. "So we're engaged, and we have a date."

He looked down at me and grinned at the look on my face. "A *tentative* date. December thirteen next year. You're all invited."

The room erupted again. Helen proposed a toast, and wine was poured all around.

Hans and I stood close and clinked glasses. I swallowed some before I noticed Hans had only raised his glass and set it down.

"Oops," I said.

He smiled, shaking his head. "You don't need to do that. It's not your job. You helped me through the hard part."

"Okay . . ." I cleared my throat. "There's something I haven't told you."

"Oh?"

"I've been drinking . . . I was. Until Tuesday."

He cocked his head, a little half smile. "Really. I never noticed."

"It wasn't much. And I was discreet. I didn't want you to know."

"And why not?" He looked down his nose at me in a parody of disapproval.

"Probably I didn't want you to know that our breaking up was bothering me in the least."

Looking stern, he shook his head. "Very immature of you."

I smiled. I liked this, that I could sometimes be the immature one.

Maybe this would be our little joke through the years.

Acknowledgments

S O MANY HAVE helped me in the journey to write and publish this book. I thank first my husband, Richard Webster, who has encouraged and supported me from the beginning. He read numerous drafts, gave valuable feedback, and even helped me come up with a key plot point.

For insightful feedback on early drafts I thank Carole Gibb, Leslie Barber, Kelley Beebe, and Paula Magar.

New eyes read the first complete draft and helped me through that stage. For that I thank Betsy Binnian, Cara Izumi, Marilyn Stark, and Falaah Jones. Carole Gibb stepped up near the end to help with technical aspects and cheer me on to the finish line. She also did a final proofing, as did Richard.

Jerry Dzugan helped me get on the right track on hypothermia, and Lance Wiskowski arranged a tour of the ship that would serve as a model for the one in my novel. Thanks for this help towards authenticity. Other friends have helped with details of ship life and travel, offered rural settings for solitary writer's retreats, and advised me on the ins and outs of their own self-publishing adventures.

And a final thanks to my publishing consultant, Beth Jusino, who smoothly navigated me through the publishing maze, and to my copyeditor, Kristin Carlsen.

Countless others have given encouragement and support.

Together you make a team to whom I'm forever grateful.

About the Author

T RAVELS TO FAR flung locations inspire Arlene Springer's writing. A trip to the Falkland Islands in 2007 was the spark that ignited *Feet First*. This is her first novel.